CODE WORD

CODE WORD

A NOVEL BY

TRACI HUNTER
ABRAMSON

Covenant Communications, Inc.

Cover image: *Girl in Tunnel* © Milos Jokic, courtesty istockphoto.com

Cover design copyright © 2012 by Covenant Communications, Inc.

Published by Covenant Communications, Inc.
American Fork, Utah

Printed in the United States of America
First Printing: August 2012

18 17 16 15 14 13 12   10 9 8 7 6 5 4 3 2 1

ISBN-13: 978-1-62108-188-3

For Diana

ACKNOWLEDGMENTS

THANKS TO THE MANY READERS who have encouraged me to write this book. I have thoroughly enjoyed writing about the Saint Squad, and your feedback and input has been invaluable.

Thank you to all of the wonderful people at Covenant who continue to support and encourage me to do what I love. A special thanks to Rebecca Cummings for helping me become the writer I am today and to Samantha Van Walraven for constantly helping me turn the seed of an idea into a complete novel.

To my family, thank you for supporting my writing and the crazy hours I often keep when I'm in the middle of my fictional world.

Thank you to the CIA Publication Review Board for your help in meeting some demanding deadlines throughout this editing process. Your efforts are greatly appreciated.

Finally, I want to recognize the members of our armed forces who sacrifice so much to protect our freedom.

PROLOGUE

CARINA CHANNING NAVIGATED HER WAY through the outskirts of Denver and listened to her two younger sisters chat about their summer plans. She had returned home a few hours earlier, and her mom had suggested they celebrate by going out to their family's favorite pizza place. It was a bit odd that her mom hadn't come with them, but Carina assumed her mom wanted to give her time alone with her sisters.

She was looking forward to the three months they would spend together before she had to leave for graduate school. Her semesters at NYU had been incredible, but she was ready for a break before she went back to Manhattan, this time to attend the Fashion Institute of Technology.

The Rocky Mountains rose to the west as the cool air whipped through the open windows of her mom's Mercedes. She had missed this during her time away at school: the open landscape of the west, the rugged beauty of Colorado. In her heart, this was home, even though she had spent her turbulent childhood in Chicago.

She beat the memories back before they could form, reminding herself that she wasn't a Perelli anymore. None of them were. They were the Channing family now. A nice, normal American family who happened to only have one parent living in their home.

"You're going to let us help you decorate your new apartment, right?" sixteen-year-old Gianna asked from the passenger seat as she tucked a strand of her blonde hair behind her ear.

"Absolutely." Carina grinned. She still couldn't believe her mother was buying her an apartment in New York and would finalize the deal in less than a month. She would no longer have to deal with messy roommates or the awkward parties that often came with them. Living the Mormon lifestyle had been a challenge in the city, but she knew it was one she would have to learn to deal with if she wanted to work in the fashion industry.

"I can't wait to see it," fourteen-year-old Bianca said from the backseat.

"Me too." Carina's eyes lit up. "Did you see the pictures the Realtor sent Mom? The place is incredible."

Gianna grinned. "I think Mom just wanted to make sure there was enough room for all of us for when we come to visit."

"Personally, I think we should spend some time in LA this summer," Bianca said.

"Let me guess, there's a swim meet you want to go to."

"It's not just any swim meet," Bianca countered. "It would be my first chance to swim in a national competition. And it's right next to the beach. You guys would like that."

Carina listened to Bianca rave about the vacation she had planned for them and her pleas that they help her convince their mom.

She turned the corner toward her mom's house, at first unaware of the two cars parked in her driveway. She was half a block away when she noticed them, the identical black SUVs, the kind the bad guys always drove back in Chicago, the kind she wanted to believe were only in the movies. But this wasn't the movies. This was real life, and the bad guys she knew were anything but fictional.

Her heartbeat quickened, her eyes searching the front of the house for any sign of the visitors. She knew the two cars parked in her driveway shouldn't have been cause for alarm. Since her mother had moved them to Colorado over eight years before, they had lived quietly in this upscale Denver suburb. Not once had they seen or heard from their father since they had run away from Chicago and the family.

She had nearly convinced herself that everything was okay when she saw the front door of their house open and a burly man in a dark suit take a guard-like stance on the porch.

Carina forced herself to look away from her house, to focus once more on the road.

"Carina, where are you going?" Gianna asked, motioning behind her. "You just passed our house."

"Call the house. See if you can get Mom on the phone."

Gianna's eyebrows drew together, but she pulled her cell phone from her pocket and hit speed dial for their house phone. "She isn't answering."

"Try her cell."

Gianna dialed once more but shook her head when again their mother didn't answer. "Nothing."

Carina took a deep breath, praying that her mother was okay, that she and her sisters would remain safe. She turned the corner and pulled over to the side of the road. "Listen to me. Something doesn't look right at the house. I want you to drive over to the Jorgensens. If I don't call or text you in the next five minutes, call the cops."

Gianna's face paled, and she shook her head. "If something's wrong, we should stay together."

"I'm just going to check on Mom," Carina said, fighting to keep her voice calm. "Your job right now is to keep Bianca safe."

Even as Bianca protested that she wasn't a kid anymore, Gianna swallowed hard and nodded.

Carina climbed out of the car, leaving the keys in the ignition for her sister. She cut through the neighbor's backyard and headed toward her own in the hopes that she could get inside through the side garage door without being seen.

Quietly, she slipped into the garage to find it empty. Light streamed in through the door she'd left open behind her. Cautiously, quietly, she moved across the concrete floor toward the entrance leading into the house. She reached for the doorknob, but her hand jerked back when she heard a gunshot vibrate through the quiet neighborhood, followed by a second and a third.

She gasped, her stomach clutching with fear. She wanted to pretend that it was a car backfiring or someone's TV blasting, but she knew better. She knew exactly what gunshots sounded like.

In that moment, she froze, afraid to move forward, too terrified to run away. She hadn't stopped to think that her father's men would never leave the garage unprotected.

Men shouted inside. Rapid footsteps sounded.

Carina's heart pounded in her chest, and panic seized her. She thought of her sisters, of the instructions she had given them. Reality flashed through her mind, the knowledge that opening the door, walking into her house, could end her life. Her hands shaking, she pulled her cell phone free of her pocket. If she called for help, the people inside might hear her, but she had to do something.

With a prayer in her heart, she texted Gianna three simple words: *Call the cops.*

1

Two years later. May 2, 2011

ADRENALINE AND ANTICIPATION. THE SCENT of sweat and greasepaint. Helicopter rotors thrumming overhead. Lieutenant Jay Wellman absorbed every detail as he studied the dark shadows of the other eleven men in the back of the Blackhawk helicopter.

The seven men sitting nearest the doors were relative strangers to Jay, all of them members of another SEAL team. This was their mission, their lead. The Saint Squad, which Jay belonged to, was part of SEAL Team Eight, but together they comprised an all-important, top-secret unit.

This was one of at least a dozen special ops missions planned for tonight, each one just as important as the next. But theirs, if successful, might not only make the news but could also make history.

The other SEALs who would accompany them tonight were aboard the Blackhawks currently flying in formation beside them. Jay didn't have to look out the window to know they were passing through the lower ranges of the Himalayas. Like the others on board, he had studied the mission plan until he knew it by heart. For two months they had trained for this, always preparing for this moment.

The helicopters transporting them were the stealth variety, specially designed to avoid detection by the local military. Even though Pakistan was currently an ally, its government hadn't been alerted that the SEALs were coming. Which meant Pakistan's military didn't know they were coming either.

Officially, the SEALs weren't in Pakistan tonight, and unless their mission yielded the desired results, no one would ever know of their presence.

In the darkness, Jay studied the other four members of his squad. Though he had only been with this unit for less than a year, Jay could now identify his teammates under any circumstances. Across from him, Tristan Crowther rolled his shoulders as though trying to get more comfortable.

His relaxed posture nearly managed to disguise the energy pulsing through him. Beside Tristan, Quinn Lambert was ready for action. Six feet tall, impatient, and built like a boxer, Quinn was always ready for a fight.

Their commanding officer, Lt. Commander Brent Miller, sat between Quinn and one of the other squad commanders. The two senior officers had their heads together over the map Brent held, a flashlight cutting through the darkness to illuminate their object of study.

The final member of the Saint Squad sat beside him. Seth Johnson's dark skin made him almost invisible in the night, but Jay knew that when there was trouble, Seth would be there to watch his back.

Over the past ten months since Jay had joined the Saint Squad, these four men had become a second family to him. On the surface, he knew he shouldn't feel like he belonged, but—somehow—he did. The other members were all married, all Latter-day Saints. The Saint Squad's nickname had come from the fact that the whole squad was Mormon. He had become the exception when the squad's former commanding officer moved up to take over the command of SEAL Team Eight.

Jay still couldn't say he really understood their religion, but he had gotten used to their idiosyncrasies. Prayers before missions were now commonplace for him, as was the expectation that going out for a drink meant a round of soda.

They had been deployed to Afghanistan for three months before returning to their home base in the States to train for this mission. As soon as they completed their objective, they would head back to Virginia Beach, where they would go back to life as usual—or at least what passed for usual for Navy SEALs.

"Two minutes until target." The copilot's voice came through Jay's headset.

Grips tightened on the automatic weapons they all held, and Jay felt his stomach pitch with apprehension for several seconds before his adrenaline pushed it aside. This was routine, he reminded himself. He could no longer count how many times he had jumped out of a helicopter or worked his way through the darkness in search of the enemy. He had been trained for nights like tonight. They all had.

He visualized his target, the one-acre property in Abbottabad surrounded by eighteen-foot walls. The helicopter was so close to the ground as they approached that he could feel the vibration of the houses shaking beneath them.

The one-minute countdown started, and the smell of anticipation kicked up another notch. Jay heard someone let out an obscenity as a spark of light illuminated the sky.

"Incoming!" someone shouted as the helicopter jerked hard to the right.

A rocket-propelled grenade flashed past them, and the helicopter spun around as the pilot fought for control. Instinctively, Jay tightened his harness. The other Blackhawks fired on their target to clear their landing zone, but not before another grenade burst into the air.

The impact and the subsequent explosion rocked the helicopter again.

"Hang on!" The pilot's voice was clipped.

Jay gripped the edge of his seat, and he felt the Blackhawk start to vibrate awkwardly.

The world seemed to stop in that instant. Reality crashed over him, the certainty that he was very likely about to die. He thought he'd been prepared for the possibility that he might give his life serving his country. But not like this. Not while strapped into a helicopter, the safety still engaged on his weapon.

The seconds ticked by in slow motion, like a replay on a football game being shown frame by frame. Obscenities erupted from the other squad on board, contrasting sharply with the silence from his own squad.

With his night vision goggles already in place, Jay could see his teammates clearly. Fear, concern, alarm. Those expressions were written on everyone's faces, but beneath those most basic emotions, the rest of his squad seemed calm, accepting of the chaos surrounding them.

Didn't they understand that they were rapidly hurtling toward the ground? Didn't they realize their wives could become widows in the next ten seconds—wives who were waiting at home for them, who would miss them when they were gone?

Jay didn't have that, had never really had that.

Before he could finish the thought, the Blackhawk impacted hard on the ground, and his body jerked forward. A shower of sparks at the rear of the helicopter accompanied the crunch of metal.

The next voice over the communication gear was the commander's, who was sitting beside Brent. "Helo One has landed. We are a go."

Instantly, everyone sprang into action. Two by two, the SEALs exited the helicopter while the rest of the assault squad slid down ropes from the other helicopters hovering overhead. The initial burst of gunfire, the sound of the guards on the roof shooting at the SEALs overhead, was expected.

More gunfire sounded as Jay's feet touched the ground. Immediately, he dropped to the dirt, a tremor working its way through his body. His brain shut down for a dangerous second, his reality adjusting from almost dying to now trying to stay alive.

He caught a glimpse of Seth out of the corner of his eye. That was enough to remind him why he was here. He was part of a team, and his team needed him.

Quickly, he checked his teammates' positions and then returned fire. After squeezing off a couple of quick bursts, the shooter retreated into the house. Jay didn't speak Arabic, but it didn't take much to figure out the gist of the man's frantic shouts of warning.

The mission commander gave the signal for the planned assault to begin, and the SEALs entered the main structure in waves. Children cried out, and a woman's scream pierced the air. Rapid footsteps sounded in several directions as they moved steadily forward. Then the rat-a-tat-tat of automatic weapons punctuated the night.

Tristan led the way into a stairwell, with Seth bringing up the rear, as they made their way up one level and then another. They cleared the first several rooms, finding only some rumpled bedding and stray clothes. Cautiously moving forward, Jay heard more gunfire from the level below, followed by someone whimpering in a room close by.

Quinn and Tristan searched the rooms across from them, Brent holding his position in the hall. The whimpering grew louder as they continued forward. Jay touched his ear and signaled to Seth before pointing to the room where the sound had originated.

Seth nodded and moved into position. Using the wall as a shield, Jay pushed the door open. Then he and Seth entered in tandem, their weapons drawn as they stormed in. Three children ranging in age from six to ten were huddled with a woman in the corner. Seth spoke to them in Arabic while Jay checked the room for explosives or weapons.

He spoke quietly into his headset. "This room is clear, but we've got prisoners. Where are we holding them?"

Before Brent could answer, gunfire sparked in the hall. Jay pressed up against the wall by the doorway. "Status?"

"We've got a shooter two doors down on the right," Brent told him. "Give us some cover fire. He's got us pinned down. And Seth, secure the prisoners. We'll come back for them."

Seth quickly tied up the woman and the three children to the low-lying wooden bedpost. Jay didn't have to look to sense their fear. He could smell it. Seth's face held a look of distaste as he completed the unwelcome task, ensuring that the woman and children would stay safely out of the battle zone.

As soon as Seth moved into position, Jay squatted down and then swung his weapon into the hallway, sending off two quick bursts. The gunman returned fire, bullets impacting the wall and doorframe.

Jay fired again, his shots quickly followed by his teammates' rounds. The minutes drew out, neither side able to gain an advantage.

"I've had about enough of this," Seth grumbled beside Jay.

Brent's voice was clipped. "Quinn and Tristan, clear the roof. See if you can reach the window and flush him out from the other side."

"You got it." Quinn's impatience hummed through the headset.

Several more minutes passed, the bursts of gunfire growing shorter as their target presumably began conserving his ammunition. Finally, Tristan's western drawl told them what they wanted to hear. "We're in position. Tell us when."

Seth shifted beside Jay. Brent squatted in the doorway across from them and held up his hand, signaling the countdown with his fingers. When he reached one, he gave the order to Tristan and Quinn. "Now!"

Gunfire and the sound of shattering glass vibrated through the air. A moment later, Quinn's voice came through the headset. "Shooter is down."

They could hear through their headsets that another squad was working their way through the hall parallel to them and encountering heavy resistance.

"Quinn, stay with the prisoners. Tristan, search these rooms for intel," Brent ordered. "Jay and Seth, let's move. We'll see if we can give these guys some help."

Jay and Brent took the lead, and Seth fell in behind them. They reached the end of the hall, where they could see two gunmen positioned between the two doors. One guard was already down, but the other was rapidly shooting bullets toward the adjoining hall. Brent shot twice, taking out the second guard.

Four members of the other squad emerged from the hall opposite them. Through hand signals, the other squad prepared to charge the room behind the closed door to the left. The Saint Squad positioned themselves to storm the one on the right. Brent held up a hand to hold everyone in position and nodded to Seth. Seth shouted out in Pashto then repeated himself in rapid Arabic, and again in Urdu.

A chance to surrender. They were ordered to give the man in charge that chance despite his horrific crimes against the United States and her citizens. Angry voices shouted back. Jay looked to Seth inquisitively for a translation. Seth shook his head in response, and bullets sprayed at both doors to punctuate the meaning. They weren't surrendering.

Brent counted down on his fingers before one of the other SEALs and Seth kicked in the two doors in unison. Bullets immediately sprayed toward them. Seth stepped out of the line of fire and held up four fingers indicating the number of targets inside. Brent motioned to Seth and Jay, indicating the plan of action.

"We got him!" A voice shouted from the other room. Jay didn't have time to wonder if the *him* was the man they had come for. His focus was entirely on the gunfire still sparking toward him and his squad.

When Brent gave the signal, the three members of the Saint Squad moved as one. Two armed men were to the right of the door, and another man stood behind them. The moment the SEALs entered the room, Brent fired at the figure on the right as Seth took out the one on the left.

Jay's eyes swept the sparsely furnished bedroom to see only one man still standing, his hands free of any weapons. A woman sat a few feet away, her expression an odd combination of shock and indignation. Seth shouted out in Arabic once more, another offer to surrender.

The man in front of them shook his head and reached down for a weapon that had fallen to the floor.

Jay pulled his trigger as the woman screamed and jumped in front of the man, directly into his line of fire. Jay saw the sheer hatred in her eyes as his bullets struck her body. A split second later, Brent fired his weapon and ended the man's life.

"Clear the room," Brent ordered Seth and Jay. Brent then pulled out a camera and started snapping photos to document the mission and confirm their targets' identities. The photos would be filtered through facial recognition software to make sure everyone was accurately identified.

Seth started on the far side of the room, pulling open the doors to the wardrobe cabinet to make sure no one had hidden inside. Jay moved into the center of the room and kicked a fallen weapon away from one of the men who was now sprawled on the floor. He looked down at the bodies and got his first good look at the person he had shot. The woman he had shot.

Her long dark hair covered her face, and Jay pushed it aside to check for any sign of life. Then he looked down at where her loose clothing was already saturated with blood, indicating that at least one of his bullets had nicked an artery.

Her eyes stared up at him, half open. Jay pressed his fingers to her neck, but he suspected he wouldn't find a pulse. The color had already started to fade from her face, confirming what he had dreaded. He had killed an unarmed woman.

"It's not your fault." Seth's hand came down on his shoulder, his southern drawl attempting to soothe. "You didn't kill her," Seth continued and pointed at the man she had tried to protect. "She died because of him."

"I pulled the trigger."

"And she made her choice."

Outside, an explosion rocked the ground, followed quickly by another.

Brent stepped beside them. "We're going to have to double up on the other helicopters. They're destroying what they can of the one we came in on."

Jay's eyes were still on the woman, his chest tightening.

"Come on, Jay." Seth nudged his arm. "We have work to do. We still have to search this place for intel."

Jay nodded, forcing himself to stand. Then rapid chatter down the hall pierced his thoughts. The words echoed through the night, words everyone had waited to hear. "Bin Laden is dead. We have confirmation. Osama bin Laden is dead."

2

Pete Wellman stood on the pool deck in the early morning light, his cell phone gripped in his hand. His eyes were on the swimmers in the water, on the few elite athletes he had agreed to train. He made a mental note to talk to Bianca about her hand placement on her freestyle even as he willed his phone to ring.

The news spread everywhere—the radio, the Internet, the newspapers. Osama bin Laden was dead. A group of Navy SEALs had killed him. SEAL Team Six to be exact.

The patriot in him rejoiced over the successful mission. The Marine in him wondered about the details. The father in him just plain worried. His son Jay was assigned to SEAL Team Eight, but Pete knew that the difference between reality and what was in the news was often a lot wider than most people realized. Even though the press claimed that SEAL Team Six had carried out the successful mission, Pete knew from his time with the Corps that the unit unofficially known as "Team Six" had been renamed years ago and its new designation remained classified.

Pete had already calculated how long it would have taken the SEALs to extract from the assault mission and then go through the initial debriefings. Barring a communications blackout, he estimated that the earliest any of those involved with the mission could get to an open-source phone or computer was twenty minutes ago. And, of course, there was no reason he should think that Jay had been on this mission. Except for the silence.

Pete looked down at his phone again. Jay should have called by now. Or texted. Or something. Always before when the SEALs had been in the news, Jay had found some way to let him know that he was okay. Typically, his communication method was a text message that included a code embedded among the letters. The simple misspelled word would go unnoticed by anyone but him and would confirm that it wasn't someone else sending him the message.

Approaching footsteps distracted him momentarily, and he turned to his right to see Bianca's older sister heading toward him. As always, Carina looked like she belonged in a window display in Milan instead of on a pool deck, her designer dress accenting her tall, willowy frame. Her dark, chin-length hair was perfectly styled, hanging straight except for a few soft curls that complemented her high cheekbones. Carina glanced over her shoulder at the parking lot behind her before closing the distance between them.

"Good morning, Coach." Her dark eyes narrowed slightly, and she motioned to the phone he held in his hand. "Is everything okay?"

"Fine," Pete said gruffly before stepping closer to the pool, where Bianca had just come to a stop. She rested her arms on the side of the pool, a strand of her red hair poking out of her swim cap, her long body dangling in the water. Pete's voice was brusque when he motioned to her right arm. "You're still pulling wide on your freestyle."

Her dark eyes met his, and she nodded toward the phone. "You expecting a call?"

"Ten two-hundred freestyles." Pete's eyes swept over the seven swimmers in the water before he waved toward the far end of the pool. "Go."

Bianca gave a little shrug of her shoulders. Then she dipped down in the water and pushed off to start the new set behind Amber, the only other girl in the group.

Beside Pete, Carina folded her arms and stared after her younger sister. "I wish she'd move that fast when I ask her to do the dishes."

Some of the tension eased out of him, and Pete fought to keep his lips from curving up. "You might try telling instead of asking."

Carina shook her head. "That doesn't work very well either."

He swallowed a chuckle and shook his head as she moved to one of the poolside tables and pulled out a chair. As she did each morning, she pulled her laptop out of her sleek computer bag and started tapping away on the keys.

He didn't know much about the Channing girls' living situation, except that Carina had been granted custody of her two younger sisters at some point before they had shown up on his pool deck. The middle sister, Gianna, had returned to college shortly after the girls had moved from Phoenix to Miami, leaving Carina alone to care for sixteen-year-old Bianca.

Pete hadn't expected to get to know Carina any better than the rest of his swimmers' families, but over the past few months, he had come to realize she didn't scare as easily as most people.

Generally, the parents and family members of his athletes steered clear of him. Personally, Pete preferred it that way. If he was being paid to make these swimmers the best they could be, the least the families could do was stay out of his way and let him do his job. Yet his gruff manners and no-nonsense military attitude didn't seem to affect Carina. She acted like he was the most cordial person in the world, and she always took the time to offer a greeting and some lighthearted conversation.

Pete still wasn't quite sure how Carina had convinced him to take on the responsibility of training her sister. He hadn't planned on picking up any new athletes, especially since three of his six athletes had already competed in the world championships and had the potential to make the Olympic team.

He supposed the call he'd received from CJ Whitmore had been the thing that ultimately swayed him. If it hadn't been for CJ, Pete never would have come back to coaching. They had gone to the Olympics together, swimmer and coach, despite some overwhelming obstacles.

More than once during those Olympic games, he had watched her step up onto the podium to receive a medal. He had stood on that podium himself a few decades ago, but receiving his own gold medal hadn't prepared him for watching his athlete stand in the spotlight. The feeling of awe had been overwhelming, the knowledge that he had played a part in her success.

From that point on, he'd been hooked. CJ had stepped away from serious competition a short time later, but it hadn't taken long before some of the nation's top athletes had sought Pete out, choosing to train in Miami so he would be their coach.

Originally, Pete had planned to work with no more than six athletes at a time to make sure they all received the personalized attention he felt they deserved. Planning three practices a day, six days a week, was a daunting task even before considering his athletes' demanding competition schedule.

Carina's determination and CJ's persistence had ultimately persuaded him to take Bianca on as the seventh. After four months together, he couldn't say he was sorry. Already he was seeing significant progress, even more than he had expected.

Bianca wasn't likely to go to the Olympics, but he was pretty certain he could help her achieve her goal of winning a swimming scholarship to college.

She was starting her fifth two hundred when his phone finally vibrated in his hand.

Pete lowered his eyes to the screen, a sigh of relief when he saw that the text message was from Jay. Then he saw the code embedded in the short message, confirming that Jay was okay. Pete went over the time line in his mind once more. Even though his son would never admit whether he was one of the men who had gone in after bin Laden, Pete was starting to wonder if SEAL Team Six had really been the only SEAL squad on the assault mission in Abbottabad.

* * *

Jay struggled to surface from the edges of the dream. He was standing in the hallway in bin Laden's compound, his finger on the trigger as he prepared to storm into the bedroom. He knew what was coming and tried desperately to stop it. He willed himself to shift his weapon, to keep from firing when the woman threw herself into the path of his bullets.

He thrashed against the lightweight covers on his bed, twisting and pulling until he could get his arms free. The woman's face flashed in front of him, her eyes bright with hatred.

His finger pressed against the cold metal of the trigger. He moaned out loud as he tried to stop it, tried to prevent the spray of bullets from leaving his weapon. Then the scene shifted, and he felt the vibration of the helicopter on its way down. He saw the ground coming toward them, felt that falling sensation despite the harness holding him in his seat. They were going to crash, only this time he was certain the controlled landing wasn't going to work. This time the impact was going to kill him and all of his friends.

Another moan escaped him, this one jarring him awake. Abruptly, he pushed himself up, a sheen of sweat on his face, his heart pounding.

It took him a minute to find his bearings in the sparsely furnished room of his apartment in Virginia Beach. His duffel bag leaned against the wall, the same place he had dropped it when he arrived home the day before. His shoes lay haphazardly by the door because he'd been too lazy to put them away.

Jay pushed himself out of bed and made his way down the hall to the bathroom. He splashed water on his face but didn't look in the mirror. Instead, he used his sleeve as a towel and headed for the kitchen.

In contrast to the bedroom, the simple L-shaped kitchen and adjoining living room were spotless except for the layer of dust that had accumulated during his three months in Afghanistan and the time spent training for the bin Laden mission. A well-worn couch stretched along the far wall and was nearly long enough to accommodate his six-foot-six frame. Opposite the couch, a flatscreen TV hung on the wall, and a cherry coffee table sat between them.

A single bookshelf leaned against the wall across from the front door. Framed photographs and a few hardbacks occupied the shelves, as well as five copies of the Book of Mormon, all gifts from his various teammates. He was going to get rid of them eventually. He just hadn't gotten around to it yet.

He considered the irony that the only copy of the Bible he owned was the miniature one Seth had given him shortly after he had joined the squad. Each of his teammates had one just like it, along with their extra set of scriptures. Of course, they all made it a point to go to church every Sunday that they could manage. Jay believed in God, but he didn't understand what the big deal was about belonging to an organized religion.

He ran a hand over his face once more, still struggling to push aside the remnants of his dream. He stepped into the kitchen and pulled open the refrigerator. More out of habit than hunger, he started lining up ingredients. He dumped some spinach, strawberries, and orange juice into his blender. Then he added some protein mix and two bananas before putting the top on and hitting the puree button.

A minute later, he poured his breakfast into the large cup he had bought from the local smoothie place and stuck a straw in it. He skirted the counter and sat down on the barstool closest to where his computer was charging on the kitchen counter. His normal routine was to look over the morning news while drinking his breakfast, but today he pushed the laptop aside.

He already knew what the headlines would say. He had seen them all, even though he hadn't wanted to. *Osama bin Laden Is Dead. Osama bin Laden Killed by Navy SEALs in Firefight. The Secret Team that Killed bin Laden.*

For the past five days, the media had probed and prodded, eagerly trying to reveal the details of the assault as well as the identity of the men who had conducted it. The mission was being hailed a success, but Jay didn't feel successful.

After three sessions with the unit psychologist, he'd been cleared for duty again, but talking about what had happened in that upstairs bedroom in Abbottabad hadn't changed the reality. Bullets from his weapon had killed a woman who was in the wrong place at the wrong time.

The memory of those blank eyes staring up at him still haunted his thoughts, but the images were becoming less frequent. Unfortunately, his memories of those moments before the helicopter crashed were both constant and vibrant.

Jay had told the shrink what he had wanted to hear, confessing some uneasiness about the events that had taken place on the mission, showing a willingness to try to work through the tangle of emotions that wouldn't let him go.

But the nightmares weren't going away, and Jay wasn't sure if they ever would. Of course, he hadn't told the good doctor that or about the fact that he found himself struggling to face each new day. The one thing Jay did know was that lying on a couch talking about the past wasn't going to do him any good. Somehow, he had to figure out a way to care about his future again.

His squad had returned to Virginia Beach the afternoon before with the contingent from the SEAL team that had been on the mission with them, the team the press had dubbed "SEAL Team Six." Their arrival had appeared routine to everyone at the airfield. But it wasn't routine. They were the men the media were looking for, the men whose identities, if revealed, could not only end their careers but could also endanger both them and their families.

A retaliation attack by al Qaeda was a very real possibility, and none of the SEALs wanted to see their loved ones become targets.

Jay glanced at the clock on the wall and then out the window at the early morning light. He wasn't due on base for another two hours. Maybe a long run on the beach would give him the chance to clear his head and help him remember what he was fighting for.

3

CARINA PULLED HER SLEEK LITTLE Mercedes into her typical parking space between a battered old pickup truck and an ancient minivan. She knew it wasn't practical to keep such an expensive car, but it had been her mother's, and she couldn't bear to sell it.

A local judge in Denver had administered her mother's will shortly after her murder, leaving Carina in charge of her possessions as well as custody of her sisters. The economic downturn had erased any profit she might have previously made out of the house, and the real estate agent had told her she was lucky to break even. She had kept the car, however, as well as some of their old furniture.

She stepped out of the car, satisfied that the two larger vehicles would help hide it from view of anyone driving by on the main road. This area of town wasn't exactly known for a low crime rate. The fact that her car had yet to be stolen out of this run-down neighborhood was a miracle in itself, although she had a feeling Lou was the main reason she continued to find her car untouched every morning.

As if on cue, Lou edged out of his apartment, his expression serious. Her grandfather had assigned him to be her mother's bodyguard shortly after Bianca was born. Although Carina knew he had been paid to watch over them, in her mind, he had been the uncle she wished she had. He had always been there to bandage a scraped knee or teach them to ride a bike. More often than not, family outings had included Lou rather than her father. Right after her mother's death, Lou had arrived again, insisting that he stay nearby to keep them safe.

Carina looked closely at him now that he was facing her. His once dark hair was completely gray, his heavy brow furrowed in concentration. Three fingers were missing off of his right hand, a souvenir from his last days working with the family. She remembered too well the day he had shown up after her mother's death, his fingers still wrapped in bandages.

Despite the injury, he had taken care of a number of details during that trying time, ultimately helping her and her sisters sell their old home and move to Phoenix. He was still somewhat secretive about his source of income, and Carina could only assume he was living off of the money he had saved while working for her family. Even though he hadn't held any kind of traditional employment since her mother's death, Carina knew he was still every bit their bodyguard.

He took a step toward her with a pronounced limp and addressed her in Italian. "Everything okay?"

Carina nodded, automatically slipping into the language of her father. "Everything's fine. I just dropped Bianca off at practice, and I want to get a little work done before I go back to get her."

His eyes softened. "You work too hard."

"So you keep telling me." Carina granted him a small smile, noting that his dusky skin looked a bit paler than usual. "You should go get some rest. I'll see you later."

He gave her a curt nod, but he waited until she unlocked the apartment next to his and went inside before he closed his own door.

Carina flipped on the light in the living room and tried not to wince. Even after five months of living in this hole-in-a-wall, she still couldn't quite believe this was now her home. She let out a sigh and reminded herself that this was what she wanted. She wanted to be free of her family and the evil that surrounded them. She wanted Bianca and Gianna to have normal lives and be sheltered from their family's business.

Her sisters still didn't know much about their father or his side of the family. Bianca had been six years old, Gianna only eight, when their mother had taken them to the mall for back-to-school shopping and hadn't stopped driving until Chicago was only a distant memory in their rearview mirror.

Her mother had made their escape seem like an adventure, one filled with promise. For eight years it had been exactly that. They had made a new life in a high-end suburb in Denver, making new friends and ultimately finding a new way of life. As the new kid in school, Carina had felt lost for the first few days, but then she had met Beth Jorgensen.

Beth and her five siblings had lived right around the corner from Carina's new house. Her father was a pediatrician and, at the time, had also been the bishop at their church, The Church of Jesus Christ of Latter-day Saints. The Jorgensens had invited them over for dinner within a week and then to various Church activities over the following few months. When they'd suggested that Carina and her family meet with the missionaries, Carina's mother had been surprisingly willing to listen.

Carina had listened too, eager to find the unwavering sense of peace the Jorgensens had. Bianca and Gianna might have been too young to know about their father's involvement in the Chicago mafia, but at fourteen, Carina had known far too much. And she didn't want to ever be like her father or her uncle. She supposed it was a bit ironic to think that the family of a mobster was LDS, but their conversion had been surprisingly simple.

Shaking her head, Carina pushed aside the images of the past, avoiding the memory of what had brought her here. She was an adult now, and she was determined to stay in control of her own life. She set her laptop bag down on the desk by the window, the smooth leather of the case contrasting against the cheap particle board. A French-style bulletin board hung on the wall beside the desk, sketches and photos tucked into the ribbon that crisscrossed it.

Even though her fingers itched to pick up her sketchpad and work on her designs, Carina dutifully pulled out her laptop and powered it on. She logged into her work's website and started going over the current inventory levels. She knew that scoring a job as a district buyer for a local department store had been a stroke of luck. At only twenty-four, she was the youngest buyer for Classy Deals, a high-end discount store, but the fact remained that she was buying other people's designs instead of creating her own.

Still, the income was decent—enough for her to continue creating her own designs in her free time while also covering Gianna's tuition at BYU and Bianca's swimming expenses. She also had the added bonus of her job being flexible enough to allow her to work from home most of the time. The trade-off had been the apartment, but she and Bianca had agreed. Now that Gianna was away at college, they were willing to live in a dive if it meant all three of the Channing sisters could follow their dreams.

* * *

Jay was on his fourth mile before the dream from the previous night finally faded. He hadn't bothered with shoes this morning, and his toes sank slightly in the wet sand as he jogged along the surf. He passed a woman walking her dog, the little terrier pulling at his leash to try to get closer to

Jay. Farther down the beach, a man relaxed on a lounge chair with a newspaper in his hands.

The rumble of a helicopter sounded in the distance, and Jay instinctively looked out over the water, where he could see it coming into view. He slowed his pace long enough to watch the training exercise underway and saw a squad of Navy SEALs jump out of the helicopter into the surf.

Jay could imagine the jolt of adrenaline they were feeling right then, the shock of the cold water as they sank below the surf wearing nearly one hundred pounds of gear, the sense of satisfaction when they surfaced to see that everyone was where they were supposed to be. He watched as the group of seven started swimming toward the beach together. Jay wasn't sure what to think about the fact that he was relieved to be standing on the shore today instead of being one of the SEALs in the water.

A wave washed up over his feet, and he continued to splash through it. What was wrong with him? Why wasn't he looking forward to the next adventure with his squad instead of dreading it? And why couldn't he get the image of that woman out of his mind?

She had chosen to live with bin Laden, to live with men determined to take innocent lives. So why was her death hitting him so hard?

He had killed before, more than once over the course of the past year with the Saint Squad. The reality that he had taken a life was unsettling, but knowing that he had been defending himself each time had helped him justify the outcome. He wanted to believe what Seth had told him right after he'd shot the woman, that bin Laden and his men had been responsible for her death, that she had chosen her fate. Unfortunately, he still hadn't been able to come to terms with that.

He continued down the beach for another quarter mile before circling back toward his apartment. The breeze coming off the water stopped once he cleared the buildings along the oceanfront, the air becoming thick and muggy. His face dripped with sweat by the time he turned onto his street.

He was nearly to his building when he noticed the two men standing beside their bicycles, both of them wearing white shirts and ties. The fair-skinned, red-haired man was leaning heavily against the side of a building as the other shoved a water bottle into his hands. Even from half a block away, Jay recognized the signs of heat exhaustion.

Though he considered heading straight to his apartment, somehow he found himself walking toward the two men.

"Are you okay?" Jay asked, now realizing the struggling man couldn't be more than about nineteen or twenty years old.

"I think he's a bit overheated," the older one answered. He wasn't much older, Jay noted, reminded of one of the preppy baseball team jocks from his high school days—the kind of guy all of the girls followed but who was too busy concentrating on his sport to take the time for a girlfriend.

Jay read the little black name tag on his shirt. *Elder Smith. The Church of Jesus Christ of Latter-day Saints.*

"You're missionaries," Jay stated simply. He caught the earnest looks on their faces and found himself wondering if any of his SEAL teammates had ever looked this eager. With a resigned sigh, he motioned toward his building. "Come on. I live right over there. You can come inside for a while so he can get out of the heat."

"That would be great. Thanks." Elder Smith gave him a goofy smile. Then he locked their bikes to a lamppost and put a steadying arm on his companion, Elder Thompson. "I'm sorry. I didn't catch your name."

"Jay Wellman." Jay led them inside his apartment and headed straight for the kitchen. "Go ahead and sit down. I'll be right back."

He dampened a washcloth with cool water and then returned to the living room, where both missionaries were now sitting on the couch. He handed the washcloth to Elder Thompson. "Here, put this on your forehead. It will help you cool off."

"Thanks," Elder Thompson muttered.

"No problem." Jay went back into the kitchen to get both missionaries some water.

"We really appreciate your help," Elder Smith told him when he returned with their drinks.

Jay sat in the chair across from them, suddenly aware of the thick layer of dust everywhere. "Sorry for the mess in here. I just got back last night after being gone for a few months."

"Are you military?"

"Yeah, navy."

Elder Smith nodded politely, his eyes sweeping over the room until they landed on the bookshelf. He pointed at the stack of Book of Mormon copies. "Are you LDS?"

"Me? No." Jay glanced at where the missionary was pointing and shook his head. "I work with a bunch of Mormons. They keep giving me those."

Elder Thompson lowered the cool cloth from his face, his color much improved from when Jay had first seen him. His voice was a bit shaky when he asked, "Have you ever read the Book of Mormon?"

Again Jay shook his head.

The two elders looked at each other. Then Elder Smith spoke again. "You really should. There are a lot of answers in there, everything from how Jesus Christ died for us to our Heavenly Father's plan of happiness."

Jay's eyebrows shot up, and he looked at them skeptically. "Plan of happiness?"

"Yeah." Elder Smith nodded. "God wants us to be happy. The Book of Mormon helps show us the way. We'd love to tell you about it."

Something in their earnest faces made him teeter between wanting to hurry them along and hearing if this happiness they talked about might explain that intangible calmness he had sensed in his teammates when their helicopter was about to crash. He glanced at his watch and realized time had decided for him. "I'm afraid I don't have time right now. I have to be on base in less than an hour."

Elder Thompson straightened slightly. "Is there a time we can come back?"

Jay shrugged. He could only imagine what his teammates would think if they found out he was talking to the missionaries. "I don't know."

"Can we get your phone number?" Elder Smith pulled a little notebook from his pocket. "We can call you later, after you've had some time to think about it."

"I guess that would be okay." Jay recited his number and watched Elder Smith scribble it down in his little book.

Both elders stood up.

"We'd better let you get ready for work. Thanks again for your help," Elder Thompson said.

"You're welcome."

Elder Thompson pulled a business card from his wallet. "Here's our number in case you have any questions or if you want to set up a time for us to come back."

Jay took the card and then accepted Elder Thompson's outstretched hand.

"It was good to meet you, Jay," Elder Smith offered as he shook hands with him as well. "I hope we can talk again soon."

Jay nodded politely. As soon as the elders left, he glanced at his watch again. Realizing he was running late, he quickly headed for the shower, all thoughts of the missionaries quickly forgotten.

4

Carina couldn't stop a smile when she walked into the pool area and saw CJ Whitmore standing on the deck beside Pete Wellman. CJ held a towel in one hand and was rubbing at her damp hair. She looked tiny besides Pete, standing almost a foot shorter than him. Not for the first time, Carina wondered how someone with her petite build could be so fast in the water.

Watching CJ chat with Pete, it was hard to believe she had once been in the Witness Protection Program or that she had a collection of Olympic medals in her home. Her unique circumstances had actually been the impetus of how they had met. CJ had been asked to speak at a fireside in Phoenix, the city where she had grown up.

Carina and Bianca had been in the audience that night, and they had been able to chat with CJ at a reception afterward. When Bianca started quizzing CJ about swimming, the ensuing conversation had resulted in Bianca's insistence that she wanted to train with CJ's old coach, Pete.

Carina's smile widened when she got close enough to hear the banter between the former coach and trainee.

"Pete, you can hardly expect me to get the same times now as I did when I was in the Olympics."

"Yeah, but couldn't you have at least embarrassed these guys a little more? I mean, really. Amber only lost to you by two seconds."

"Tell you what. After Amber has had three kids and takes a few years off, we'll have a rematch. Then it will be a bit more even."

Pete shook his head and grumbled. "You and your excuses."

"Good morning." Carina greeted them as she stepped up beside CJ. "I didn't expect to see you here this morning."

"Pete wanted to torment me so he convinced me to come swim against these guys this morning." CJ gave Pete a wry look. "I remember now why I retired from competitive swimming."

Carina chuckled. "I gather he's always been a slave driver."

"Oh yeah." CJ nodded. "And when he coached me, I was the only swimmer in the pool. Talk about intimidating."

Pete pulled his eyes away from the pool and looked down at them. "You know I'm standing right here?"

"Yeah." CJ waved toward the pool. "Why don't you go yell at them for a while? We're going to sit down and talk."

"You're getting lazy in your old age."

CJ rolled her eyes. "Yeah, I'm practically ancient."

Carina pulled out a chair and watched Pete move closer to the pool as his swimmers came to a stop on the edge. "So how are you doing? I haven't seen you at church for a couple of weeks. Relief Society has been so boring without you."

"Matt was on a three-week road trip," CJ told her, referring to her husband, who played for the Miami Marlins. "We've been flying out to meet him on the weekends."

"You've been flying all over the country with three kids? By yourself?"

She nodded. "Yeah, but it wasn't really that bad. Kailey loves to fly, and she can be really helpful when she wants to be."

"I assume Matt must be home now since you don't have the kids with you."

"Yesterday was an off day, and his game is late today, so he doesn't have to go in until eleven," CJ told her. "Everyone was still asleep when I left, but if I know my family, I'll probably get home to find them all in my bed eating Pop Tarts and watching cartoons."

Carina smiled at the image, finding herself a little wistful. CJ was only a few years older than Carina, but she was living the dream that Carina had hoped to find for herself someday. Not that she needed an enormous house like CJ's or a famous husband. Rather, she wanted to find someone to love, someone who loved her the way Matt loved CJ.

She had been to their home often over the past few months, and she was always amazed at the absolute joy CJ and Matt found in being together and in spending time with their children. Carina knew Matt's schedule was hard on their family life, but she had never heard either of them complain about it. Matt loved his job, and CJ supported him completely.

In a way, it was probably Matt's job that had allowed Carina and CJ to become such close friends. Matt had left for spring training a couple of months after Carina and Bianca moved to Miami. Bianca had instantly become CJ's favorite babysitter, and they had quickly started sitting together in church so Bianca and Carina could help CJ with the kids while Matt was out of town.

CJ had even picked Bianca up a couple of times so Carina could attend the singles branch. After only a few weeks, Bianca had insisted that Carina start coming with her to the family ward again. She said she missed having her to sit with, but sometimes Carina wondered if her younger sister just didn't trust her to get to church on her own. Sure, she had missed a couple of weeks when Bianca had gone with CJ's family, but it wasn't like it was that big of a deal. Besides, she would have plenty of time to check out the singles branch again in a couple of years when Bianca left for college.

"It really does feel like we haven't talked in forever," CJ commented, breaking into Carina's thoughts. "How is everything going with you?"

Carina's shoulders lifted. "I was just thinking how weird it's going to be when Bianca goes off to college."

"I can imagine. You'll have to learn how to think of yourself for a change."

Her eyebrows drew together. "What's that supposed to mean?"

"Everything you do now is for your sisters," CJ said, stating the obvious. "You don't date, you don't even socialize unless it has something to do with Bianca." CJ's eyes narrowed as though looking at her from a new perspective. "Do you even have any friends who aren't married?"

"Sure," Carina said automatically.

"Who?"

Carina thought for a minute. "There's Keisha from work. She's single."

"Isn't she the one with all of the piercings and tattoos? The one you said is always talking about partying?"

Carina nodded.

"Then she doesn't count." CJ shook her head. "I'm talking about someone you actually might be friends with, someone you can go out with."

"I went out to dinner with you just last month."

"Carina, going to Chuck E. Cheese's for my son's birthday party doesn't count."

"Of course it counts," Carina insisted, humor lighting her eyes. "I happen to have a soft spot for Spencer and Chuck E. Cheese."

"Yes, well, Spencer loves you too, but I think you might consider going out with someone who's a little older than three. Maybe even someone your own age," CJ pressed. "I heard there's a young single adult event coming up in a few weeks. You could let Bianca come spend the night with me so you can go enjoy yourself for a change."

Carina shook her head. "I don't know . . ."

"Carina, don't you think it's time you get more involved in church?" CJ asked gently.

"I am involved. I make sure Bianca goes to Young Women every week. I go to church every Sunday."

"Okay, but are you really going for yourself?" CJ asked perceptively.

The question hit home. Lately Carina had been going through the motions of attending church. It wasn't that she didn't believe in God. She just wasn't so sure she liked Him at the moment. A sense of unfairness pressed to the forefront of her thoughts. Why had she been forced to put her dreams on hold because her sisters' needs always rated as a higher priority?

Every time she talked to Gianna on the phone or received a text, Carina could tell how much she was enjoying college. And Bianca was thriving here in every aspect of her life. Yet, so often, Carina felt like she was simply existing.

She didn't answer CJ's question, instead turning her attention to Bianca, who was walking toward them. She had her damp hair pulled into a messy knot on top of her head, and she was already wearing her street clothes.

Bianca greeted CJ before turning to her sister. "Hey, Carina, are you ready to go? I have a yearbook meeting this morning."

"Sure." Carina stood up and put a hand on CJ's shoulder. "I'll see you later."

CJ stood as well and waited for Carina's eyes to meet hers. "Promise me you'll think about it."

"Okay, I'll think about it. But no promises," Carina said, even though her mind was already made up.

She crossed the pool deck behind Bianca, but when she approached her car, she noticed the plain white envelope tucked beneath the windshield wiper. Carina pulled it off, prepared to throw it away. Then she noticed her name printed in red ink across it. Curious, she opened the envelope and pulled out the card. A picture of New York City graced the front, a city scene near Central Park. A number was written beneath it: *995 5*. On the inside, there was a simple message scrawled in the same red ink. *Remember who you really are.*

Carina's heart immediately picked up speed. She looked around the parking lot and at the street beyond. Two girls jogged by on a nearby sidewalk. Cars flowed by, interrupted only by the traffic signal at the corner. The parking lot remained vacant, except for the half dozen cars parked there. She stared down at the words again, her mind trying to wrap around the potential implications.

She shook her head, fighting against the paranoia that always seemed to be just beneath the surface. Surely this was just a note from some friend from church, some kind of inspirational message. It couldn't have anything to do with the fact that she was the daughter of a convicted mobster, a man who had pled guilty to murdering her mother.

Instinctively, she reached into the outside pocket of her briefcase to make sure her semiautomatic pistol was in easy reach. She had learned to shoot early in life, but her hatred of guns had prevented her from owning one until after her mother's death. Since then, she had never gone anywhere unarmed.

She looked at the front of the card again, at the red numbers written beneath the picture. There weren't enough digits to be a phone number or a zip code. A sense of uneasiness crept over her once more as she stared at the buildings of Central Park. Could this have anything to do with her mother's visits to New York right before her death? Could this be some kind of message from the family? And if so, who was it from, and what did it mean?

"What's that?" Bianca asked, startling Carina out of her thoughts.

"Nothing." Carina tucked it into her briefcase and repeated the words in the hopes of convincing herself. "It's nothing."

5

"Have you seen this?" Seth asked from across his shared office with Jay.

"What?" Jay unfolded his long, lean body from his oversized desk chair. At his height, the standard-issue variety just didn't accommodate him. He dropped a hand on Seth's chair, identical to his own, and looked over his shoulder.

A news article filled the computer screen on Seth's desk, the headline much like the others they had seen over the past few days. "Look here."

Jay read the sentence Seth had pointed to, and his eyes widened. The article spelled out the organization of the SEALs, specifying their command structure and several acronyms and code words he had never seen or heard outside of a classified environment. Until now. "How in the world did that leak out?"

Seth shrugged and let out a frustrated sigh. "The White House and Congress are so busy playing politics that someone is leaking classified information."

Brent Miller appeared in the doorway. "I gather you've seen the news."

"Yeah." Seth nodded, his expression dark. "Do we know where the leak is?"

"It looks like it came from the top," Brent said. "The White House doesn't believe that releasing code words will have any damaging effect."

"We know better," Seth grumbled.

"Yeah, well, we weren't elected to the Oval Office." Brent motioned to Jay and nodded toward the hallway. "Jay, Kel wants to see you."

"What about?"

Brent shrugged. "I don't know. He didn't say."

Confusion still evident on his face, Jay nodded and headed down the hall toward the office of SEAL Team Eight's commander. Prior to being wounded in action, Kel Bennett had commanded the Saint Squad. It was because of his injury that Jay had received his Saint Squad assignment.

The door was open when he arrived, and the commander waved him in.

"Good morning, Commander." Jay remained just outside the threshold. "Brent said you wanted to see me?"

"That's right." Commander Bennett nodded to the door. "Come on in and close the door."

Jay did as he was told and then took the chair the commander motioned toward. He noted the unusually serious expression on his leader's face and asked, "Is everything okay?"

"I hope so." His eyes were direct, and he studied Jay for a moment before speaking again. "I talked to the unit psychologist last night."

Jay's eyes narrowed, the commander's tone adding weight to his impression that something wasn't quite right. "And?"

"He's expressed some concerns."

A little sense of panic skittered through him. "I thought I'd already been cleared."

"You were, but I wanted to talk to you myself. The doctor can't tell me what you discussed with him, but I've seen the mission's after-action report," Commander Bennett told him. "My guess is that the woman who died is troubling you."

"I'm fine," Jay said a little too quickly.

"No one said you aren't." He leaned forward, resting his arms on the edge of his desk. "But the fact remains that this is the first time you've shot someone who wasn't actively trying to kill you."

Something lodged in Jay's throat, and he remained silent.

His boss studied him for a moment. "How is everything working out for you with the Saint Squad? Are you happy there?"

Confused, Jay nodded. "Well, yeah. I guess."

"I'm just asking since you're about to hit your one-year mark with them. I know they have a different dynamic than the other squads on the team," the commander explained. "I'm getting ready to make some adjustments because of some new recruits coming out of BUD/S training. There's also a guy over on another team who might be interested in transferring into the Saint Squad. Would you like a change, or would you prefer to stay where you are?"

Jay looked at him suspiciously. "You're giving me a choice?"

"A say in the matter, at least."

"I guess I never really thought about being with another squad." He tried to visualize what it would be like to be with people who were more like him, guys who didn't have wives waiting for them at home, men who didn't all belong to the same church. A hollowness settled into the pit of his stomach at the thought of going out drinking with one of the other squads or hanging out at a bar and trying to pick up women. He missed women, but he couldn't say he particularly missed the bar scene.

Slowly, Jay shook his head. "I think I'd prefer to stay where I am."

Commander Bennett nodded, and he pushed to a stand. "I've been over all of the reports, and the woman's death wasn't your fault. The sooner you come to terms with that, the better."

Jay simply nodded and stood too.

"One other thing," Commander Bennett said before Jay could reach for the door. "My wife and I are blessing our baby on Sunday. I've invited the rest of the guys in your squad to come. We'd love for you to be there too."

Startled by the casual invitation, Jay nodded. "Sure."

"Great." The commander motioned toward the door. "Can you let Brent know I need to see him?"

* * *

Carina sat down on one of the two pieces of furniture in Lou's living room, a brown plaid couch he had picked up from a local thrift store. She waited for Lou to take a seat beside her before handing him the card she had discovered on her windshield an hour earlier.

"What's this?" Lou asked in Italian. He pulled the card free of the envelope, his dark, bushy eyebrows drawing together in concentration. "Where did you find this?"

"It was on my windshield this morning. I found it after I picked up Bianca at the pool." Carina responded in his native language and hoped he didn't notice the waver in her voice. "Lou, I was only in the pool area for about ten minutes. At first I thought maybe it was a note from someone at church, but I called both of my visiting teachers and CJ. None of them knew anything about it."

Lou shook his head, considering. "You haven't heard from your father, have you?"

"No. I don't even think he knows where we are."

"Could Gianna have told him?"

"I doubt it. Why would she contact the man who killed our mother?"

"She still doesn't believe he's guilty."

"Gianna only sees the best in people. Unfortunately, the courts said differently," Carina reminded him. "What do I do about this?"

"Nothing. You're untouchable. The family won't let anything happen to you."

"I thought you said the family doesn't know where we are. Besides, if you didn't think there was any danger, why were you so eager for us to move after Dad was convicted?" Carina asked pointedly.

"We moved because Bianca wanted this new coach," Lou insisted. "You know that."

Carina studied him, unable to decipher the older man's emotions. "Lou, why do you always do that? Why do you always try to protect me? I know what my family is like. I've seen what they've done."

His face reddened, and he stood up. "You've seen nothing!"

"I have!" Carina's temper flared just as quickly as Lou's. She stood and faced him. "I may not know everything, but I know what happened in my father's office. I saw the guns and the cash. I saw the government officials who came over for dinner but who were really there to collect their payoffs. And I know what happened when Leone Hamilton came to meet with Dad and Uncle Marciano at our house but didn't leave there breathing."

Lou's eyes widened. "How do you know . . . ?"

"I was there!" Carina shouted. She took a steadying breath. "The cops might think that mob hits don't happen anymore, but I know someone in my family killed Leone and then made it look like he drowned in Lake Michigan. I even know the name of the doctor who got paid off after doing the autopsy."

"How? How would you know this? You were only a child."

"I stopped being a child when I was ten, the first time I saw Uncle Marciano pull a gun on Aunt Clarice for asking too many questions." Carina raked her fingers through her hair and dropped her hands to her side. "Lou, I know you've been protecting us for all of these years. What I don't understand is who you're protecting us from or why."

Lou tapped the card against his hand, his eyes remaining on Carina. "It's enough to know that I'm on your side."

"Lou . . ." Carina began, but Lou moved to the door.

"This is nothing more than a reminder from your past," Lou insisted and handed her back the card. "Don't you worry. I'll look into it."

Carina closed her hand over his on the doorknob. "Why won't you tell me what I need to know? I need the truth. I need to understand how I fit into this mess that I call my family."

"You think you want the truth, but sometimes the truth doesn't set you free. Sometimes it only anchors you in the past." He shook his head. "Go to work and trust me on this, *cara mia*."

Carina opened her mouth to argue further, but she caught the determination in Lou's eyes. With a sigh, she released his hand and let Lou open the door. "Promise me you'll let me know what you find."

Lou nodded, but his eyes didn't meet hers.

A weight still on her heart, Carina walked outside and wondered if she would ever truly be free of a past she barely understood.

6

"WHAT AM I DOING HERE?" Jay asked from the backseat of Seth's car. The parking lot beside the Mormon church was crawling with families making their way into the building, and Jay still wasn't sure how Seth had convinced him to join them.

"You're going to church. The whole squad is here to support Kel. You should be here too."

Jay clenched his jaw for a moment. Ever since the bin Laden raid, Seth had become more insistent that Jay spend time with them. Barbecues and fishing trips, he could handle, but going to church with Seth and his wife made him feel like he was an alien who didn't know what planet he had landed on.

Jay noticed a man in his late twenties cross the parking lot toward them carrying a toddler. Beside him, a pretty blonde cradled a newborn. The man couldn't be more than a year or two older than him, and he already had a family of four. Again, Jay shook his head. "Seth, this is crazy."

"Come on, Jay. It's not like I'm trying to convert you."

"Since when?" Jay asked, sarcasm dripping. "You've given me three copies of the Book of Mormon in the past six months."

Seth's wife, Vanessa, shifted in the passenger seat to look back at him. "Jay, I hate to say it, but he's going to keep giving you copies until you break down and read one of them."

"Look, I just really don't know about this." Jay shifted his attention to Vanessa. Maybe she would get that he didn't belong here. "I know Commander Bennett is blessing his baby today, whatever that means, but I hardly know the commander."

"He obviously knows you or he wouldn't have invited you." Seth pushed open the car door and climbed out. "Come on."

Muttering under his breath, Jay climbed out to stand beside Seth. He looked him in the eye and shook his head skeptically. "This is just weird."

"If you tell me you're afraid to walk into a church, I'm going to be really disappointed in you."

"You aren't seriously trying to dare me to go inside, are you?"

"Whatever works." Seth gave his arm a friendly punch. "Come on."

Jay sighed heavily. Resigned, he fell into step beside Seth and Vanessa and headed toward the double glass doors.

* * *

Carina walked out of the Relief Society room into the crowded church hallway. Four different people had approached her about going to the upcoming young single adults' activity. The more people who told her about it, the more Carina dug her heels in, determined not to go. Couldn't everyone understand that three hours of church a week was plenty? The last thing she wanted was to be hanging out with a bunch of people she didn't know and get preached at.

Associating with the other young single adults always made her feel so out of place, so isolated. They were all so cheerful, their lives so uncomplicated. Sure, she knew they all probably had some minor trials in their lives, but worrying about finding a date for Saturday night seemed pretty insignificant compared to being related to the Chicago mob.

Besides, she was tired of feeling like everyone's charity case. It wasn't like she hadn't dated at all since her mother's death. Admittedly, she hadn't gone on many second dates, but she didn't have time for that kind of stuff anyway. Every time someone asked her out or set her up, she couldn't help feeling like a huge fraud.

CJ knew a little about her past. At least, she knew her father had killed her mother. Yet somehow, despite their close friendship, Carina had never been able to confide in her about the rest of her family.

How would she even start such a conversation? *By the way, CJ, did I ever mention that my father is the top man in the Outfit, also known as Chicago's mafia?* Yeah, she couldn't see those words coming out of her mouth. Besides, the fewer people who knew about her past, the safer everyone would be.

Carina managed to work her way through the crowded hallway until she reached the foyer, where she could at least breathe a little while she waited for Bianca. The anonymous note still on her mind, Carina moved to the window and stared out into the parking lot.

The cars outside ranged from beat-up station wagons to luxury cars, a tribute to the eclectic neighborhoods that made up her ward. Most ward members lived in the beautiful neighborhoods in Miami that boasted mansion-sized houses and private ocean access through a series of canals that led to the ocean. A few members, like herself, lived in the little slice of the ward made up of low-income housing in crime-infested apartment complexes.

She tried not to resent her current housing situation as she continued to search the cars. She didn't realize what she was looking for until she was sure it wasn't there. No dark SUVs, no men who looked like they were fresh in from Chicago.

Lou hadn't seemed too concerned about the note left on her car, and she wondered now if she was just being paranoid. Maybe it really had been from some random friend. Surely she was overreacting to think it was possibly time to relocate again.

Lou's instincts had served them well over the past two years, and Carina couldn't begin to imagine what it would be like to truly be out on her own without Lou around to keep an eye on them. Even though she had, in essence, been taking care of her sisters since their mother's death, Lou's presence continued to make her feel safe.

Carina thought of Bianca and how well she was doing with her new coach and knew she would be devastated if she had to start over somewhere else. She also knew she didn't have the money for a move right now, especially since Gianna had decided to stay out at BYU for the summer. Despite living as frugally as she could, they were living paycheck to paycheck, and Carina didn't see that changing anytime soon.

"Hey, Carina."

She turned to see Matt Whitmore standing behind her. "Hi, Matt. Welcome home."

"Thanks." He glanced around the hall before turning his attention back to Carina. "Where's your sister? I was hoping to catch her today."

"Looking for a babysitter?"

He grinned and nodded. "Yeah. CJ is supposed to be speaking at a fireside tonight and I've got a game."

"I'm sure she can help out. I'll have her give you a call to work out the details."

"That would be great. Thanks." Matt took a step toward the door. "By the way, I have some extra tickets to my game for Wednesday. I thought you and Bianca might want to come."

"Sure, we'd love that. Thanks."

Matt nodded, his face lighting up when he noticed his wife standing outside, loading their kids into their car. His focus already on his family, Matt gave her a quick nod and started for the door. "See you later."

"See you." Carina nodded, trying not to let the happiness of everyone around her aggravate her. Maybe in a couple more years, she could start going after what she wanted in her own life. Maybe then she would get her turn.

* * *

Jay noticed the two missionaries the moment he walked in the door. They weren't the same ones he had met by his apartment, but they were dressed in the same white shirts and matching black name tags. He thought a moment about the plan of happiness Elder Smith had mentioned. They had made it sound so simple. Just believe and be happy. He wished it were that easy.

Prelude music sounded softly as he followed Seth and Vanessa into one of the long pews in the center of the chapel. Jay took the seat beside Tristan and exchanged greetings with him and his wife, Riley.

"Glad you were able to make it," Tristan commented, his arm draped casually around his wife's shoulders.

"I'm glad Kel and Marilyn decided to push off the blessing until you all made it home," Riley added. "They had originally scheduled it for last Sunday."

Jay's mind immediately raced to the events of the Sunday before, the day he'd almost died in a helicopter crash. Riley must have noticed a change in his expression because she leaned forward and looked at him intently. "Are you okay?"

"Yeah," Jay said, trying to shake off the memory. He quickly turned the attention back to Riley, motioning to the hand she had resting on her slightly rounded stomach. "How are you feeling?"

"Really good, thanks." She nodded toward Tristan. "I just hope there aren't any international incidents five months from now. It would be nice for Tristan to be home when the baby comes."

"Yeah." Jay nodded, considering the strain all of his teammates must be under trying to juggle marriage and family while gone so much of the time. Jay remembered vividly when Tristan had finished video chatting with Riley in February, eager to tell them the news that they were expecting. He would be the first in their squad to become a father, and Jay was a little surprised that Riley and Tristan seemed so undaunted by the possibility that Riley might go through the birth of their first child without her husband by her side.

After growing up with a father in the Marines, Jay understood the balancing act required to be successful in both family and a military career. He looked forward to facing that challenge himself someday. Still, he couldn't help but notice the ease with which Tristan and Riley faced the uncertainty in their future. It wasn't that they didn't plan for what was to come, but rather they seemed completely accepting that some things were inevitable and that ultimately everything would work out.

It was that same attitude the rest of his squad had exhibited on the helicopter in those long seconds when Jay had been so certain their lives were about to end.

A man stood at the pulpit in front of them, the music stopped, and the quiet chatter in the congregation ceased. Jay settled back in his seat and prepared to be bored for the next hour. He had only been to church services a handful of times during his life, and most of them had been for weddings or funerals. He was pretty sure his aunt had taken him to mass once or twice when he was little, but he couldn't have been more than six or seven at the time. All he remembered was that it had lasted forever.

The first few minutes of the meeting were somewhat predictable, the man in front making some announcements, everyone singing, and then someone from the congregation saying a prayer.

When the man at the pulpit announced Commander Bennett's baby's blessing, Jay's eyes narrowed when all of his teammates stood and moved to the front of the room. They and a few other men formed a circle around the commander, who was holding his baby girl. The prayer that followed, said by the commander himself, was unlike any Jay had heard before. Rather than some sort of standard prayer, it was one filled with promise, and it appeared to be unique for the child in Kel's arms.

After the blessing concluded, Kel held little Zoe up so the congregation could see her, and then they all returned to their seats. After another song, several boys passed the sacrament. Jay followed his friends' lead and took a little piece of bread from the tray when it was offered, followed by the miniature cup of water.

Jay wasn't sure what to think of the next part of the meeting, which started with two teenagers giving talks. They were surprisingly articulate for their age, both of them quoting from scripture and offering messages of what they could do to be good citizens. The final speaker, a man of about forty, continued the theme, sharing some personal experiences from his military career.

When the man spoke of his own struggles with a mission that hadn't gone as planned, Jay was surprised to hear his conviction of how he believed the Lord had helped him overcome the past and that with His help, he had found understanding and peace. The man's eyes swept over the congregation, and Jay could have sworn he was speaking right to him.

Those memories of the woman stepping into his line of fire pressed at him, but somewhere from deep inside, he found a desire rising up in him to let the memory go, a silent prayer for peace.

It wasn't until the last speaker concluded that Jay realized he hadn't been bored during the service as he had expected. Rather, he had found himself intrigued by the speakers and at times even uplifted. When the meeting concluded, he stood up with his friends, not quite sure what to think of their meetings or how oddly comforting it was to be here with them.

7

CARINA DIDN'T NOTICE THE YELLING at first, the sound of angry voices blending into the normal sounds of the busy neighborhood; her sewing machine drowned out most of the sound. Then the words became loud enough for her to make them out, and she realized they were being shouted in Italian.

Now recognizing Lou's voice among the shouts, Carina pushed back from the sewing machine in the bedroom and hurried to the front of her apartment.

"I told you to leave!" Lou shouted. "There's nothing for you here."

A male voice answered, fury vibrating in his tone. "Don't make me hurt you, old man."

Carina pulled open the front door, immediately assaulted by the hot wall of humidity. "What's going on out here?"

Both men turned toward her, frustration evident on Lou's face, victory lighting the other man's expression.

Her eyes skimmed over the man in the expensive clothes and designer Italian shoes before she looked questioningly at Lou.

The younger man took a step toward her, and she was surprised that Lou didn't stop him. "I didn't expect to see you living in the slums, *bellisima*. You deserve better than this."

She took an automatic step back, studying him more closely. He was around her age, midtwenties, and his black hair was cut stylishly short. She saw the recognition in his eyes and tried to place where she might know him from.

"Surely you remember me, *bella*. Every girl remembers the first boy she ever kissed."

Her eyes widened, the memory of a backyard barbeque flashing into her mind. Nick Baldino had grabbed her hand and pulled her behind a thick oak tree so he could kiss her without their families seeing them. She had felt so special in that moment, knowing the boy she had liked for months had finally liked her back. That had been only two weeks before her mother had made her escape. Carina gave his face another quick study, now recognizing the dark eyes and the arrogance reflecting from them. Confusion and apprehension shot through her. "Nick?"

His laughter rang out haughtily. He closed the distance between them and took her face in his hands, kissing one cheek and then the other.

Stunned by both his presence and the overly friendly welcome, Carina stepped back. "What are you doing here?"

"I came for you."

"I don't understand." She glanced over at Lou to see him glaring at Nick. Her stomach twisted uncomfortably at the knowledge that Nick clearly wasn't an invited visitor. "How did you even find me?"

"A lucky coincidence." Nick waved smugly toward Lou. "I was just asking Lou where to find you, and here you are."

"Why would you come to Lou?"

"Please." Nick sneered and rolled his eyes. "Everyone knows that he kept in touch with your mother after she ran away." He motioned at Lou's mangled hand. "Or didn't he ever tell you how he lost those fingers?"

Carina paled, her eyes darting to Lou's face. He looked down at the ground but not before she saw the truth in his eyes. Luigi Rizzoni, the man who had always been like a treasured uncle to her, had been tortured by her family and had still protected them. She didn't have to ask to know that Nick had been there when it happened.

"Tell me why you're here, Nick," Carina demanded with a deceptively calm voice.

"Your father sent me."

"My father and I aren't exactly on speaking terms. What does he want?"

"He's worried about you." Nick seemed to struggle for the right words. "He expressed concern that some of his former clients might try to hurt you to get to him."

Disbelief filled her voice, overshadowing her anxiety. "And you're here to protect me?"

"I'm here to bring you home," he stated simply. "It's time for you and your sisters to come back to Chicago."

Before she could respond, Lou stepped forward. "They aren't going anywhere with you!"

"I already told you, old man, stay out of this. It isn't your concern."

"The devil it isn't!" Lou took another step.

Carina stepped between the two men. She shot a placating look at Lou before turning to address Nick. "I appreciate your concern, but I can take care of myself."

"You don't know these people. You don't know what they are capable of." Nick's words carried a hard edge of truth. "Your father can't protect you now, so he sent me."

"Tell me this, Nick. How long did it take you to find me?" Carina asked perceptively. "My father has been in prison for two years."

He looked over her shoulder. "We didn't realize how serious the threats were until recently."

"You know, you never were a very good liar," Carina told him, remembering the way he had broken her fourteen-year-old heart. She had believed him when he'd told her she was the only girl for him. Then he had broken up with her only a day after that first kiss so he could go out with Liliana Minimi. She put a hand on his chest and nudged him back. "Go back to Chicago, Nick. I can take care of myself."

Nick stared down at her for a moment and then shook his head. "You think you can take care of yourself, but this time you're wrong."

Carina pointed at the shiny black Jaguar that obviously belonged to him. "Nick. Leave."

He took a step back and shot her a cocky smile. "You'll change your mind." Before Carina or Lou could protest any further, he climbed into his car and pulled out of the parking lot.

"I'm sorry, Carina. I don't know how he found me."

"It doesn't matter, and you have nothing to be sorry for."

Lou stared after Nick for a moment before turning his attention back to Carina. "Maybe we should move again."

"What?"

"I know you and Bianca like it here, but if there really is a threat against you, we may have to leave."

"You've always said the family would protect us no matter what. I believe that." Carina reached for his damaged hand, lifting it so she could see the evidence of where his fingers had been brutally and painfully removed. "My father did this, didn't he? Or was it my uncle?"

He pulled his hand free. "It's not important."

It was important to Carina to know the truth, vitally important to know if it had been her father who had inflicted such pain. She opened her mouth but couldn't bring herself to press him for details. Instead, she said, "You said my family thought you betrayed them, that that was why you left."

"The past is the past."

"Yes, but I need to understand it," Carina insisted. "I'm not like Bianca and Gianna. I've seen what my father is capable of. I know how dangerous he is." She hesitated and looked up at him, her eyes pleading. "What I don't know is how my mother managed to escape the family or where the money came from for all those years."

"The money?"

She waved toward her apartment. "I may not have been astute enough when I was growing up to wonder how my mother was able to raise us in such a nice neighborhood or pay for my college tuition, but I know now that someone was supporting us. She never had a job, and I know my father didn't know where we were."

Lou lifted his good hand to her cheek. "Leave it alone, *cara mia*. Just leave it alone."

* * *

The scent of hamburgers and hot dogs on the grill caught in the light breeze that brought with it a taste of the sea. Jay hadn't expected to be invited to the commander's house for the celebration following his daughter's blessing. Yet somehow he had ended up on Kel's back deck with the rest of his teammates, staring out at the water that edged Kel's property.

The inlet was calm; docks stretched out into it from the backyards of the various houses that bordered it. A sweet little speedboat was tethered to the long wooden dock at the edge of Kel's yard, and Jay found himself wondering how often Kel got the opportunity to take it out.

At the grill, Kel flipped the burgers and then turned his attention to the five men ranged behind him. "I talked to Admiral Mantiquez Friday afternoon. He's a little concerned with the media attention that's still following your last mission."

"It's not like we can do anything about it," Brent said with a shrug. "The attention will die down eventually."

Kel nodded. "I agree, but running training missions in Virginia Beach while the press is swarming could cause us some trouble. The last thing we need is to have them catch one of you on camera."

"What do you suggest?" Brent asked.

"Two weeks off," Kel said. "If we get lucky, this media frenzy will die down by the end of it. If not, I'll look into scheduling some training at one of the other bases for a few weeks to keep you out of the spotlight."

"I could handle a couple of weeks off," Tristan said with a lazy grin.

"Well, you've got them." Kel picked up a pair of tongs and started transferring hot dogs from the grill to a plate. "Starting tomorrow, you're all on leave."

* * *

"This is going to be more complicated than I thought," Nick said warily into his cell phone. "Not only did Carina not want to come home to Chicago, but Lou is living right next door to her."

"He has been a thorn in my side for years," Frank Tesan grumbled. "Does she know her father sent you?"

"Yeah, but she said she hasn't talked to him in years." Nick nodded to his empty hotel room, considering for a moment that his temporary living space was probably twice the size of Carina's dumpy apartment. "Any more news on the package you're looking for?"

"Nothing."

"What do you want me to do now?"

"Keep an eye on things down there. See if you can intercept the package. If it doesn't show up in the next couple of days, try again," Frank told him. "Carina will listen to reason eventually."

* * *

"What's going on?" Bianca asked Carina as they walked across the pool parking lot under the early afternoon sun.

"I don't know what you're talking about," Carina said and continued walking. She had considered herself beyond lucky that Bianca had already left to babysit before Nick had shown up, but she should have known Bianca would notice something was wrong. She always noticed everything.

Bianca grabbed her sister's arm, forcing her to stop and face her. Her blue eyes looked just like their mother's, her red hair cascading past her shoulders. Carina was surprised that the boys hadn't already started circling, but she supposed her sister's single-mindedness about swimming probably kept most people at arm's length.

"Tell me what's going on," Bianca demanded, shifting to block Carina's path. "You've stayed through every one of my practices for the past two days, and you never drive straight here anymore from our apartment. When I'm not at school or at the Whitmores' babysitting, Lou is at our apartment watching me like I'm still five years old."

Carina thought of the mysterious note left on her car last week and was now convinced Nick had placed it there. Playing down her concerns, she gave Bianca a condensed version of recent events. "I just had a visitor recently who I hadn't expected to see. I don't want you to be alone until I'm sure he's really gone."

"Who is he?"

"Just a guy." Carina motioned to where Pete was standing, the other swimmers already stretching on the deck. "Go on. You're going to be late."

"I think you worry too much about me." Bianca shifted the swim bag hanging from her shoulder.

"That's my job."

A touch of sadness illuminated Bianca's eyes. Her voice lowered slightly. "It shouldn't be."

Before Carina could respond, Bianca had started toward the pool deck. That's when Carina saw the flash of black, the sleek sports car cruising slowly past them. Her eyes narrowed as she tried to make out the driver behind the tinted windows. Was it her imagination, or did the car slow down for a moment before continuing down the road?

A sigh of relief escaped her when the car stopped a half block later and a man emerged from the adjoining building and climbed into the passenger side. Carina willed her heartbeat to slow back to its normal rhythm.

She was losing it. There was no other explanation for this paranoia she'd been experiencing lately. The note on her windshield had kicked her fears into high gear, and Nick's arrival certainly hadn't helped things any. Even though she hadn't seen him since he'd driven off Sunday afternoon, she was looking for him around every corner.

For the past two days, she had taken the long way to the pool, afraid that he might be waiting somewhere nearby in an attempt to follow her. Obviously her excuses that she had to run random errands each day hadn't fooled Bianca for a minute.

Her cell phone buzzed, and she pulled it free of her laptop bag to see a text message from Gianna. Summer semester had barely started, and already she was asking for more money. Carina just shook her head, instantly calculating how she was going to come up with the two hundred dollars for the textbook Gianna apparently needed for her Italian class.

Carina texted her back, telling her to charge it to her school account. As she was slipping the phone back into her bag, she heard the rumble of a car engine. Her heart jumped into her throat as she turned to see the car pulling into the parking lot. She relaxed slightly when she saw a beat-up coupe instead of Nick's sleek Jaguar.

Turning away from the new arrival, she started toward the pool and took a steadying breath. This was a new day, Nick was nowhere in sight, and she had work to do.

8

JAY STRODE TOWARD THE POOL, a towel slung over his shoulders, a pair of goggles in his hand. When Commander Bennett had given his squad two weeks off, the decision to visit his parents in Miami had been instant, as had his plan to surprise them.

He had driven as far as Jacksonville on Monday and had decided to spend the night at a local campground before continuing on. Not only had it made sense to break up the fifteen-hour drive, but he also knew that surprising his parents at two in the morning wouldn't go over very well. His father was notorious for keeping a loaded gun in his bedside table.

He had stopped by his parents' house long enough to drop off his gear and change into a swimsuit. He had planned to visit with his mom for a while but discovered the house empty. He wasn't sure why his mom wasn't home, but he knew exactly where to find his dad. Just the thought of squaring off with his father lifted some of the weight Jay'd been carrying for the past nine days.

Retired marine colonel Pete Wellman was gruff, impatient, and demanding. And his heart was pure gold. Those who took the time to see beyond the stern exterior knew he had a wicked sense of humor and a deep love for the three most important things in his life: his family, swimming, and the Corps.

Swimming was his focus at the moment. Jay caught a glimpse of his father, his graying hair cut military short, even though he had retired from the Marines several years earlier. He was still long and lean, no doubt from the five-mile runs he still imposed on himself every morning. And his voice still carried an edge when he was annoyed.

"Danny, if I'd wanted you to do a two hundred for warm-up, I'd have told you to do a two hundred. Now get off the wall and finish. And no lazy flip turns either. You can be lazy on your own time."

The teenager Pete had clearly been yelling at shot him a dopey grin. "Okay, Coach."

Jay dropped his bag on a lounge chair, his attention caught briefly by the stunning brunette sitting at a nearby table. She was dressed in street clothes, if you could call the tailored button-up and flippy little skirt street clothes, but she was definitely too young to be one of the swimmers' parents. If he had to guess, he figured she was a couple of years younger than him, maybe twenty-four or twenty-five. She was tapping away on her little laptop, only glancing up at him for a brief moment as he walked by.

She was even prettier up close, dark eyes framed by even darker eyelashes. Her hair was cut short, styled to accent high cheekbones. Her wary expression made him wonder if she was leery of strangers in general or if it was just him. His dad's voice interrupted his thoughts, and he shifted his attention back to his reason for coming.

"Go," Pete ordered Danny.

Jay stepped up beside his father, his voice deceptively casual. "Still never satisfied, I see."

"Well, I'll be." Surprise and a faint smile lit Pete's face. "When did you get into town?"

"Just a little while ago." Jay turned toward his father, who immediately encompassed him in a bear hug.

Pete motioned to the clock on the wall. "You know practice started five minutes ago."

"Yeah, that's what I heard." Casually, Jay lifted his arms high above his head, slowly stretching the muscles through his back and shoulders. "But you know I need a few minutes to stretch."

Pete chuckled. "You'd stretch for an entire practice if I let you." He waved toward the pool. "Well, go on. Get in."

"What lane do you want me in?"

"How about getting in behind Danny? He could use someone reminding him that if he slows down, someone might just run him over."

Jay grinned. He pulled the towel that was still hanging around his neck and tossed it over his dad's shoulder. After stretching for another minute, because he really did need to work the knots out of his shoulders, he slipped on his goggles and dove into the pool.

The water closed around him, cool and refreshing. The sense of freedom contrasted with the images that still lurked in the corners of his mind. A few dolphin kicks, a breakout freestyle stroke as he surfaced, and he managed to find a name for this forgotten sensation flowing through him—home. He was finally home.

* * *

Carina was trying not to stare. The new arrival cut through the water gracefully, if the term *graceful* could be applied to a man like him. He was tall, a couple of inches taller than Pete, his dark hair cut short like several of the other swimmers in the water. He had a swimmer's body: long, lean muscles, with broad shoulders that tapered down to a narrow waist.

His stride when he walked by was confident, almost cocky. She could only assume he knew he looked a little too perfect to be real and probably had an inflated ego as a result.

She only caught a brief glimpse of his face when he walked by. She wasn't really interested in who he was as long as he wasn't Nick. Then she had heard Pete laugh. Out loud.

In the five months she had known Pete, she hadn't ever heard that sound. Not once. Oh, sure, she caught him on the verge of smiling sometimes. In fact, she deliberately tried to put that expression on his face. Some kind of challenge, she supposed. But this guy showed up, and in fewer than thirty seconds, he had Pete grinning *and* laughing.

Still curious, she continued to watch him as he finished his warm-up and came to a stop at the wall. Several of the swimmers greeted him with surprised enthusiasm, as though he were their long-lost best friend who had finally come home. Maybe he was, Carina considered. He looked too old to be a college student home for summer break, but she supposed he could have started a couple of years late.

Pete broke up the reunion and started barking out orders for their next set. The newcomer looked up at Pete, an easy grin on his face. Then his gaze shifted, and his eyes met hers. The intensity she saw there was unexpected, a complete deviation from his otherwise easy manner. She felt her cheeks grow warm and quickly diverted her eyes back to her computer screen.

She didn't have time for silly distractions. She had work to do and tuition to pay. It didn't matter to her who this guy was. Obviously, if Pete was that comfortable with him, he must be safe.

Carina shook her head slightly, annoyed at the way she always summed up new people as though she were conducting some sort of threat assessment.

Maybe someday she would stop looking over her shoulder. Maybe a day would come when life was all about the future instead of running from the past.

* * *

One practice with Jay Wellman was all it took for Bianca to decide he was perfect for her oldest sister. Carina was way too serious all the time, and she needed to start going out and having fun. Maybe then she would relax a little and remember there was more to life than working . . . and hovering over her younger sisters.

"So, Jay," Bianca began as she stepped out of the pool beside him. "How long are you visiting?"

"About two weeks."

"Really?" Bianca's lips curved into a smile. "Come on. I want you to meet someone."

Jay looked down at her skeptically, but he let her pull him the few steps to where Carina was packing up her laptop.

"Hey, Carina, have you met Jay yet?" Bianca motioned to Jay. "He's going to be practicing with us for a couple of weeks."

Carina looked up at Jay and gave him a reserved smile. "Nice to meet you, Jay."

"You too." Jay nodded at her before looking back at Bianca suspiciously.

"Bianca, we need to get going." Carina slipped the strap of her briefcase onto her shoulder and then glanced back at Jay. "I guess we'll see you later."

"Yeah, sure." Jay nodded.

Carina started toward the parking lot, and Bianca trotted after her. "You know, you could have at least talked to him for a minute before rushing off."

"What are you talking about?" Carina pulled the keys out of her briefcase and hit the unlock button before looking up at Bianca.

"I'm talking about Jay." Bianca leaned on the passenger side of the car but didn't open the door. "I saw the way you were looking at him."

Carina's eyebrows lifted, and their eyes met over the top of the car. "What are you talking about?" she repeated.

Bianca waved a hand in the direction of the pool, where Jay was standing next to Pete. "The tall, good-looking swimmer you were staring at for half of my practice. You know, the one I just introduced you to."

"You're trying to set me up?"

"Trying." Bianca nodded. "But not succeeding."

"I can take care of my own social life, thank you," Carina said, not sure whether to be annoyed or amused. She slid into the driver's seat as Bianca dropped her swim bag on the floor in the backseat and then took her place beside her.

"Since when?" Bianca asked sarcastically. "You haven't been out on a date for two years."

"I have too. I went out with Dennis Buckner just last month."

Bianca cocked her head to one side and gave her sister a knowing look. "You gave him a ride to a fireside because his car broke down, and I was with you. That's not a date."

"He thought it was."

"That would explain why he's been moping around ever since."

"I'm just not interested in dating right now, okay?" Carina shot Bianca a meaningful look. "Just let it go."

"Fine, but it's your loss." Bianca wiggled her eyebrows and shot her sister a grin. "Jay is hot."

Carina just shook her head and laughed. "You know, eventually you're going to figure out that looks aren't everything."

"And eventually you're going to find a guy who is going to melt away this ice queen thing you've got going."

"Tell you what. You drop this sudden, annoying obsession you have with improving my social life, and I won't ask what you got on your chemistry test today."

Bianca debated for less than half a second. "Deal."

9

"You never mentioned that you took on another swimmer," Jay said casually as he carried his dinner plate to the sink. "I thought you said six was your max."

"It just kind of happened," Pete muttered.

"Those Channing girls didn't give your dad much of a choice," Sandra Wellman told her son. "Bianca is definitely persistent."

"At least she listens." Pete shrugged. "Unlike Danny. I swear if he would put any effort into his practices, he could make the Olympic team with his eyes closed."

"He has to want it, Dad. You've said so a million times. You can't help an athlete achieve something they don't want for themselves."

"Don't I know it."

"Why don't you two go relax in the living room? I'll finish up in here," Sandra said.

"No dish duty?" Jay looked at his mom, surprised. "I thought for sure you would take advantage of having me home."

"Oh, I will. Seems to me, the trim could stand to be painted."

"I get it. You're being easy on me tonight so you can put me to work tomorrow."

"Maybe." Sandra reached up and pulled Jay's face down so she could kiss his cheek. "It's good to have you home."

"Thanks, Mom. It's good to be home."

"Come on and tell me how life has been treating you." Pete led the way down the hall and into the living room then settled into his favorite recliner. "How are the teams?"

"Good," Jay said a little hesitantly.

"Is something wrong?" Pete asked, his eyes searching.

"No, I'm fine," Jay said the words, but even he could hear his lack of conviction.

"Come on, son. Spill it." Pete leaned forward. "I know you can't talk details, but I've seen enough action that I might be able to help."

Jay took a deep breath and let it out in a huff. "My last assignment didn't go exactly as planned. At least my part in it didn't go as I'd expected."

"Collateral damage?"

Jay's eyes narrowed, surprised that his father would make a correct assumption so quickly. "What makes you say that?"

"I saw your workout today. You obviously weren't injured, and you haven't mentioned any concern for any of your teammates." Pete rested his elbows on his knees, and his eyes met Jay's. "Look, I don't know what you saw, but I can tell you this. Put it behind you. Whatever it was."

"That's easier said than done."

"I know," Pete acknowledged. "I saw some things over the years that I had a hard time getting over. Sometimes I even had to get help to shake some things loose."

"You? You went to counseling?"

"A time or two." Pete shrugged noncommittally. "The career you've chosen is demanding. The physical part is easy compared to the mental side of things. Physically, you train for whatever you might encounter. Emotionally, you can't always be sure you're ready. If something's beating down on you, figure out a way to let it go. If you can't, then go get some help."

"I've already done the counseling thing," Jay admitted. "I think now I just need some time to sort things out."

"If you say so, but if you need to talk, I'm here." Pete pushed up out of his chair. "I'm hitting the sack. Morning comes early around here."

Jay's eyebrows lifted. "How early?"

"Four." Pete shot him a grin. "You are going to run with me in the morning, aren't you?"

"I think you're tougher on me than my commanding officer is."

"Don't want you to get lazy while you're on leave."

"No chance of that."

* * *

Carina stifled a yawn as she sat down at her usual poolside table and set up her laptop. For several days now, she hadn't seen any sign of Nick, and she was starting to think that maybe he had taken the hint and headed back to Chicago. She had said as much to Lou last night, but he hadn't been convinced.

A man's voice startled her out of her thoughts. "Do you work all the time?"

Carina lifted a hand to her racing heart and turned to see Jay standing behind her. She didn't know how he'd managed to sneak up on her, but she was sure she didn't like it. And she definitely didn't like the way he was looking at her, as though she were a piece of art and he was trying to decide how she would look hanging on his wall.

Annoyed at the way her shoulders had tensed, Carina willed herself to relax. Her voice was cool and a little distant when she spoke. "Just something to pass the time while I wait for my sister."

"So what do you do?"

"I'm a buyer for a local department store." Carina glanced at her watch. "It's easiest to deal with our suppliers in Europe this time of the day."

Rather than take the hint that she wanted to be alone, Jay seemed to take her response as an invitation. He pulled out a chair and sat beside her. "Sounds interesting."

Carina couldn't say why Jay's presence put her on edge, but something about him unsettled her. The fact that Bianca wouldn't stop talking about him the night before hadn't helped, and she wasn't about to admit that she had caught herself thinking about him.

She wouldn't consider that his appearance had captured her attention. Instead, she liked to believe that any thought she had given Jay was because of the way Pete had transformed with his arrival.

She also had to admit that the contrasts in him pulled at her. He seemed so carefree, so at ease with himself and everyone around him. Except there was that troubled look in his eyes. No one else seemed to have noticed it, but she had seen it yesterday in that unguarded moment before he dove into the pool.

She let her eyes skim over his attire, his plain blue shorts and his washed-out gray T-shirt. His feet were bare. Then she looked up at his face again and noticed his cocky expression. "I doubt you would find fashion interesting."

"Maybe. Maybe not." Jay gave her a half grin. "I do like your style."

Before Carina could respond, Jay stood up and stripped off his T-shirt. That same hint of vulnerability was back in his eyes when he looked down at her again. "Don't work too hard."

Carina shook her head as though she could dismiss him on a whim. Out of the corner of her eyes, she saw him drop his shirt onto a chair and walk over to the side of the pool. She heard a few moans from the swimmers when Pete gave them their warm-up. Satisfied that she wouldn't have any more interruptions, Carina forced herself to focus on her computer screen and get to work.

* * *

Jay pulled up in front of his parents' house and put his car in park before looking down at his cell phone to see the text message from Seth. He wasn't sure what to think about how consistently Seth had been checking in on him since they had all gone on leave. At least twice a day, he received a call or text message from him. Usually it was a *just checking in* type of message, but this one wasn't like the others. The message was too long for a light message, the characters scrolling into a second text. He read through it, his eyes narrowing.

This isn't an attempt to convert you, but I read something and thought it might help. Moroni chapter 7. It's on page 521 of the Book of Mormon. Read it.

Jay shook his head. Seth seemed to think that the answers to everything were within the pages of his scriptures. He started to dismiss it and then thought of the talks he had listened to last Sunday. Some of what the speakers had said made sense. With a sigh, he opened up the glove compartment and fished out one of the copies of the Book of Mormon his teammates had given him.

He opened it up to page 521 and started skimming. The first few passages didn't really make sense to him, but by the time he reached the end of the page, he found himself engrossed. The passages talked of good and evil, offering him clarity unlike anything he had experienced before. He turned the page and continued to read. Then he stumbled upon a passage that stopped him. He read it a second time, slowly absorbing the words: *For behold, the Spirit of Christ is given to every man, that he may know good from evil . . .*

Jay thought of the images of 9/11. He remembered the shock that had rippled through the nation, everyone stunned that anyone would want to inflict such harm on so many innocent people. Then the image of the woman he had shot flashed into his mind. She had chosen to die, he thought suddenly. He had no idea if she had shared Osama bin Laden's hatred for Americans or if she was a victim of circumstance. Regardless, it had been her choice to step into the line of fire, to take the bullets meant for another.

His emotions oddly unsettled, Jay closed the blue book. He heard his father's car pull up beside his and quickly stuffed the book beneath the passenger seat. He wasn't sure why he had followed Seth's instructions to read the passage he'd suggested, but he certainly didn't want to try to explain it to his father.

He climbed out of the car and glanced up at the peeling trim on the house. "Mom wasn't kidding when she said she wanted the trim painted, was she?"

"Nope." Pete slapped Jay on the back. "Come on. I'll help you get the ladder out, and then you can brood about how you're going to get that girl to go out with you."

"What girl?" Jay turned to look at his dad. "What are you talking about?"

"Carina Channing."

"I just met her."

"So?"

"So what makes you think I'm planning on asking her out?"

His father shot him a knowing look. "Because I didn't raise you to be an idiot. Besides, I saw you talking to her."

"I was just talking to her. I didn't ask her out," Jay told him. "For all I know, she might be seeing someone."

"No, she's single," Pete said with conviction. "And she could use a little fun in her life."

"She doesn't act like she's looking for fun right now. In case you didn't notice, she isn't exactly approachable."

"Maybe you need to change your approach."

"You aren't really going to give me dating advice, are you?" Jay winced. "I am twenty-seven years old. I think I can figure out how to ask a girl out without my father's help."

"Carina's a bit more complicated than the last girl you brought home."

"I'm only home for two weeks. I'm not looking for complicated right now."

"Son, trust me when I tell you that anytime you're dealing with women, life gets complicated."

10

CARINA SCROLLED THROUGH THE CALENDAR on her phone and considered whether she could have Bianca catch a ride home tonight with her friend Amber. She had a few errands she wanted to run before heading over to the office, but she wasn't sure she trusted Bianca to go straight home if she didn't take her there herself.

She glanced out at the pool, her eyes landing on Jay. He looked up at her and gave her a lazy smile. He had barely spoken to her after practice that morning, and when he had arrived for the afternoon practice, he had only offered a simple hello. After the way he had made a point to talk to her earlier, she thought for sure he was going to ask her out. Not that she would have said yes, of course.

Determined to finish her preparations for her upcoming sales meeting, Carina shifted her attention back to her laptop. She scanned through the dozen e-mails from various designers, all people pushing for her to pick up their excess products. She caught herself mentally editing others' creations and tried not to be annoyed because she knew she could do better than most of these designers. Instead, she reminded herself that she was lucky to have a job in the fashion industry at all, especially after two moves in two years.

She indulged in her brief fantasy of returning to the Fashion Institute in Manhattan, wondering what her life would be like right now if she were living in the apartment her mom had planned to give her, if she had just completed her master's degree as she had intended.

Pete's voice interrupted her little daydream, and a glance at her watch told her practice would end shortly. She pulled her focus back to her work, putting the final touches on her report as Bianca and the other swimmers climbed out of the pool and headed for the locker room.

She was so engrossed in the latest sales data for accessories that she barely noticed the sound of another car pulling up. Then she heard a car door slam. Her heartbeat quickened when she glanced toward the parking lot and saw Nick standing beside his car, his eyes searching.

Behind her, she could hear the swimmers emerging from the locker room, followed by Bianca's carefree laugh. *Bianca!* Nick wouldn't necessarily recognize Bianca, not unless he saw her with Carina.

Carina quickly packed up her bag, leaving the side pocket open for easier access to her handgun.

Before Bianca could approach her, Carina started for the parking lot without looking back at the pool. She crossed to where Nick was now standing beside his car so she could keep as much distance as possible between him and her younger sister.

"What are you doing here?" Carina asked in Italian.

"I wanted to talk to you. Without Lou around."

"Why?"

"I told you before. Your father sent me here to protect you."

"From whom?" Carina asked. "Who are these former clients of my father's? What are their names?"

"I can't tell you that."

"Then I don't have any reason to talk to you."

"Carina, your grandfather is dead."

"What?" Carina's stomach clutched. She thought of the man who used to swing her up onto his shoulders when she was a little girl, his thick Italian accent filled with laughter. Logically, she knew he had a darker side. She had even seen the way others cowered when his voice took on that hard edge when he wasn't pleased. For now though, all she chose to remember was the good. "What happened?"

"He hadn't been well for a long time." Nick motioned to his car. "Look, it's time you come back. Things have changed, and you need to take your place in the family."

Carina's jaw clenched, and she could feel her face pale. "I don't need to do anything with that side of my family. They're all dead to me now."

"That's not how they see things." Nick stepped closer and gripped her arm. "Don't make things difficult. Be a good girl and come with me. Your uncle can explain everything once we get there."

"Let go of me," Carina said evenly. "Or you'll have plenty of explaining to do after I call the cops."

Nick's eyes darkened, his stance now threatening. His voice was low, even when he leaned forward and spoke with certainty. "You wouldn't dare."

Despite the ripple of fear that crept through her, Carina called his bluff. "Won't I?" She pulled out her cell phone and punched in a nine and a one. She could hear Bianca approaching, her voice filled with humor as she talked animatedly with one of the other swimmers. Urgency filled her, a sense of panic snaking through her as she prayed she could get Nick to leave before Bianca gave herself away.

Nick snatched the phone out of her hand and immediately cleared the numbers she had punched in. Then he looked at her with an annoyingly amused expression. "You've changed, Carina. More than I expected."

"It's been ten years," Carina reminded him, trying to sound confident and casual, fear still twisting her stomach. "Now, would you please leave? Just leave me alone."

"You may think that's what you want, but it isn't." Nick ran a hand down her arm. "Trust me."

"Hey, Carina." Bianca stepped beside her and looked at Nick with curiosity. "Who's your friend?"

"Bianca, you've grown up," Nick said smoothly before Carina could answer, now switching to English.

"How do you know my name?"

"Our families are old friends, from a long time ago." Nick glanced down at Carina's phone and started tapping on the touch screen. Then he handed the phone back to Carina. "There. Now you have my number."

Carina snatched it out of his hand. "Good-bye, Nick."

Nick winked at her flirtatiously and slid behind the wheel of his car. "See you later."

Bianca waited until Nick had pulled away before turning to look at Carina suspiciously. "Are you going out with him?"

"No." Carina shook her head vehemently. "Definitely not."

"He sure acted like you are."

"That's all it was. An act."

"You know, you are allowed to have a life," Bianca said in her straight-forward way. "I'm only two years from going to college. Maybe you should stop worrying about taking care of me and Gianna and start thinking about what you want in your own life."

"I have what I want."

"Please." Bianca rolled her eyes. "Living in a tiny apartment, creating designs that no one ever sees, except when you're wearing them. That's not the life you want, and you know it." Bianca shot her a knowing look and added, "I don't even think you would go to church anymore if it weren't for me."

Desperate to change the subject, Carina noticed Pete heading their way with Jay. "What's the deal with Jay practicing with you guys? Did he used to train with Pete?"

"He's Pete's son," Bianca told her. "He's just home for a visit."

Carina looked over at him again to find him staring at her. She felt her cheeks flush, and when she spoke again, her words were a little sharper than she intended. "Come on, Bianca. We need to get home. I have work to do."

"What else is new?" Bianca muttered and climbed into the car.

Ignoring the comment, Carina set her briefcase in the backseat and slid the key into the ignition. Her little run-in with Nick had put her behind. Now she was going to have to hurry if she was going to be able to drop Bianca off at their apartment before her sales meeting with the area store managers and her boss, the district manager.

She turned the key in the ignition but nothing happened. Her eyebrows drew together and she tried again, her heart dropping when again the engine failed to start. Even though her boss was usually great about letting her choose her own hours, their Wednesday meeting was the one thing that was set in stone. She had to be there.

With a silent prayer, she looked heavenward and tried once again. Her heart sank even lower. First Nick and now this. Today was just not her day.

11

JAY WATCHED CARINA AND BIANCA get out of their car. They were quite a pair, the stunning brunette and the willowy redhead.

"Looks like they're having some trouble," Pete commented after he saw where Jay's attention was focused. When Carina struggled to open the hood of her car, Pete started toward them and called out, "Hey, Carina. Is everything okay?"

Disappointment and frustration showed on her face, her eyes darting to meet Jay's for a moment before she responded. "It won't start."

"Let's take a look." Pete reached under the hood and released the latch so he could open it wide. "You've met my son Jay, right?"

"Yes, we've met," Carina said politely, even though her attention was still on her car.

Jay stepped beside his father. He winced when he caught a glimpse of what was beneath the hood. Corrosion covered the battery, and he doubted the car had had an oil change, much less a tune-up, for at least a year.

"What do you think? The battery?"

"That's where I'd start." Jay nodded and looked over at Carina. "I can try cleaning it off first. If that doesn't work, we can run out and get you a new battery."

"Thanks." Carina glanced down at her watch, clearly distressed.

Jay glanced to where his car was parked a few spaces away. It was the first car he'd ever purchased on his own, a simple coupe he had bought used while he was at the Naval Academy. Still, it was in decent shape, and it could go from point A to point B. "Can I give you a lift somewhere?"

Carina looked up at him, seeming a bit stunned by the casual offer. "No, no that's okay. I have to run a lot of errands before Bianca's practice tonight. I can just call a cab."

"You don't need to do that." Jay fished his car keys out of his pocket. "Here. Just take my car. If you leave me your keys, I'll see what I can get done on your car before your sister's next practice."

Carina looked at him like he'd just told her he was taking a trip to Mars. "Why would you do that?"

Jay shrugged. "Because I can." He motioned to the engine. "Look, I'm pretty good with cars, and it's going to cost you way more than it should if you take it in to a mechanic. If you don't really need a new battery, it'll probably only cost a few bucks to get your car up and running again."

"That's really sweet of you to offer . . ."

"Let me just grab my tools out of the trunk," Jay said before she could finish what was likely to be a polite refusal. He popped the trunk as he crossed the few spaces to his car and retrieved the small toolkit he always kept there, along with a couple of rags. He then walked back to Carina and pressed his keys into her hand. "My car isn't anything fancy, but it's got a full tank and it will get you where you're going."

Pete put a hand on Carina's shoulder. "Go on, now. Jay will take care of your car."

"Okay. Thanks." Still looking stunned, she handed over her keys. "Let me give you my phone number in case you run into any trouble."

She and Jay exchanged phone numbers, and then Carina turned to Bianca. "Come on, Bianca. I don't have time to run you home, so you'll have to come with me to my meeting."

"It's so boring at your office," Bianca complained. "Can I stay and help Jay instead?"

Jay gave a casual shrug, noticing the wariness in Carina's eyes once more. "It's fine with me, if you don't mind."

"I guess that would be okay."

In response, Jay pulled a screwdriver out of his toolkit and waved toward Bianca. "Come on, Bianca. I'll show you how to clean a battery in case this ever happens to you."

"I've got to get home," Pete said, "but give me a call if you don't get the car started, and I'll come back and get you."

"Thanks, Dad." Jay nodded in his direction and then looked up to see Carina still watching him with wary eyes. "Carina, I'll call you as soon as we know anything."

"Thanks." Carina gave him a reluctant nod and slowly crossed the parking lot.

* * *

"That's really all that was wrong with the car?" Bianca asked. "A few minutes of cleaning the battery, and it's good as new?"

"Well, not good as new, but at least it's running." Jay closed the hood and then packed up his tools. "Let's drive over to the auto supply store and pick up a few things. This car is in desperate need of a tune-up."

Bianca narrowed her eyes. "Do you like working on cars or something?"

"Actually, yeah." Jay fished a plastic bag out of his swim bag and stuffed the oily rags into it. Then he looked over at Bianca. "Why do you ask?"

"I don't know. I just didn't expect you to do all of this stuff for someone you just met."

"It's my job to do things for people I don't know." Jay put his tools and the rags into the trunk of Carina's car.

"What's your job?"

"I'm in the navy." Jay pulled open the driver's side door. "Come on. We can swing by my house and grab some dinner after we finish at the store."

"I'd rather go to McDonald's. Your dad is always on me to eat healthy."

"Welcome to my world." Jay chuckled. "And don't think for a minute you're going to get me involved in eating contraband. If my dad found out, he'd kill me."

"Chicken," Bianca taunted.

Jay shot her an easy grin as the weight lifted from his shoulders. "Yep."

* * *

Carina listened to one of the local store managers complain about a missing shipment of T-shirts. Or at least she tried to listen. Her mind was still on Jay Wellman and the way he had handed her his car keys like they had been friends for years instead of casual acquaintances for days. And they were barely acquaintances, at that.

A little seed of worry was still lodged in her stomach, but it wasn't concern about her car; it was concern about her sister. Had Jay not been Pete's son, she never would have agreed to let Bianca stay with him. She wanted to refuse anyway but hadn't been able to find a way to say the words without seeming ungrateful.

"What am I supposed to do about this?" the manager demanded. "I sell dozens of these shirts every day, and there's no way I'll be able to last until the next shipment comes in."

It took a couple of seconds for Carina to realize that the woman was speaking to her. She tapped a couple of keys on the laptop in front of her. "Pamela's store has extra stock of those items right now. I can arrange for an interstore transfer to hold you up until the shipment comes in. I've been assured it will arrive by next Thursday."

The two managers debated for a moment before they came to an agreement. Carina glanced at her watch, annoyed that this meeting was dragging out because of the petty bickering among the managers. Her phone vibrated in her pocket, and she barely resisted the urge to check to see who it was. Another five minutes and she hoped to be out of here.

Fifteen minutes and three minor crises later, Carina finally walked out of her boss's office and checked her phone for messages. A text from Jay informed her that her car was fixed. Another from Bianca told her that she had eaten dinner at Pete's house and that she would see her at the pool.

Carina stared at the messages, amazed. Two hours ago, she was certain she was going to have to figure out a way to juggle finances to pay for car repairs, and now it looked like the problem had been solved completely without any involvement from her. She couldn't remember the last time that had happened.

She climbed into Jay's car and dropped her briefcase on the front seat. The bag toppled forward, her gun and a few pens spilling out onto the floor. Carina quickly scooped the weapon up and tucked it back into her case. She then reached down to gather the pens that had fallen out. That's when she caught a glimpse of blue.

Curious, she reached under the seat and picked up the softcover book. Her eyes widened when she realized it was a Book of Mormon. She knew Pete wasn't Mormon, and she never considered that his son might be a member of the Church. Wasn't that an interesting possibility?

Her cell phone vibrated again. She looked down at the screen and scowled. Nick. He must have figured out her cell phone number when he'd grabbed it from her earlier. The message was simple, almost identical to what he had been telling her since he'd arrived in town. *We need to talk. You're in danger.*

12

"I can't believe you were able to fix the car *and* change the oil before practice," Bianca said as Jay slammed the hood shut.

"I've had lots of practice with this kind of stuff," Jay told her. "If you're ready for practice, we can take the car for a quick test drive before we head over to the pool."

"Sure."

"I'll be right back." Jay walked to the front door, pulled it open, and called out, "Dad, Bianca and I are heading out. We'll see you at the pool."

"Okay. I'll be right behind you," Pete called from the kitchen.

Jay headed back to Carina's car and pulled open the door. "Let's go."

"Are you going to practice with us again tonight?" Bianca asked as she climbed into the passenger seat.

"Yeah." He nodded. "I'm only home for a couple of weeks. I figure I'll give my dad as much opportunity as possible to boss me around."

"He definitely looked like he enjoyed it at the last practice."

Jay shot her a grin. "He did, didn't he?"

He started the car, satisfied that the engine purred smoothly. He backed out of the driveway and asked, "Where to? We have fifteen minutes before we have to go to the pool."

"McDonald's?" Bianca suggested hopefully.

Jay shook his head. "Nice try. Besides, we already had dinner."

"We had a smoothie. With spinach in it," Bianca said pointedly. "I can't believe you convinced me to try that."

"It's healthy, and it'll give you lots of energy."

"It was green."

Jay chuckled. "Which way? You're navigating."

"Turn right. We can swing by my sister's work and see if she's done yet." Bianca waited until he started down the road before adding, "Maybe *she'll* buy me some french fries."

"I wouldn't get your hopes up. If she knows my dad, there's no way she would buy you that stuff right before practice."

Bianca motioned for him to make another turn. "She's not scared of your dad, but you're probably right that she wouldn't get me anything fast food. She's a health nut too."

"What about your parents? Are they like you or your sister?"

The easygoing look on her face faded. Her lips pressed together before she said, "They aren't in the picture."

Jay glanced over at her, surprised by her sudden mood change. "I'm sorry."

"It's okay." She stared straight at the road rather than looking at him. "Turn into that parking lot on the right."

He turned where she indicated and parked. A quick scan revealed that his car wasn't there. "She must have already left. I don't see my car anywhere."

"She might have parked in the back lot." Bianca reached for the door handle. "I'm going to go check. Do want to come?"

"That's okay. I'll just wait here."

Bianca nodded and climbed out of the car. She jogged across the parking lot, returning fewer than three minutes later. "You were right. She's already gone."

Jay waited for her to clip her seat belt into place before pulling back out into the street. Traffic was thick with the tail-end of evening rush hour. Jay noticed a black sedan emerge from the parking lot across the street and take position behind them, but he didn't pay it any attention until they approached a busy intersection and the light turned red.

"It might be faster if you take the freeway," Bianca suggested as Jay pressed on the brake pedal and prepared to stop.

Instinctively, he checked his mirrors to analyze his surroundings the way he had been trained. His eyes widened when he saw the black car and realized it wasn't slowing down. In fact, it looked like the car was speeding up as it headed toward them.

Jay honked his horn, hoping the driver would look up and see the red light, but still, it continued to gain speed. A truck had already come to a stop in front of him, blocking his forward path, but the sidewalk beside him was clear. "Hold on!"

He whipped the wheel to the right, jumped the curb, and laid on the horn in case any pedestrians might be coming from the other direction. Bianca screamed, but Jay blocked out the sound. He focused on the through traffic going the other way, hitting his brakes momentarily before aggressively turning the wheel once more to cross one lane of traffic and merge into the other, narrowly missing the two cars he cut off.

Tires squealed and horns blared. Out of the corner of his eye, Jay saw the black car, now parked crookedly behind the truck. He couldn't tell if the driver had come to a screeching halt when he finally realized that traffic had stopped or if he had been unable to decide whether or not to pursue them. Surely the driver hadn't really planned on hitting them deliberately.

"Are you insane?" Bianca yelled, one hand gripping the door and the other pressing hard against the dashboard.

Jay's heart pounding, he forced himself to slow down to go with the flow of traffic. An angry driver pulled up beside him, waving a fist. Jay assumed correctly that he was in one of the cars he had narrowly missed hitting when he had merged into traffic.

"I think we'll just go the long way," Jay announced, turning at the first intersection.

Bianca's grip loosened on the dashboard, but her voice was breathless when she asked, "What were you doing?"

"The car behind us was going to hit us." Jay nodded back toward the way they had come. "If he'd hit us full speed, I don't know if either of us would have survived the impact."

She blinked twice in disbelief. "So you're telling me that you were driving my sister's car like a complete maniac because you were trying to save my life?"

"Yeah." Jay glanced over at her, feeling a little embarrassed by her analysis. "Something like that."

"I'm not sure if I should thank you or vow to never get in a car with you again," Bianca muttered. "Where did you learn to drive like that anyway?"

"Let's just say that I've had lots of practice." Jay checked his mirrors, taking random turns for several minutes before starting toward the pool. "We should be able to make it on time. No one will ever have to know."

"You don't want me to tell my sister what happened?"

"You can tell her whatever you want. Just do me a favor and don't tell her about it in front of my dad." Jay gave her a cynical look. "He already worries about my driving."

"Gee," Bianca's eyebrows lifted in mock surprise, "I wonder why."

* * *

Carina looked around the parking lot, surprised that her car wasn't there. Jay had said it was fixed, and Pete was already standing on the pool deck. Why wouldn't Jay and Bianca already be here too?

Practice wouldn't start for another ten minutes, but Carina had seen the way Pete looked at swimmers who were right on time. Clearly, he considered five minutes early right on time. *Make that ten*, Carina thought to herself when Danny walked in and earned a hard stare from his coach.

As she approached Pete, Carina did a quick head count to see that all of his swimmers were on deck except for Bianca. "Where are Bianca and Jay?"

"I don't know." Pete's shoulders lifted. "They left the house before me."

"I hope the car didn't break down again." Carina grabbed her cell phone out of her bag and texted Bianca. A little sigh of relief escaped her when an immediate response came back that said simply, *Almost there*.

Sure enough, a minute later she saw her car turn into the parking lot. Bianca and Jay both jumped out of the car and jogged toward the pool. Bianca headed for the locker room as Jay closed the distance between them.

"Is everything okay?" Carina asked when he stopped beside her and dropped his towel and swim bag on a chair.

He hesitated briefly before nodding.

"What was wrong with the car?"

"Nothing a little maintenance can't fix." Jay stripped off his shirt and looked at her. "I cleaned off the battery and changed the oil, but your car really needs a tune up. If you don't mind letting me hang onto it for another day, I can take care of that for you."

"Oh, I couldn't ask you to do that," Carina said, trying to keep her focus on his face and not on his well-muscled chest.

"You aren't asking. I'm offering." Jay nodded toward his dad. "I'm on two weeks' leave, and I can guarantee my dad is not going to let me sit around all day. I'd much rather work on your car than paint the trim on the house."

Her eyebrows lifted. "Let me guess. You don't like heights."

"It's not the heights that bother me. I just hate painting." His eyes sparked with humor.

Carina smiled in response. "I guess if fixing my car will save you from painting, it's the least I can do to help you out."

"Great." Jay motioned to the pool. "I'd better get going before my dad starts his usual rant."

As if on cue, Pete turned toward them. "Are you going to swim tonight or what?"

"Thinking about it."

Carina watched him move toward his dad. He stretched for a minute, apparently waiting for Pete to order him into the pool. Then he rolled his shoulders once more, shed the baggy shorts he wore over his suit, and dove into the water.

* * *

Jay stroked through the water, his muscles protesting a bit at the pace his father was demanding of him. Swimming a mile or two wasn't uncommon for a SEAL, but swimming at sprint pace wasn't expected of them frequently and certainly not three times a day.

He glanced at the swimmer in the next lane, almost expecting to see one of his teammates. Most of them had left town for their two weeks off, with the exception of Seth and Vanessa. An instructor for the CIA, Vanessa had been scheduled to teach a class this week so they had decided to remain at home. The rest of the squad had scattered within hours of receiving the news that they not only got to take some time off but Commander Bennett wanted them to keep a low profile.

He thought of the multiple invitations he had received from his teammates. Tristan, Quinn, and Brent were all heading to northern Virginia to visit their various family members after taking a few days to enjoy romantic getaways with their wives. Amazingly, they had all offered to let him tag along on their trips to northern Virginia, always acting like he wouldn't be a third wheel.

When he had first joined the squad, he had spent most of his leave visiting his old girlfriend in Annapolis, but that relationship had ended when his visits started getting shorter and his deployments grew longer. After seeing his teammates with their wives, he could admit now that while the break-up had stung at the time, he knew the relationship had been destined to self-destruct eventually.

He and Darcy had enjoyed all of the same things, swimming, fishing, sailing. They had also been better suited to be friends. When he had deployed, he had always been so busy, so focused on the job, that he had never really missed her. At least he had certainly never missed her the way his teammates missed their wives. The idea of scheduling time for a video chat or a phone call with Darcy never would have occurred to him, and even sending e-mails to her had usually been in response to one she had sent him.

When he came to a stop at the far end of the pool, he looked up and his gaze landed on Carina. She was a vision sitting there in the evening light. Bianca came to a stop beside him, and he nodded toward Carina. "So what's your sister's story?"

"No story, really. She's just a workaholic."

"Boyfriend?"

"Nope." Bianca looked at him speculatively. "She's pretty good at shooting guys down when they ask her out."

Jay considered Bianca's assessment, noting that it was similar to what his father had told him about Carina. He wasn't sure why she had caught his interest, but something about her, something beyond her cool, classic beauty, had planted her firmly in his thoughts.

He couldn't say exactly what it was that made him want to scale that almost tangible wall she had built around her, especially since everything about her practically screamed *keep your distance*. But for whatever reason, Jay wasn't seeing those invisible walls as a deterrent. He saw them as a challenge.

"Are you thinking about asking her out?"

Jay's shoulders lifted. "Maybe."

"Then you're going to need some help," Bianca stated matter-of-factly.

"Excuse me?" Jay's eyebrows shot up. "No offense, Bianca, but I'm not in the habit of having teenagers set me up on dates."

Bianca rolled her eyes. "I'm telling you, if you just go up and ask her out, she'll say no out of habit." Her eyes shone mischievously. "But I do have an idea that should work in your favor."

Both amused and intrigued, Jay nodded. "Okay. Let's hear it."

13

"WHAT DO YOU MEAN YOU don't want to go to the game?" Carina shook her head in disbelief. "You're the one who's always saying we never get to do anything together and now you're too busy to go?"

"Carina, I'm sorry, but I thought I would have my English paper done by now." Bianca looked at her apologetically. "You can still go without me."

"I don't want to go by myself," Carina said, frustration evident in her tone. "Besides, I don't want you home alone."

"Actually, Amber and I were hoping I could spend the night at her house. We were going to work on our papers together, and her mom said she can drive me to practice in the morning."

"I don't know . . ." Carina started, her attention shifting slightly when she noticed Jay come out of the locker room dressed in cargo shorts and a plain blue T-shirt.

"Carina, go out and have fun for a change." Bianca motioned to Jay, who was now standing by them as he packed his swimsuit and towel into his duffel bag. "Why don't you take Jay with you? I'm sure he'd like to go."

Jay looked up. "Go where?"

"The Marlins game," Bianca told him.

Jay glanced down at his watch, confirming that it was a little after seven. "Hasn't the game already started?"

"It starts at 7:30," Bianca told him. "We were going to go right after practice, but I have too much homework."

Jay looked from Bianca to Carina, his eyes meeting hers. "I'd love to go." He gave a nonchalant shrug. "That is, if you don't mind me tagging along."

"See, this will be perfect. I get to spend the night at Amber's, and you can take your first night off in two years." Bianca beamed at both of them. "I'll see you later. Amber's waiting for me in the parking lot."

Carina looked helplessly at her sister, not quite sure how she had been so neatly maneuvered into a corner. Bianca took two steps before Carina thought to call after her. "Text me when you get to Amber's house."

"I will." Bianca lifted a hand and sent them an absent wave. "Have fun!"

Carina turned back to Jay, looking up at him hesitantly. "Did you really want to come tonight, or were you just being polite?"

"No, I'd love to go," Jay assured her. Then a slow smile crossed his face. "In fact, it will give me something to tease my commanding officer about. His brother-in-law plays for the Marlins."

"Really?" Carina managed a smile of her own. Before she could say anything further, Jay motioned to Pete.

"Let me tell my dad where I'm going."

"Okay." Carina picked up her briefcase. "I'll meet you out in the parking lot. I want to double check with Amber's mom to make sure it's really okay for Bianca to spend the night tonight."

"All right." Jay nodded. "I'll only be a minute."

* * *

Jay headed for the parking lot, feeling rather pleased with how perfectly Bianca's plan had worked. Bianca had confided in him that she was worried about her older sister and her lack of a social life. He had a hard time believing Carina wasn't dating anyone, but he liked the idea of changing that for the next couple weeks. He had no idea if they would even have anything in common, but he looked forward to finding out.

Jay was at the edge of the parking lot when he saw Carina wave good-bye to Bianca as she drove off with Amber. That was when he noticed the man a short distance away, the same man he had seen talking to her earlier. At first Jay considered that maybe Carina was involved with someone after all, someone Bianca clearly didn't know about. Then Jay saw the violence in his expression.

He shot Jay a warning look, one that was obviously intended to scare him off and ensure some privacy. Carina noticed Jay too, apparently still unaware of the visitor. Then she turned and saw the man heading toward her. Her expression instantly changed and indicated that this confrontation wasn't going to be a welcome one.

Instinctively, Jay ran toward them. He came to a skidding stop when Carina reached into her briefcase and, in one fluid movement, pulled out a gun.

She aimed the compact little pistol at the man, her stance as steady as a veteran Navy SEAL on a routine op. The shock of seeing her armed lasted for only a moment and turned quickly into a sense of admiration. Why she was armed and what this guy had done to warrant this display was a mystery, one he hoped to unravel immediately.

He heard the words being exchanged between them, and it took him a moment to realize they were speaking in Italian. Italian wasn't his strong suit, but Jay's knowledge of French and Spanish helped him catch the gist of the conversation.

Carina's voice was defiant, her dark eyes determined when she insisted, "I will not go to Chicago with you."

"You don't have a choice. You're in danger if you don't leave this place."

"No, you're wrong. *You're* the one in danger if you don't leave." She nodded toward his car. "Leave now. And don't come back."

"You're making a mistake."

"Maybe I am, but that has nothing to do with you."

"This isn't over."

"It is over. The sooner you accept that, the sooner we can both get back to our own lives."

Jay watched the man shake his head and then take a wide path around Carina as he made his way to his car. Carina's hands trembled from the weight of her weapon, but she didn't lower it until he got into his car and pulled away.

"I hope you don't have to use that thing often," Jay said casually as he stepped beside her.

Her eyes whipped up to meet his, her cheeks flushed.

"Who was that guy?" Jay asked.

"Nobody." Carina secured her weapon and tucked it back in her bag.

"You obviously knew him. Have you had problems with him before?"

"He's nobody," Carina repeated, a little more sharply this time.

"Sorry. I didn't mean to pry." Jay laid a hand on her shoulder, and his eyes narrowed in speculation. "Are you still up for going to the game?"

She seemed to consider for a moment. Then she took a steadying breath and nodded. "Yeah. Actually, I would still like to go. I'd rather not be home alone right now."

He wanted to know more. He needed details, but Carina's expression was already guarded, and Jay suspected she wasn't about to explain anything to him right now. Reluctantly, he nodded, and they walked together to his car.

Carina handed him his keys so he could drive, and a moment later they started for the stadium. They drove in silence for the first few minutes, Jay concentrating on his rearview mirror and the black SUV that followed them for several blocks. He took the time to make a few wrong turns, noticing the way Carina glanced behind them a few times as if to see if they were being followed.

When he made yet another wrong turn, Carina's eyes narrowed and she asked, "Where are you going? The stadium is the other way."

"I'm just making sure no one is behind us," Jay told her. He corrected his path once more and then zigzagged through town toward the stadium. "Do you want to talk about it?"

She shook her head. "Not really."

Jay swallowed his urge to press for information and forced himself to change the subject. "So how is it that you're taking care of your sister?"

Carina stiffened, but her voice was nonchalant. "My mother died a couple of years ago. I've been taking care of my sisters ever since."

"Sisters? How many do you have?"

"Two. Gianna's away at college right now."

"Where's she going to school?"

"BYU."

Jay's eyes narrowed. Brigham Young University. A Mormon school. "Does she like it?"

"Actually, she loves it there." Carina nodded. "After seeing some of the challenges I had at NYU, she decided she wanted to try something a little more suitable to a Mormon lifestyle."

"Those are both top-notch schools."

"Where did you go to college?"

"The Naval Academy." The corners of his lips lifted slightly. "My dad went to the Academy too. He wasn't thrilled when I chose the navy over the marines, but I think he's adjusted."

Her voice was wistful when she shifted to look at him. "You're close."

"Yeah, I guess. I mean, I don't get to come home much, but my dad's the same now as he's always been."

She nodded, obviously lost in her thoughts for a moment. "You know, I had never heard him laugh before you showed up." Her shoulders lifted. "I can tease that little half smile out of him every once in a while, but that's about it."

"He must like you, then," Jay said, amused. "Most people are scared of him."

"His swimmers aren't. I think they just want to please him," Carina said. "Although I think Danny likes to slack off just to get a rise out of him."

"Oh yeah." Jay grinned. "Dad's demanding as a coach, but no one can argue with the results."

Jay glanced into the rearview mirror and took a couple more quick turns before making his way into the stadium parking lot with the other late arrivals. He climbed out of the car and circled to Carina's door just as she was pushing it open. As soon as she got out, she turned and looked around the parking lot.

"Don't worry. I made sure we weren't followed." Jay locked the car and reached for her hand. "Come on. I think we both need to go inside and forget about everything but the game for a while."

Carina looked up at him with dark eyes and slowly nodded. "You know, I think you're absolutely right."

* * *

Carina let Jay lead her out to his car, her hand warm in his. A breeze cooled the air, bringing a chill to the night. Fans filtered out of the stadium in droves, but Jay didn't seem to mind the people pushing past them. Instead, he appeared to be content to walk at a leisurely pace as though he wasn't in any big hurry to leave.

"Thanks for letting me tag along with you tonight," he said when they reached his car. He opened the passenger side door and grinned down at her. "I was wondering how I was going to get you to go out with me."

"This isn't exactly a date."

"Why not?" Jay stood beside the door, now staring at her with the intensity she had seen a few times before.

"This was just two people going to a game together."

"Then maybe you should let me take you out tomorrow so you'll know that we're on a real date."

"I don't know if that's a good idea," Carina managed to say, even though she didn't sound convincing.

"Of course it's a good idea." Jay edged closer until they were standing only a breath apart. "This doesn't have to be complicated."

"My life *is* complicated."

"Maybe it's time to simplify." Jay leaned toward her, and for a moment, Carina thought he was going to kiss her. A flutter of panic shot through her, and she froze as she struggled against her conflicting feelings.

She found herself drawn to Jay, but the idea of getting involved with someone, of trusting someone, terrified her.

As though sensing her apprehension, Jay simply squeezed her hand and lifted it to his lips. Then, without a word, he stepped aside and waited for her to climb into the car.

He circled to the driver's side, and she tried to remember what it was like to date. Would she ever be able to simplify her life enough to let someone into her limited circle of friends and let herself care for someone new?

Jay slid into the seat beside her and gave her a quick grin that caused her stomach to lurch with a forgotten sense of anticipation and friendship. Carina managed to smile but wondered at the same time if maybe she had misjudged Jay. Maybe he wasn't so safe after all.

14

"WHAT'S TAKING SO LONG?" IMPATIENCE hummed through the cell phone Nick held to his ear as he listened to the other man talk.

"Carina won't listen to reason," Nick said warily, a bead of sweat trickling down his back. "She doesn't believe she is in any danger, and she obviously doesn't have a clue that she's the key to the organization right now."

"And she isn't going to know," Frank Tesan said hotly. "If she finds out about her inheritance, she could unravel everything her family has worked for."

"You don't really think Alex would try to kill her, do you?" Nick asked hesitantly.

"If she receives that package her father sent her, I think that's exactly what he'll do," Frank insisted. "We have to find it and make sure Alex knows she never received it. Otherwise, Carina Perelli is going to end up just like her mother."

Nick gripped the phone tighter, afraid to consider the way the fabric of the Outfit had started to tear, to think that he might very well end up right at the heart of the battle that seemed inevitable. "What do you want me to do? Do you want me to bring the Perelli girls to Chicago by force? I haven't even seen Gianna yet."

"Maybe it's time to make sure they don't have a reason to stay in Miami," Frank stated simply. "Besides her sisters, what matters most to Carina? Boyfriend? House? Job?"

Nick thought for a moment. He hadn't seen any evidence of a boyfriend, and certainly she wouldn't care if something happened to the rundown apartment she lived in. The job was with a discount store. Discount. He shook his head as he tried to reconcile the facts he had gathered with the knowledge that Carina came from one of the wealthiest families in Chicago. Then he considered his first encounter with Carina.

"Lou," Nick said. "Lou is the most important thing to her right now."

"Try reason one more time. If that doesn't work, you know what needs to be done."

* * *

He was back in Pakistan. The acrid smell of spent explosives mixed with the smell of lingering curry from what must have been that night's dinner. A burst of gunfire sounded, and he heard a woman's scream. He saw the door in front of him. The bedroom door in bin Laden's compound.

The scene changed before he could relive the moment he wanted so badly to forget. Now he was in the helicopter, strapped in with his teammates, the message coming over his headset that they were hit and going down.

Jay turned away from the men in the back of the helicopter, instead focusing on his squad. He searched their faces for answers. How could they be so calm? Were they really ready to die? Or did they know something he didn't?   .

The helicopter jerked hard when it impacted the ground, and Jay shook himself awake. His heartbeat was rapid, as though he really had lived through the crash again, but the images didn't hang in his mind as they so often did. He rubbed a hand over his face, rolling over in the hopes of chasing away the nightmare by falling asleep quickly.

He started to doze only to find himself back in the helicopter right after impact. Seth put a reassuring hand on his shoulder and then held out his other hand. Jay looked down at what he held, surprised to see a Book of Mormon resting in his palm. It wasn't like the other ones Seth had given him. This looked like Seth's own copy, the miniature-sized scriptures that he kept in a pocket of his utility vest.

Oddly compelled to take a closer look, Jay saw himself reach out to take the book. The moment his fingers closed around it, the image changed. He was at church with his squad, everyone dressed in suits, Kel holding his little baby girl. Jay turned to look around and felt a hand clasp his. He looked beside him to find Carina sitting there smiling up at him.

Somehow comforted by the image, Jay felt himself settle into a deep sleep.

* * *

Carina sat at the table by the pool and glanced back at the parking lot. She was relieved that she didn't see any sign of Nick and was slightly disappointed that Jay hadn't arrived yet. He hadn't been at practice that morning when she had arrived to pick up Bianca, and so far, he hadn't called or texted to let her know what was going on with her car.

After returning home from their impromptu outing, Carina's thoughts had continued to dwell on the time she had spent with Jay. Except for the moment when she thought he was going to kiss her, Jay had been easygoing and friendly, never pressing her for information about her past or even about Nick and the incident in the parking lot. He had also been surprisingly easy to talk to and always stayed on safe topics like baseball and swimming, his dad, and her sister.

When he had driven back to the pool so he could pick up her car, he promised that he would have it ready for her today. He hadn't mentioned anything else about taking her out again, and she found she was a bit disappointed that he hadn't pressed her to say yes.

She still couldn't believe he was doing so much for her, but with the way Pete had taken Jay's offer in stride, she imagined Jay was the kind of guy who wasn't a stranger to helping someone in need.

She saw her car pull into the parking lot and felt a smile play on her lips when Jay climbed out and headed toward her. He gave her an easy smile as he dropped his towel over the chair beside her.

"Hey, Carina. How's it going?"

"Good, thanks." She watched him strip off his T-shirt. "Is everything okay with you? I didn't see you at practice this morning."

"I slept in." He shot her a grin. "And I wanted to get to the auto shop early."

"Did you find something else wrong with the car?"

"No, you're all set." He reached into the pocket of his shorts and pulled her keys free. "Here you go."

"How much do I owe you for the parts and everything?" Carina asked, preparing inwardly for an amount that she likely couldn't afford.

"You don't owe me anything."

Relief and surprise swept through her. She did some quick calculations in her head and said, "At least let me pay for the oil."

"Just consider it a trade for my ticket to last night's game."

"I got those tickets for free," she told him as Pete glanced in their direction.

"I'd better get in the water." He pulled off the baggy shorts he wore, revealing his Speedo swimsuit covered only by a drag suit. "I'll talk to you later."

He tossed his shorts on the chair with his towel and moved toward the pool. Carina watched him greet the other swimmers and chat with his dad for a minute. Then he looked back at her. Their eyes met, and he gave her a smile that made her feel like she was the most important person there. A second later, he rolled his shoulders and then dove into the pool.

* * *

Jay stretched his arms above his head in an attempt to work the tightness out of his shoulders. Bianca came to a stop beside him and grinned.

"So how was your date last night?"

Jay laughed and let his arms fall to his side. "Your sister still isn't sure she wants to consider it a date."

"Close enough."

"How was your sleepover?"

"Amber's mom actually made us do our homework before she would let us watch a movie." Bianca let out a sigh. "And she made us go to bed at nine."

"You did have a five a.m. practice."

"Yeah, but still . . ."

Jay leaned back against the wall and looked across the pool. Carina was still sitting at one of the poolside tables, her laptop open in front of her. Even from this distance, he could see the way her brow furrowed as she concentrated on the screen in front of her. "How far away do you live from here?"

"Three or four miles. Why?"

He rolled his shoulders again. "Just wondering."

His dad shouted from across the pool to start them on their next set. Jay pushed off beneath the water and considered that maybe he should go for a run after practice.

* * *

Lou sat in his chair facing the window, the parking lot in his view. Nick and his buddies from Chicago hadn't been around for a couple of days, but he was sure they were still here. Even though he hadn't seen anyone besides Nick, he knew there were more. There were always more.

He was still furious that Nick had found the girls through him. He had worried that something like this might happen when they found these apartments. The place they had found in Phoenix right after Donna Perelli's death had been smaller than they were used to, but at least it had been in a decent neighborhood. Everything had seemed to be going smoothly enough until Giovanni Perelli was finally convicted.

The trial had been long and drawn out, Giovanni's conviction not coming for a full eighteen months after Donna's murder. Lou had convinced Carina and her sisters to leave Denver immediately after their mother's death for fear that the family would pressure them to go back to Chicago, the one place Donna had been so determined to protect them from.

The girls had all been in shock, losing their mother so unexpectedly, so tragically. Lou had felt their sorrow. He had shared it.

Carina had understood more than the others, and he hadn't been able to prevent her from attending her father's trial. She had seen more of the dark side of her heritage than she should have. She didn't know everything, of course. It was too risky for her to know what had really happened the day her mother had died, but for now, her hatred of her father was serving her and her sisters well. She knew enough of her family's business to understand the danger, and the loss of her mother had brought out her protective instincts when it came to those closest to her.

Lou hated the burdens she carried now, but unfortunately, that couldn't be helped. When they had first relocated to Phoenix, money had been plentiful enough for him to hire a bodyguard, even though the girls didn't realize the guy down the street was more than just a helpful neighbor.

The move to Miami had taken a toll on the little money he had managed to stash away before all of the family's bank accounts had been frozen. Carina's job had been a godsend, but he felt useless knowing that she was now helping support him instead of the other way around.

He wished he was the one drawing a paycheck, but his age and his health were starting to catch up with him. He didn't want to admit that he wasn't moving as fast as he used to, but he knew it was the truth.

Carina and Bianca had arrived home earlier, but Lou hadn't managed to catch them before they'd disappeared into their apartment. He had been watching for them for hours, worried that something was wrong. The girls hadn't come back to the apartment between practices, and it wasn't like Carina to break her routine without telling him. And even more strange was that a few minutes later, they had headed out again, and then Carina had returned by herself.

It was then that he finally caught her at the door, expressing his concern that she hadn't checked in with him. She had brushed away his fears, certain that Nick had followed her request and was leaving them alone.

Lou shook his head. Carina might think she knew what her family was capable of, but she had only been a girl when she had escaped. She had only seen glimpses of what her uncle was really like.

Lou's eyes narrowed when he saw the tall, dark-haired man jogging toward their complex, and he did a quick assessment. He was wearing shorts and a T-shirt and didn't appear to be armed. The man slowed as he approached, eyeing the faded numbers painted on the outside of each door.

Immediately suspicious, Lou hauled himself out of his chair and pulled open his front door. "Can I help you?" he asked in English, the flavor of the old country hanging in each word.

"I hope so." He nodded and motioned to the girls' apartment. "Is this Carina Channing's apartment?"

Lou's eyes narrowed, and he took a protective step forward. "Why do you want to know?"

"I lent her my car while I was fixing hers, and she left today before I got my keys back from her." He offered his hand, apparently unaffected by Lou's protective stance. "I'm Jay Wellman. My dad coaches Bianca."

"Oh." Lou studied Jay and considered. He didn't look like one of the goons the Perellis normally employed, and if Jay was lying, he was extremely convincing.

Jay's eyes were direct and honest, and he didn't appear to have any ulterior motives. Slowly, Lou nodded. "That's Carina's place right there."

"Thanks." Jay took another step forward, his eyes still on Lou. "I didn't catch your name."

"I'm Lou."

"Nice to meet you, Lou."

Lou nodded and stepped back inside. Then he angled his chair so he could make sure this Jay fellow was really a welcome guest in Carina's home.

15

JAY APPROACHED CARINA'S DOOR, FULLY aware that the older man's gaze followed him. His curiosity was piqued as he tried to reconcile the rundown neighborhood with Carina's shiny little sports car. Surely if she was able to drive a Mercedes, she could afford someplace to live that didn't include bars on the windows.

He rapped on the door twice and listened to the hesitant footsteps approaching from the other side. A moment later, the door swung open.

Carina looked at him, clearly stunned by his presence. A faint flush of embarrassment crept into her cheeks and she asked, "What are you doing here?"

"I forgot to get my car keys from you." Jay could almost see the wheels turning in her mind as she replayed the moment he had returned her keys but neglected to mention retrieving his own.

Her cheeks reddened, and she motioned him inside. "I am so sorry. Come on in, and I'll get them for you."

Jay followed her into the tiny living room, surprised by the décor. Elegant furniture contrasted sharply against the shabby carpet. Tasteful artwork brightened the dingy walls that were in desperate need of a fresh coat of paint. In fact, the whole room looked like it belonged in a model home but had somehow been misplaced in this rundown apartment.

Carina motioned to the brown leather couch. "You can sit down if you want. I'll go grab my purse."

"Thanks." Jay lowered himself onto the couch, his eyes drawn to the bulletin board across the room. Pencil sketches and swatches of fabric were tucked into the ribbons crisscrossing the corkboard. Little sticky notes lined the edges of the board, and more stuck out on the desk. A partially finished dress hung from a headless mannequin, and swatches of fabric were piled on a bookshelf.

Jay had planned this meeting so he could get a glimpse into Carina's life to see if she might share some of the details of what it was like to be responsible for her two younger sisters and just maybe to convince her that living the life of a parent didn't mean she couldn't go have some fun for herself.

Faced with her unexpected living conditions, Jay felt a new sense of admiration and determination. Like Carina, he was the oldest of three children, but he could barely fathom the idea of being responsible for his younger siblings and certainly not if he lived in this kind of neighborhood. He also now understood why Bianca had been so eager to help Carina get out where she might have some fun. He suspected that Carina didn't often put herself first on her list of priorities.

She reemerged from the short hallway that presumably led to the bedrooms, his keys jingling in her hand. "I really am sorry about this. I thought I had given these to you when you gave me mine back."

"No big deal." Jay held out his hand and curled his fingers around the keys she handed to him. "I needed to go for a run anyway."

"You ran here?"

"It's only a few miles."

Carina sat down on the other end of the couch and shifted so she was facing him. "You say that like it's no big deal."

"It isn't." Jay shrugged. "I do a lot of running for work."

"You're in the navy, right?"

He nodded and looked around the apartment once more. "Where's Bianca?"

"She's babysitting for some friends from church," Carina told him. "She's supposed to call me when she's heading home, but it probably won't be for about an hour. Do you want me to drive you back over to the pool to get your car?"

"That's alright. I don't mind running."

"That's really not a good idea in this neighborhood, especially after dark."

As if on cue, a siren sounded nearby, growing fainter as it moved down the street. Jay looked at her, amused.

"Besides, it's the least I can do after you fixed my car."

"If you insist, but I actually had another idea."

"What's that?"

"I thought maybe I could take you out to dinner tomorrow night," Jay suggested.

Carina looked at him warily. "I don't know . . ."

"Bianca can come along too." Jay shot her a mischievous look. "It wouldn't hurt for her to learn to like the food that's good for her."

The corner of Carina's lips lifted. "You mean eat dinner without begging for french fries or brownie sundaes?"

"Exactly." A knock sounded at the door, and Jay didn't miss the concern illuminating Carina's face. "Is something wrong?"

"I just don't normally get visitors, except for my home teachers or visiting teachers, and they always call first." She stood and crossed to the door to look out the peep hole. To Jay's surprise, instead of opening the door, she turned back toward him.

"Who is it?"

"His name is Nick," Carina said, her voice low. "He's the guy who was bothering me at the swimming pool yesterday. I'm afraid he isn't getting the message that I want him to leave me alone."

Another knock rattled the door, Jay stepped toward the entrance, and a shout echoed through the room.

* * *

Carina cringed when Nick called out in Italian, his voice heavy with annoyance and frustration. "Open the door, Carina! I know you're in there."

Jay put a hand on Carina's arm and nudged her farther away from the door. "Maybe you should let me handle this guy."

"Jay, really, it's okay. He'll go away eventually." Her lips pressed together, a little ball of fear curling into her stomach. Even as a teenager, she'd seen the way her uncle had taken Nick under his wing and molded him to take part in the family business. The last thing she wanted was to see what would happen if Nick and Jay squared off for a fight. And with Nick, there was little doubt that a confrontation would result in a fight.

"Come on, Carina. Open the door!"

This time Lou's voice answered at full volume. "I told you I didn't want to see you back here. Leave Carina alone. She doesn't know anything."

Jay moved to the door and leaned down to peer through the peep hole. Carina shifted to the side in an attempt to see through the gauzy drapes covering her window. The two men grappled, and Nick shoved Lou to the ground. Then she saw Nick's hand disappear under the back of his shirt in a practiced move she recognized too well.

"No!" Carina shouted, but before she could react, Jay yanked the door open and rushed outside despite the gun that Nick now held in his hand.

One of Jay's long legs kicked out, knocking the gun to the ground. Surprise and fury melded together on Nick's face, his fist clenching and then swinging toward Jay. Jay ducked and delivered a counterpunch that left Nick groaning.

For a brief moment, Carina thought the fight was going to end with only a single punch thrown. She should have known better.

Nick straightened and steadied himself, his eyes now lit with rage. Jay reached for the gun, but Nick surged forward. Jay stumbled backward when Nick's fist connected with his jaw, but he regained his footing quickly.

The expression on Jay's face was one of determination, and Carina saw a look of concentration there she hadn't expected. He balanced on the balls of his feet like a boxer, his fists clenched and lifted to defend and to strike.

Jay waited for Nick to swing again, countering his move with another well-aimed blow.

"Nick, stop it!" Carina shouted, her attention torn between the two men grappling and Lou, who was still on the ground, his hands pressed to the sidewalk as he struggled to stand.

"Get back!" Jay ordered Carina, but she couldn't move. She could only stare from the open doorway as punches flew, the deadly gun gleaming on the sidewalk at their feet.

Lou finally managed to get to his feet, one hand lifted to his temple where blood was oozing from an open wound, the other hand pressed against the wall as though he wasn't quite steady enough to stand without help.

Jay landed another punch and sent Nick reeling. As they continued to scuffle, Jay managed to kick the gun out of Nick's reach. Hoping to end this madness, Carina started forward, glancing briefly at the car idling in the parking lot.

Even though Jay was facing away from her, he must have sensed her presence. "Get back inside!"

Carina ignored him, leaning down with the intent of scooping up Nick's gun. Then she heard a squeal of tires and glanced up to see the car at the other end of the parking lot veering toward them, the barrel of a weapon visible from the passenger side.

Jay cursed under his breath and moved in a blur. He released Nick and dove toward her. One arm hooked around her, and he shoved her back into her apartment. One of his legs must have kicked the door because it slammed closed as he pulled her into the space between the front door and the window. A split second later, gunfire rang out.

Her body jerked in surprise, surprise from the gunfire and from finding herself plastered against this man she barely knew. His hands were at her waist, firmly holding her in place, his breathing surprisingly steady. His eyes were focused outside where Nick jumped into the open back door of the car a moment before it sped away.

As soon as the car was out of sight, Jay looked down at her, concern showing in his dark eyes. "Are you all right?"

Slowly, she nodded and took a shaky step back. "I need to check on Lou."

Jay followed her outside, one of his hands sliding from her waist to the small of her back as though he was afraid to release her completely. He lifted a finger to where a bullet had impacted in the doorframe, several other bullet holes visible in the wall where he had been standing a few minutes before. Lou was on the ground behind one of the shrubs in front of his apartment.

Jay released her now, abandoning her to tend to the older man. "Are you hit?"

Lou shook his head. "I'm okay."

Jay helped him stand and then looked from Lou to Carina. "Are you going to tell me who that guy was and why people were shooting at you?"

"They weren't shooting at her," Lou interrupted. "They were shooting at you."

Jay's eyes narrowed. "Why?"

Carina looked from Lou to Jay, an unsteady breath shuddering out. Had Nick's friends been shooting at Jay? Had they somehow mistaken Jay for whoever it was that Nick thought was a threat to her? Her shoulders lifted. "I'm not sure."

"Maybe we can sit down and you can start with explaining who that guy was," Jay said as he helped Lou into Carina's apartment.

Carina's instinct was to hide her past and keep the walls she'd built around her and her family firmly in place. Then she thought of the Book of Mormon she had found in Jay's car and the way he had so quickly rushed to defend her and Lou. Maybe he really was someone she could trust. Carina's eyes met Lou's, and she saw his subtle nod. "I can try. But it's complicated."

"That's okay. I'm an expert at complicated."

Carina lowered herself onto the couch, searching for a good place to start. Before she could get a single word out, sirens sounded, growing louder as they drew closer.

16

JAY LISTENED TO CARINA GIVE her statement to the police, waiting the whole time to hear the real story behind Nick and the men who had shot at them. Carina explained that Nick was an old family friend of her father's and that he was trying to convince her to move back home. When the police questioned her about why their "friends" had shot at them, both Lou and Carina had insisted that it was just a scare tactic.

Jay thought of the spray of bullets that had come from the car and the evidence in the outside wall of Carina's apartment. Carina and Lou clearly knew these men, and yet, for some reason, they were protecting them. Going over the incident in his mind again, Jay considered Lou's earlier comment that he had been the target rather than Lou or Carina.

Admittedly, if these men had wanted Lou dead, he wouldn't be breathing right now. They had definitely had a clear shot at him when they had first opened fire. The bullet holes in the wall had all impacted in a line about six feet off of the ground, which was admittedly above Carina's head. Had these men really been shooting at him? And if so, why?

The minute the cops left, Jay turned to Carina. "Why are you protecting those guys?"

"I'm not." Carina sighed and looked over at Lou as though asking his permission to talk to Jay. Lou nodded, his eyes troubled.

"Tell me what's really going on. Why do you think they were shooting at me?"

"They thought you were someone else."

"Who?"

"I don't know."

Jay merely lifted one brow and waited.

Carina let out another sigh and ran her fingers through her hair impatiently. "Nick showed up last week, insisting that I go back to Chicago with him."

"Yeah, I already figured that out."

"He said my father sent him, but I haven't seen or heard from my father since my mom died," Carina told him.

"Why didn't your father just come see you himself?"

"He's in prison," she said flatly. She raked her fingers through her hair again before letting her eyes meet his. Jay didn't miss the way her hand trembled or the way she bit her lower lip as though trying to fight back her emotions. "Look, I'm sorry those guys shot at you, but this really was one of those situations of someone being in the wrong place at the wrong time." Carina sighed. "Nick thinks one of my father's enemies is trying to get to him through me."

"Your father's enemies carry guns?"

"They aren't exactly the law-abiding types," she said dryly.

Across the room, Lou shifted in his seat, wincing in pain. "Carina, after what happened today, I think it may be time to move again."

"Lou, I can't keep running. We have a life here now. Bianca's happy with her coach, and I have a decent job," Carina said with a shake of her head. "Besides, it's not like the family to put hits out on people these days."

Jay was still trying to decipher Carina's reference to "the family" when Bianca rushed inside, her eyes alight with worry. "Why is there a cop car parked outside? Is everything okay?"

"Everything's fine," Carina insisted, her eyes shifting to the woman who followed Bianca inside.

Jay's brows drew together when he looked at the slender brunette whom he knew to be in her late twenties. "CJ?" Jay stepped forward. "CJ Whitmore?"

"Jay?" CJ's eyes widened as she stepped into his outstretched arms for a friendly embrace. "Oh my gosh! I didn't know you were in town."

"It was a last-minute thing. I'm just around for a couple of weeks."

"Well, it's good to see you." CJ looked from him to Carina. "How do you two know each other?"

"I had some car trouble after one of Bianca's practices. Jay was nice enough to help me out." Curiosity was visible on her face, as though she was trying to put a puzzle together. "I gather you two know each other through Pete."

CJ nodded. "When Pete was coaching me for the Olympics, Jay came to practice a couple of times and gave me some competition." Amusement filled her voice. "I never did beat him in freestyle."

"And we don't talk about breaststroke. Those results are still classified," Jay added. Then he glanced over at Carina and considered. "CJ, you still live in the same house, don't you? The one with all of that enhanced security?"

CJ nodded.

"Any chance you would be up for a couple of house guests?"

She shrugged. "I've certainly got extra space. Why? Aren't you staying with your dad?"

"Not me." Jay motioned to Carina and Bianca. "Them."

Before CJ could answer, Carina shook her head and gave a pointed look toward Bianca. "Jay, we're fine here."

Bianca looked at her sister suspiciously. "What aren't you telling me?"

Lou slowly rose from his seat. "Bianca, can you help me back over to my apartment? I think I need to get some rest."

Bianca hesitated, but then she gave him a reluctant nod. "Sure, Uncle Lou."

As soon as Lou and Bianca left, CJ narrowed her eyes and studied Carina. "What's going on? And why *were* the cops here?"

"Someone just shot at us," Jay announced before Carina could respond. "I don't think it's safe for Carina and Bianca to stay here."

"Someone shot at you?" CJ reached out and laid a hand on Carina in understanding, concern visible on her face.

Carina sighed and gave CJ the abbreviated version of what she had just told Jay. As soon as she finished, Jay was relieved to see CJ side with him.

"Jay's right. You shouldn't stay here, at least for a few days," CJ said with a definitive nod. "My house has plenty of room."

"CJ, we can't stay with you. I don't want to take the chance that we might put your family in danger."

Jay's eyes narrowed as the puzzle pieces started falling into place. He thought of Lou's mangled hand. That combined with Carina's words created an interesting picture, one he definitely hadn't expected to find. *The family doesn't put out hits. Father's enemies. Not exactly the law-abiding types.* "Exactly how involved are you with the Chicago mob?"

Jay watched Carina's cheeks redden and CJ's jaw drop.

"The mob?" CJ glanced over at Carina before her eyes fixed on him again.

Carina's lips pressed together for a moment, and she took a steadying breath. "I'm *not* involved with the mob."

"But your father is," Jay finished for her.

Slowly, she nodded. "Look, I haven't talked to him since the day my mother died, and before that, we hadn't seen him for years. My mother left him when I was fourteen, and we never looked back."

"How much does Bianca know about this?"

"Not much. She knows our father killed our mother, but Lou and I have tried to protect her from the truth about the rest of the family."

Jay swallowed the words of comfort that burned on his tongue. "And the truth is . . . ?"

"My family isn't just involved in organized crime in Chicago. They *are* organized crime in Chicago. My grandfather headed the Outfit for as long as I can remember. My father and uncle were being groomed to take over."

"Is your grandfather still in charge?"

Carina shook her head, and her voice lowered. "According to Nick, he's dead."

Jay noticed the combination of confusion and grief in her voice. "You think your uncle is in charge now?"

Carina nodded.

"How does Lou fit in?"

"He was assigned to be my mother's bodyguard when we were kids. He showed up in Denver right after my mother was murdered and insisted on helping us relocate. He's been with us ever since."

Jay absorbed her words, trying to realign his understanding of who she was and where she had come from. He reminded himself that she hadn't chosen her family, that she hadn't asked for this to happen. "Look, one way or another we have to get you out of here. Whether those guys were aiming for you or me, this apartment isn't safe."

"Maybe we should contact the FBI," CJ suggested. "They might be able to protect you."

"Don't you understand?" Carina's voice broke. "The family is already protecting me. Those guys shot at Jay because they thought he was a threat. Bringing the government in will only make things worse."

"At least spend the night somewhere else tonight," Jay said gently. "I can help you get to CJ's without anyone knowing where you are."

"Jay's right. Come home with me," CJ insisted. "Things will look brighter in the morning. Besides, Matt wants me and the kids to go on his next road trip with him. We're supposed to leave tomorrow, and we'll be gone for about a week. You can house sit for us." She nodded toward Lou's apartment. "At least, you can tell Bianca that's why you're coming over."

"Great." Jay pointed toward the bedrooms. "Carina, why don't you go pack whatever you need. We can swing by the pool to pick up my car on the way to CJ's house."

"Why are you going to go to CJ's?" Carina looked at him with a baffled and wary expression. "Besides, I didn't say I was going to stay there."

"You can't drive your car anywhere you might be followed until I'm sure there isn't a tracking device on it. I'm coming with you to CJ's to look over the security system," Jay said, countering her retort methodically. "And you know you don't want to stay here, not until that Nick guy and his friends leave town."

Carina stepped toward him and straightened her shoulders. "You know, I'm not in the habit of having other people decide what's best for me."

"Then make an exception," Jay suggested mildly. When Bianca walked in, he stepped toward the door. "I'm going to go talk to Lou for a minute while you two pack."

"Are we going somewhere?" Bianca asked.

"Yes," Jay said simply and walked out the door.

17

CARINA STOOD IN THE MIDDLE of CJ's enormous kitchen and stared out the back window, where floodlights illuminated two swimming pools and the gardens surrounding them. She had always loved this house, the openness of it, but right now the emotions churning through her were keeping her from enjoying the atmosphere. "You know this is ridiculous, right?"

"I know that's what I thought when Pete helped install all of this fancy security equipment when I was in the Witness Protection Program," CJ countered easily. "And I kept thinking that right up until someone showed up here looking for me."

"CJ, that was different. You were a witness in a high-profile case, and you knew someone was after you." Carina sighed and looked over at her friend.

"Yes, it was different. And I was lucky enough to be able to leave WITSEC after I testified the last time. That isn't typical, but your situation isn't either. What do you have to lose if you start over? Especially if it will keep you and your sisters safe?"

"No one is really trying to hurt me. They wouldn't dare."

"Carina, I know the mob isn't like it used to be. Killing people probably isn't in your family's normal course of business, but that doesn't mean that there isn't some truth to what that guy Nick said about you being in danger. After all, your father is in prison and your grandfather is dead. There's no way to be sure how that might have changed the dynamics of your family and their involvement with the mafia."

"But there's no reason for anyone to come after me or my sisters. We haven't been around the family or their business for years." Carina threw her hands out in frustration. "My mom took us away from all of that so we wouldn't ever have to deal with this kind of thing again. I don't want Bianca and Gianna to think of themselves as daughters of a crime boss."

"But that's exactly how you're thinking of yourself right now, isn't it?" CJ asked. Her tone softened when she continued. "I know you don't like to talk about it, but is there any chance your mother's death had anything to do with your father's criminal activities?"

She shook her head, not to deny the possibility but because she didn't want to consider it. "I've never been able to understand why my dad came looking for us or why my mother had to die."

"I'm sorry, Carina. I know it's a hard memory to deal with."

Carina let out a shuddering breath as she fought against the images of that day, of the moment she had heard gunshots, of what she had found once silence had returned. Her throat closed up as she clamped down on a sudden urge to cry.

She caught sight of Jay and Bianca walking on the pool deck between the traditional backyard pool and the twenty-five-yard lap pool. "How well do you know Jay?"

"I only know him through Pete," CJ admitted. "He was attending the Naval Academy when Pete started coaching me. I've only seen him a few times over the years when he's come home to visit."

"With the way you greeted him, I thought you were good friends."

"We are."

"But you just said . . ."

"That I only know him through his dad." CJ nodded. "Jay is one of those guys who is easy to be friends with. When I first met him, Matt and I were already married, but we weren't allowed to live together for fear that someone might find me. The only people I considered friends at the time were the US Marshalls protecting me and the FBI agent assigned as my handler."

"And you had Pete."

"Pete was my coach, but I didn't see him as my friend. At least not at first," CJ corrected. "When he brought Jay in to work out with me, Jay helped me see Pete differently. I finally got it that Pete cared about me as a person as well as a swimmer. We've kept in touch ever since."

"I can't get a handle on Jay."

"What do you mean?"

"Look at him." Carina pointed out the window. "I'd never even laid eyes on him before a few days ago. But in those few days, he's already fixed my car, lent me his car, and tried to protect me from a shooting. He even came with me to Matt's game last night. Now he's out there checking out your security system to make sure I stay safe. Kind of odd for a complete stranger to do something like that, don't you think?"

"Maybe for some people." CJ shrugged. "I don't know much about what Jay does for the navy, but I do know that he and Pete don't talk about it. I've been around the government enough to know that their lack of conversation about his job probably means he has some kind of security clearance."

"So you think I can trust him."

CJ nodded. "I'm sure of it."

* * *

"What do you mean you don't know where she is?" Frank demanded in a booming voice.

Guido Manchione shifted his weight and hoped his job as messenger wasn't about to get him shot. "There was an incident at her apartment."

Frank's eyes narrowed. "What kind of incident?"

"Nick went there to try to talk to her, and some guy was there."

"Who?"

"We don't know. Tony thought it was one of Alex's men." He hesitated a moment before pushing on. "When a fight broke out between the guy and Nick, they tried to take him out."

"The boys killed some kid who was hanging out with Carina?"

"Tried to." He shook his head.

"Figure out what hospital this guy is in and find out who he is."

"He's not in a hospital. He wasn't hit," Guido said hesitantly. "Apparently, he saw them coming and jumped out of the way."

Frank's jaw clenched. "Find out who he is. And book us on the next plane to Miami. It's time we get the Perelli girls. I'm tired of playing Alex's games."

Guido nodded as he took a step back. Then, quickly, he hurried from the room.

* * *

Jay watched the monitors on the wall and clicked on a button to zoom in on the car turning into the driveway. A glance at his watch revealed that it was already one o'clock in the morning. Despite the impressive security system in CJ's house, Jay hadn't been able to bring himself to leave until he was sure CJ's husband was home.

Pete had volunteered to go to the underground garage where he had parked Carina's car to check it out for tracking devices. He hadn't found any, but he had indulged Jay and followed his request to install a signal jammer. Jay wasn't sure who might be trying to track Carina, but after the incident when he was nearly hit while driving with Bianca, he figured it wouldn't hurt to play it safe.

Jay verified the license plate of the approaching car to make sure it was indeed Matt pulling into the garage. Then he headed down the stairs.

CJ and Carina were both sitting in the living room, and he could see the signs of exhaustion on both women's faces as well as the strain on Carina's. He had to imagine that Bianca had already gone to bed in one of the two guest rooms situated on the main floor.

The door leading from the garage into the kitchen opened, and a man walked in with a duffel bag over his shoulder. His blond hair was cut short, his blue eyes questioning when he spotted Jay standing in the wide kitchen.

"Matt." CJ stood up and moved from the living room into the kitchen. "We have company."

"Is everything all right?" Matt looked at his wife inquisitively. Jay considered how he might feel if he got home after midnight to find a strange man standing in his kitchen. He noted that Matt's expression held concern rather than suspicion.

"Not exactly." CJ nodded toward the living room, where Carina was now standing. "There was a shooting outside of Carina's apartment today. I hope you don't mind, but I told her that she and Bianca can stay here while we're gone."

"Of course that's fine with me." Matt nodded a greeting to Carina. "You're welcome to stay as long as you want."

CJ motioned to Jay. "Matt, this is Jay Wellman. He's Pete's son."

"Good to meet you." Matt dropped his duffel bag on the kitchen table and extended his hand.

"You too." Jay's eyes narrowed as he tried to place why Matt looked so familiar. Then recognition dawned. "Wait a minute. Your dad is Senator Whitmore from Virginia."

Matt nodded, surprisingly unaffected by the observation. "That's right."

"And your brother is dating Kendra Blake, the singer?"

Again Matt nodded.

"And Amy Miller?"

Now confusion flickered over Matt's face. "She's my sister."

"Talk about a small world." Jay shook his head, a look of amazement crossing his face.

"I'm not following. How do you know my sister?"

"I work with her. Your brother-in-law is my commanding officer."

"Wait a minute." CJ shifted to look at him with wide eyes. "You're a Navy SEAL?"

Jay sensed everyone's surprise. He hesitated briefly, his eyes sweeping over to meet Carina's before he nodded and said, "Yeah. I'm a SEAL."

18

Carina ran a hand through her hair, trying not to think about how little sleep she had gotten before the alarm clock went off this morning. She had gone to bed right after Matt had arrived home last night, but even her exhaustion hadn't been able to help her shut off the thoughts racing through her mind.

The memory of gunfire aimed in her direction continued to punctuate her thoughts, as did her newfound knowledge that Jay was a Navy SEAL. Beneath it all was the constant concern that Nick could be right, that someone might really know who she was and be planning to use that information against her or her sisters.

She deliberately averted her eyes from the mirror hanging on the wall in the guest room. She didn't need to look to know that her eyes were puffy from lack of sleep and that no amount of makeup was going to disguise the tough night she had experienced. She probably looked like a teenager with her jeans and T-shirt, her dark hair pulled back, away from her face, but she simply didn't have the energy to get ready for work yet.

She felt like her brain was in a fog as she tried to think through her schedule for the day. With the events of yesterday, she wanted to stay with Bianca through her early morning practice. She had already decided to push back her morning appointment at work so she could come back and change after she dropped her sister off at school. She hesitated at that thought, wondering if perhaps she should keep Bianca home just in case Nick tried to pay her a visit, or worse, snatch her from school to force her hand. Of course, practice could be just as risky.

Maybe CJ would be able to give her some advice on what to do. After all, she had lived through threats far worse than just her family trying to get her to come home. Carina slipped her shoes on and grabbed her laptop case, anticipating trying to get some semblance of work done this morning at Bianca's practice. She checked her weapon, making sure it was within easy reach, and then stepped out of her temporary bedroom into the short hallway that led to CJ's living room. To her surprise, she heard several voices coming from the kitchen despite the early hour.

When she emerged into the living room, she looked across the wide room to see CJ standing at the kitchen counter, serving breakfast to Bianca and Pete. Matt and Jay were sitting at the kitchen table talking quietly.

"What's going on?" Carina's eyes swept the room, finally landing on Pete. "Pete, what are you doing here?"

"Eating." He finished off a piece of toast and pushed back from the table. "I'd better get going." He nodded at CJ. "Thanks for breakfast."

"You're welcome," CJ said before turning her attention to Carina. "Can I fix you something, Carina? I have some scrambled eggs and toast, but I can make you something else if you want."

Carina watched Pete exchange good-byes with Jay and head for the front door before she managed to pull herself back to CJ's question. Rather than respond, she shook her head. "What's going on here?" she repeated. "Why is everyone up so early? And why was Pete here?"

Jay stood up, and Carina didn't miss the silent exchange between CJ and him. "My dad was here to drop off a workout for Bianca. CJ is going to coach her here this morning, and Matt and I were just going over some details for while they're gone."

"Bianca's practicing here this morning?"

Jay nodded. "We don't want you anywhere that your friend Nick can reacquire you."

"Reacquire me?" Carina repeated, feeling like she had just been dropped into the middle of a bad action flick.

"Nick has been by the pool a couple of times, and we have to assume he's still looking for you."

Even though Jay was verbalizing her thoughts, something about his take-charge attitude put her on edge. "I already told you he wasn't after me or Bianca."

"You also told me you don't know why he's really here," Jay reminded her. "Until we know what he's doing in Miami, we need to take precautions."

"What about when Bianca goes to school?"

"I'm working on that."

Carina let out a frustrated sigh as Jay pulled a chair out for her and CJ slid a plate of food in front of her.

"Sit down and eat," CJ said gently. Then she turned to Bianca. "Come on, Bianca. Let's get your practice started."

Bianca grabbed another piece of toast off of her plate with one hand and an oversized beach towel with the other. "Any chance you have some more of those chocolate chip cookies you made on Sunday?"

CJ rolled her eyes and led the way outside as Carina reluctantly sat down.

As soon as the back door closed behind CJ and Bianca, Matt spoke. "Carina, I've asked Jay to stay here at the house with you while we're out of town."

"What?" She shifted to look at him, immediately noticing the concern in his voice. "Why?"

"We're worried about you." He motioned toward Jay. "And I'll feel a lot more comfortable having someone with Jay's training here to make sure no one manages to follow you here."

Carina sighed. "I shouldn't even be staying at your house. I don't want to take a chance that your family will be put in danger."

"CJ and I understand what it's like to know that someone is after you and feel like you'll never be safe again," Matt reminded her. "Jay and I both think you should stay here for a few days to give Jay the chance to do some digging on this Nick guy."

Too tired to argue, Carina nodded.

"Any chance you can work from here today?" Jay asked, motioning toward her laptop case.

"I have a shipment coming into the store in Coral Gables today that I will need to verify, but I was planning on pushing it back to this afternoon. Although with everything that's going on, maybe I'll just see if the store manager can take care of it for me."

"Great." Jay motioned to her plate. "After you eat some breakfast, we can start digging into Nick's background so we can figure out what he wants with you."

* * *

Jay jotted down notes on a legal pad as Carina outlined the players for the Chicago mafia, or the Outfit, as she called them. He was amazed that her memory was so keen after ten years away from that life, but she described family members, neighbors, and friends with detail that would have led him to believe she had visited with them last week.

He also didn't miss the way her voice changed when she spoke of her grandfather. She was trying hard to act like the news of his death hadn't affected her, but Jay knew better. Though Carina clearly didn't approve of her family's illegal activities, Jay could see in the way she spoke of them that her past had contained a decent number of positive memories.

Matt and CJ had left for the airport with their kids almost an hour before. His father had returned shortly after his practice had concluded to escort Bianca to school. He had already made arrangements with a friend of his to cover his early afternoon practice so he could stay focused on keeping Bianca safe.

Jay knew it was up to Carina and him to put the pieces of the puzzle together to figure out why Nick Baldino was really here. He looked down at the list of names Carina had already given him and considered his options.

If he was at his office in Virginia Beach, running background checks on these people would be simple. Unfortunately, research from the Whitmores' home would be limited at best, and most certainly inadequate. He considered his options and ultimately decided he was going to have to call in a favor.

"Out of the names on this list, who do you think would be in charge now that your father is in prison?"

"My uncle," Carina answered without hesitation. "It's hard to say who is in his inner circle right now, but I have to believe Nick is one of them since he's here and says he's representing the family."

Jay nodded and pulled his cell phone out of the pocket of the cargo shorts he wore. "I'm going to see if I can call in a favor to get some background information on these guys."

"Okay." Carina motioned to her laptop. "In that case, I'm going to see if I can get some work done."

"If you need to use the Internet, let me know before you try to connect."

"I do need to use the Internet to log into my company's website." She looked at him inquisitively.

Jay reached his hand out and slid her laptop closer to him. "I'll get you on."

"I think I'm capable of logging in by myself."

"You're capable of logging in so that someone could track your location." Jay nodded without looking up. He typed in several keys, not looking up for several minutes. Then he slid the laptop back toward her. "You should be okay now, but try not to stay on longer than thirty minutes."

"Why? What did you do?"

"Let's just say that if someone tries to track your signal, they'll think you're in Tampa Bay." Jay shrugged and his lips curved up slightly. "Or Hong Kong."

"Hong Kong?"

Jay pointed at her computer screen. "The clock is ticking."

Carina stared at him for a moment before shaking her head and pulling up her company's website.

Jay stood up and walked into the living room before he pulled up Seth's number and pressed the talk button.

"Hey, Jay. How's your vacation so far?"

"Interesting," Jay said, his eyes shifting to look at Carina. "I need a favor."

"Sure. What do you need?"

"I have a friend here who is having some trouble, and I need a background check on the guy who's hassling her, along with a few other people."

"I can go on base and run some names for you. How many people are we talking about?"

"About forty."

"Forty?"

"Yeah." Jay walked to the front door and looked out the window. "If I e-mail you the names, can you run them for me? I'll put the ones I'm most concerned about at the top of the list."

"How deep do you want me to go?"

"Deep. I need everything. Friends, assets, arrest records, names of their attorneys—"

"I get it. You need everything," Seth interrupted him. "Are you going to tell me what's really going on?"

"I don't want to get into it on the phone," Jay said apologetically. "I'll give you the gist in my e-mail. I was planning on encrypting it anyway."

"All right. How soon do you need this?"

"Yesterday."

"I'll head into the office right now," Seth said without hesitation. "And let me know if you need me to head down there. Vanessa's class ends today or tomorrow. We can catch a flight and be there by tomorrow night."

"Thanks, Seth. I'll definitely let you know."

19

CARINA PACED ACROSS THE LIVING room, listening for any kind of sound to prove that Jay hadn't left her here by herself. She had forced herself to focus on work for the thirty minutes that Jay had allowed her on the Internet. Make that twenty-eight minutes. Jay had set an old kitchen timer for her so she would know when she had to get off, and Carina was pretty sure he had robbed her of at least two precious minutes of her Internet allowance.

She had listened halfheartedly to him talk to one of his friends on the phone, his wary tone putting her already strained nerves into overdrive. After using his own laptop to send his friend an e-mail, an exercise that took a lot longer than she would have expected, he told her he was going to double check the security system and take a look around. She hadn't seen him since.

When the timer had gone off a few minutes later, she had dutifully logged off of the Internet and then gone to look for Jay. She had expected to find him in the bedroom upstairs that had been fashioned into a security observation room, but she only found a wall of television screens and a bunch of equipment she didn't understand. A quick study of the monitors didn't reveal any sign of him outside so she continued her search of the upstairs.

The single upstairs guest room didn't appear to have been disturbed, and all of the kids' bedrooms were empty. Carina leaned down and picked up one of Spencer's toy cars off of the floor and dropped it into a bin on a shelf that was labeled "cars."

Continuing on to the master bedroom, she hesitated before crossing the threshold. Even though she knew Matt and CJ weren't home, she felt like she was invading their privacy by entering their room. She called out Jay's name only to be answered by more silence.

She walked farther into the master bedroom, crossing to the French doors that led to a balcony. She pushed the curtains aside and stared out over the expanse of yard beneath her. The two swimming pools dominated the backyard, but a wide patch of grass gave the kids ample room to play. Beyond the grassy area was a wall separating the yard from the canal that bordered their property.

Carina knew from her conversations with CJ that the canal was one of a series of waterways that afforded the residents in her community access to the Atlantic Ocean. A speedboat was tethered to the dock at the edge of the Whitmores' property, and Carina tried to remember if she had noticed it there this morning when she had looked outside.

Restless and now a little concerned that she couldn't find Jay, she headed back downstairs, again calling out his name. Again there wasn't a response.

She crossed to where she had left her briefcase on a kitchen chair and made sure her weapon was still safely inside. As expected, it was exactly where she'd left it, as was her design sketchpad and her latest inventory reports. She knew she should try to get some more work done, but she also knew there wasn't any way she was going to be able to concentrate.

She tried to tell herself that it was the incident with Nick that had caused this uncommon inability to focus, but she had to admit that her curiosity about Jay was just as distracting. Besides wondering where he had disappeared to, as hard as she tried, she still couldn't comprehend his complete selflessness.

When they had first met, she had wondered if perhaps he had been so quick to help her with her car because he was trying to impress her. It had happened before, guys showing her extra attention in an effort to get her to go out with them. Realizing that most guys rarely saw past her outside appearance, she had never had any trouble refusing their advances.

She could also admit that her family background had always made her overly cautious when it came to any kind of relationship. Even though she tried to fight it, she was always afraid that she might start to care for someone only to have them find out the truth about where she came from and decide they wanted to steer clear of the complications of her life. After all, what kind of guy would want to get involved with the daughter of a mobster?

Clearly, that reality hadn't chased Jay away. Not that he was acting romantically interested in her at the moment, at least not that she could tell. Currently, he reminded her more of a controlling older brother.

Still unable to find any sign of him, she crossed to the front door and looked outside to see that his car was indeed still parked in the driveway.

The front yard was quiet, except for a hint of a breeze rustling through the fronds of the two large palm trees that flanked the front door.

Certain that he must be here somewhere, she went upstairs again, this time sitting down in the security room to watch for him outside. After ten minutes passed without any movement, she started a search of the house again. Again, she couldn't find any trace of Jay.

Her stomach grumbled in protest, reminding her that it was past time for lunch. She made her way down to the kitchen to consider her options. That's when she caught a glimpse of Jay through the window. He looked completely relaxed, a pair of pliers in one hand and a roll of some kind of wiring in the other. She watched him walk toward the back door and found herself wondering again why he had volunteered to help her.

After seeing his genuine friendship with CJ, as well as his easygoing way with Bianca, Carina was starting to think that he really was just a nice guy who wanted to help. But at what cost? He might be a Navy SEAL, but she doubted that even his extensive training could possibly prepare him for facing the Chicago mafia.

* * *

Jay skirted the edge of the lap pool and looked up to see Carina staring at him through the window. He let himself stare back, amazed that she could look even more incredible than usual wearing only a plain T-shirt and a pair of faded blue jeans. The jeans seemed out of place in this weather, over eighty degrees with humidity of at least a thousand percent. Of course, she was standing behind the glass in the air conditioned house, not hanging out in the bushes checking for weak spots in the Whitmores' security system.

She seemed different today. Not the "someone shot at me yesterday so now I'm freaked out" kind of different. Something more subtle. Maybe it was the lack of make-up and the casual clothes that made her seem more approachable. Or maybe it was that the circumstances of the past two days had helped him chip away at her polished exterior.

The look of relief he had seen on her face a moment ago shifted to annoyance. He supposed it was odd that he liked the way she seemed to always bristle when she felt he was ordering her around.

He had to admit that it was easier to deal with her when she was irritated than when he saw that raw vulnerability in her eyes. He thought of how exhausted she had been last night and his surprising urge to stay with her to make sure she was okay.

His initial interest in spending a couple of carefree weeks with her had disappeared, replaced by something he couldn't name, a depth of feeling he didn't understand. Despite their limited time together, he could already see beyond the façade, beyond the expensive car and classy clothes. He saw her now as a curious mix of characteristics: responsible and vulnerable, generous and ambitious.

He walked in the door, and she immediately shifted to face him. "Where have you been? I've been looking everywhere for you."

He heard the biting edge of irritation in her voice and ignored it. "I told you I was going to check out the security system."

"That was over an hour ago."

"I had to make a few adjustments."

She continued to look at him skeptically. "What's the wire for?"

"Just a little insurance."

She motioned to the window. "Was that boat there this morning?"

Jay shook his head. "No. I put it in the water a little while ago. I wanted to make sure we had another way out of here if we need it."

Her eyes met his, and he saw a hint of trepidation before she managed to gloss over it. "Whose boat is it?"

"Matt and CJ's." He glanced down at his watch to see that it was past noon. "Any chance you made us some lunch?"

"Why would I make lunch for someone I couldn't find?"

"Just asking." Jay set the wire and pliers on the table and moved to the kitchen sink to wash his hands. He looked up at her. "Have you eaten?"

She shook her head.

Jay opened the refrigerator and gave the contents a quick study. They were going to need to go grocery shopping soon. The freezer was more promising: homemade rolls in plastic freezer bags lined one shelf, and some various leftovers had also been packaged and stored inside. He pulled a bag of rolls from the freezer and set it on the counter and then moved to the large pantry.

"Are tuna sandwiches okay with you?"

She gazed at him as though she was trying to put together a complicated puzzle. "You're going to make me lunch?"

"Sure, unless you'd rather make something yourself."

"No, that's okay." Carina shook her head. "I'm not complaining. I'm just surprised. I didn't expect that you were the type of guy who knows his way around a kitchen."

"I live alone. That means I either cook for myself or starve," Jay told her. Then he thought of his teammates and how they were always inviting him over for dinner. Not to mention how their wives were constantly sending leftovers home with him. "Although, having married teammates has definitely improved my meals the last year or so."

"What do you mean?"

"My whole squad is Mormon, and everyone except for me is married." Jay opened a can of tuna and drained it. "Sometimes I wonder if they have a calendar floating around that says whose turn it is to feed me." He looked up at her and grinned. "Or maybe Mormon women just like to cook."

Carina's look was a cross between indignation and laughter. "I'm a Mormon woman, and I definitely don't cook unless I have to."

"I figured you were probably LDS since your sister is going to Brigham Young," Jay said, wondering how he seemed to be constantly stumbling across Mormons everywhere he went. He mixed up the tuna salad and defrosted a couple of rolls in the microwave. "Any chance Bianca likes to cook?"

"She loves to cook."

Jay looked up at her hopefully. "Really?"

"Yeah. She loves to make brownies and cookies. Chocolate cream pie."

Jay chuckled. "I'll bet she knows how to heat up frozen french fries too."

Carina shook her head. "No, but she is anxiously awaiting the day she gets her driver's license so she can go through the drive-thru by herself."

"That I believe." Jay handed Carina one of the sandwiches. "Here you go."

"Thanks." Her eyes met his, and the laughter faded from her face. "And thanks for everything you've done for me the past couple of days."

"You're welcome."

"I have to admit that most guys would have run for cover when they found out that my father is involved with the mob."

"I'm not most guys." Jay reached over and put a hand on hers. "And you aren't responsible for your father's choices."

"No, but I have to live with them."

Jay felt the pull of attraction as he stared down at her. He could lean down and kiss her. The look in Carina's eyes told him she wouldn't stop him, but he also sensed her doubts. As much as he wanted to take a step beyond friendship, something told him she wasn't quite ready.

"You're making a good life for yourself and for your sisters." He gave her hand a squeeze and then edged back.

"I'm trying."

Jay considered the lifestyle she had chosen, the complete contrast between Mormons and the mafia. "I have to ask, how is it that you and your sisters ended up Mormon?"

"My best friend in Denver introduced me to the gospel," Carina explained. "Her life was so foreign to everything I'd ever known, but I was fascinated by the way she and her family lived. It only took me about six months to read the Book of Mormon. My friend challenged me to pray about it, to see for myself that it was true."

"And you did it?" Jay asked, thinking about how many times his teammates had given him that same challenge.

"Yeah." Carina nodded and seemed to find some kind of inner peace. "It was almost like I knew the answer before I ever asked the question. Every time I read part of the Book of Mormon, it made sense. Not just the stories, but the way it made me feel." She shrugged her shoulders. "I was baptized a few weeks later."

"What about the rest of your family?"

"They all got baptized when I did," she told him. "What about you? What's your story?"

"What do you mean?"

"How did you find the gospel?"

Jay's eyebrows drew together in confusion. "I'm not Mormon."

"You're not?" Carina looked at him, surprised. "But I saw a Book of Mormon in your car. I just assumed . . ."

"One of my teammates gave that to me."

"Oh." Carina looked at him as though trying to readjust her image of him. "Have you ever read it?"

"I read a little bit a few days ago." He admitted. He wasn't sure why he felt the need to confide in her, but something about the way she had shared so much of her past with him made him feel like she might understand his confusion. "My last mission had a few glitches in it. It's been a bit of a struggle to sort some things out, but when I read some of that book, it seemed to help. Kind of like finding a peaceful spot in the middle of a lot of noise. I guess I never really thought about it the way you just said, that it makes sense."

She was quiet for a moment. Then she spoke softly. "You should read some more."

"Maybe I will."

20

SETH READ THROUGH THE BACKGROUND reports for the third time. He didn't know what Jay had gotten himself mixed up in, but these guys he was researching were serious trouble with a capital *T*. Marciano Perelli was believed to have taken over as the head of the Chicago mafia after the death of his father, Sergio Perelli. Marciano had been arrested eight times but never convicted. Nick Baldino was only twenty-six years old and already had three arrests, but he too hadn't ever been convicted.

A handful of the people on the list had done time behind bars, but most of them had résumés similar to Marciano and Nick. Others weren't in the criminal system at all and appeared to be upstanding citizens.

Seth compiled all of the reports on his computer and then encrypted them so he could e-mail them back to Jay. As an afterthought, he CC'd his wife and then deleted the e-mail Jay had sent as well as his response so it couldn't be traced back to him. After clearing the trash file from his e-mail account, he picked up his office phone to call Jay.

He had only dialed the first three numbers when a knock sounded at his office door. Seth's eyebrows drew together, and he considered who would be looking for him since his whole squad was on leave. He crossed to the door to find a suit-and-tie type standing on the other side of the threshold. "Can I help you?"

"Are you Seth Johnson?"

"That's right."

"I'm Special Agent Curtis Graham." Graham pulled out a badge and flashed it, identifying him as FBI. "You need to come with me. I need to ask you a few questions."

"What is this about?" Seth asked, instinctively taking a step back.

"We can talk about it at my office."

"I'd rather talk about it here." Seth motioned inside. "This is a secure office. I'm sure anything you want to ask me can be taken care of here on base."

The agent narrowed his eyes and then reluctantly moved into Seth's office. With an air of annoyance, he reached out and closed the door to ensure some privacy.

"Why don't you tell me why you're here," Seth suggested mildly.

"Our records indicate that you were logged into the FBI database this morning," Graham began.

"That's right." Seth circled behind his desk and sat down.

"Can you tell us why you were interested in the Perelli family?"

"No, I can't," Seth said with complete sincerity.

Graham stared, clearly surprised by his answer. "I beg your pardon?"

Seth leaned back in his chair. "I honestly don't know why I was asked to look up those names this morning."

"Who asked you to look them up?"

"I'm not at liberty to say."

"Look, you're going to have to answer my questions one way or another." Graham put his hands on Seth's desk and leaned forward. "You can either answer them here, or I can take you back to my office and we can spend some time in interrogation."

Seth recognized the intimidation technique. He had used it plenty of times himself. Though his instinct was to stand up and use his size as his own source of intimidation, he forced himself to stay relaxed. He kept his eyes on Graham's face and shrugged. "I am answering your questions."

"Do I need to speak with your commanding officer in order to get you to cooperate?"

"My immediate supervisor is on leave, but Commander Bennett should be in his office down the hall," Seth offered helpfully with a wave toward his door. "It's three doors down on the right."

Graham glanced down at the stack of background checks on Seth's desk. He reached out and lifted them, flipping through the papers. "I'm going to ask you again. Why is the navy interested in the Perelli family?"

"And I'll tell you again: I don't know." Seth stood now but remained behind his desk. "I also don't know why an FBI agent from Virginia would be concerned about a family in Chicago." Seth reached a hand out for the background checks, surprised when Graham held them out of his reach.

"I think I'll hang on to these," he said smugly. He turned to the door. "I guess I'm done here." He glanced back at Seth. "For now."

Seth watched him leave his office, his eyebrows drawing together in confusion. Instinctively, he pulled his cell phone free of his pocket to call Jay but quickly reconsidered. Obviously, he had triggered some kind of alert when he had used the FBI database. What he didn't know was why the FBI had found it necessary to send an agent rather than just having someone pick up the phone to ask their questions.

He considered what he would do if he found out the Feds were interested in one of his ops. Looking down at his phone, he tucked it back into his pocket. For all he knew, someone was already scrubbing through his e-mail account and tapping his phones.

Always cautious, Seth turned off the wireless modem on his computer, and then he downloaded the file he had created for Jay onto a flash drive. He then printed a hardcopy for himself, deleted the document, and removed all of the temporary files. Satisfied that his research couldn't be traced back to Jay, he turned his modem back on. Instantly, an alert sounded.

A few quick keystrokes confirmed what Seth had already suspected. His friends at the FBI had accessed his e-mail account. His concern for Jay heightened. He headed down the hall to Kel Bennett's office to find the door open and Kel sitting at his desk. "Hey, Kel. Do you have a minute?"

"Sure, come on in." Kel waved him inside. "What are you doing on base today? I thought you would be off somewhere with Vanessa by now."

"She had to teach a class this week." Seth closed Kel's office door and took a seat across from the commander. "Did an FBI agent stop in to see you?"

"No," Kel said, drawing the word out as his eyes narrowed. "Why?"

Seth explained the phone call he had received from Jay and the subsequent visit by Special Agent Graham, as well as the search of his e-mail account.

"Do you have any idea why Jay was asking for the background checks?"

"Not really." Seth shook his head. "He said he was trying to help out a friend. The two people he was most concerned about were Marciano Perelli and Nick Baldino."

"What do you know about them?"

"They're both from Chicago, both have been arrested several times but never convicted. They share the same lawyer, and both are suspected to have ties to the mafia. The FBI believes Marciano Perelli is the top man right now since his father died a couple months ago."

"I don't understand how any of this would tie in with Jay. His background check didn't show any friends with ties to Chicago, much less the mafia."

"I was thinking of heading down to Miami for the weekend. I thought maybe I could help him out with whatever's going on."

"I'm not sure that's really a good idea unless we want the FBI involved." Kel shook his head. "For all we know, the FBI might try to follow you to him."

Seth raised an eyebrow. "I would hope you trained me well enough that I can get from here to Miami without being followed."

"Point taken." Kel chuckled. "I'm guessing that you want to check out a couple of secure phones."

Seth nodded.

Kel opened a drawer in his credenza and pulled out five cell phones and a logbook. He jotted down the phone numbers and then slid four of the phones toward Seth. "I don't know how many you'll need, but it's easier to have too many than not enough." Kel held up the fifth phone. "I'm keeping this one so you can check in and let me know how things are going."

Seth nodded and scooped the other phones off of the desk.

Kel pocketed his secure phone and asked, "What are you going to do about a car?"

"I haven't gotten that far yet."

Kel punched a couple of keys on his computer. "We've got a supply transport heading down to AUTEC at thirteen hundred tomorrow. You should be able to check out a car from their motor pool for a couple of days."

"That should work. You don't have a problem with me giving one of these secure phones to Vanessa, do you? I have a feeling I might need her to use her CIA connections to do some digging for me."

"That's fine," Kel agreed. "Is she staying here in Virginia, or is she going with you?"

"She'll come with me, but I want to make sure she has access to a secure line if we're ever separated."

"Just make sure you keep me in the loop. I don't want us to end up in the middle of some interagency territorial dispute."

"I'll call you as soon as I talk to Jay," Seth agreed. "I'll feel a lot better when I've had the chance to talk to him and find out what's really going on."

21

"I DON'T UNDERSTAND WHAT YOU need all of this for." Carina picked one of the computer printouts up from the kitchen table and then dropped it back down again. She had spent the past several hours trying to work with very limited resources and was finding herself increasingly frustrated with her situation. Not only would Jay not let her on the Internet for any length of time, but he had also banished her from using any kind of phone.

He had turned her cell phone off last night before they had driven to the Whitmores', insisting that she couldn't use it for fear that someone might use the GPS signal in it to find her. Bianca's phone had also been confiscated and turned off after a great deal of protesting on her part.

Carina could understand her sister's frustration, but with Pete staying with her all day, at least she had someone right there in case of any problems. Her own frustrations had surfaced after lunch when she had tried to use CJ's house phone to check in with her office. Jay had banned her from that form of communication as well, convinced that somcone might try to locate her by tracing her calls. Other than giving her another twenty-eight minutes on the Internet, he had completely cut her off from any kind of communication with the world outside of CJ's house.

"Don't you think all of this is overkill?" she asked when Jay didn't respond.

"It's research," Jay said without looking up. His plain blue T-shirt had smudges of dirt on one sleeve, and she could see the slight bulge at the back of his waistband that she recognized as a holstered handgun. Except for the gun, he looked like someone she might have seen walking along the beach, one of those guys who started his days with a surfboard in hand, one eye always on the waves.

She skimmed through the background report on her uncle and shook her head. "I already told you about the family."

"Yes, but I want to know what they've been up to since you left Chicago. Did your uncle express any concerns when you talked to him at your father's trial?"

"Just that he wanted us to come home to Chicago." Carina shrugged. "I said no, and that was the end of it."

Jay looked up at her, and Carina didn't know what to think of the understanding she saw in his eyes. "Other than Marciano and Lou, it's been over ten years since you've had any contact with your family or any of their associates. Is that right?"

Carina nodded.

"So Nick would have only been a teenager back then."

"He might have been a teenager, but he was already involved in the business." Carina motioned toward the stack of papers. "Does he have a criminal record yet?"

"Yet? You say that like it's inevitable."

"It is." Carina let out a sigh. "My mother took me and my sisters away from Chicago to protect us from that life, but I was old enough to know what was going on. And I already knew where Nick was headed."

"Well, he hasn't ever been convicted, but he has been arrested a couple of times."

"If he's managed to stay out of jail for the past ten years, that pretty much proves that I'm right about him being close to my uncle," Carina told him.

"Why do you say that?"

"The family protects those close to them. Orders are given through several layers of management to make sure that if anyone gets arrested, they won't be able to tie anything to the people at the top. At least that's what my father did to make sure nothing could be traced back to him," Carina said. "Besides, when Nick first showed up, he said my father had sent him. Only an insider would have any contact with my dad."

"You know, we might want to consider talking to your father. He might have some answers for you."

Carina's eyes met his, darkening as she spoke. "He killed my mother."

"*Why* did he kill your mother?" Jay asked without hesitation.

His bluntness surprised her. Slowly, she shook her head. Hadn't she asked herself that same question a million times? Hadn't she wondered if she had come home sooner if things might have turned out differently? "I honestly don't know."

"Did you ever speak to him about it?"

Again, she shook her head. "Why would I? He never denied it." She felt the tears welling up and blinked them back. "Besides, I saw him."

Jay's eyebrows lifted, surprise and sympathy evident on his face. "You saw him kill your mother?"

She let out a ragged breath, not wanting to relive the memory but unable to stop it from forming. She shook her head again. "I was too late."

"I know it must be hard to talk about, but can you tell me what happened? I think it might be important." He reached out and put a hand on hers, an offer of comfort that seemed foreign to her.

Carina stared down at their hands, Jay's tanned and long-fingered, hers narrow, almost delicate. "My sisters and I had borrowed my mom's car and gone out together." She shook her head at the triviality, the idea that they had been eating pizza and laughing together, not a care in the world just moments before their mother's life had ended. "When we came home, I saw two SUVs outside my house."

Jay shifted in the seat beside her to face her, but he didn't speak.

"I knew something was wrong. I'm not sure how, but I knew it." She pushed out of her chair and crossed to the window. A gentle breeze rustled the palm tree leaves in the backyard and sent ripples through the water in the swimming pools. "I drove past my house and pulled over a few houses away. Then I had my sisters go to a friend's, and I doubled back to my house. I was in the garage when I heard the gunshots."

She didn't try to fight the tears now. "I made it to the door, but I couldn't bring myself to turn the knob. I was afraid of what I was going to find on the other side, and I was just as afraid of who I might find inside. It wasn't until I heard the police sirens that I forced myself to go into the house."

"What did you find?" Jay asked gently. He was standing behind her now, and she forced herself to turn to face him.

"My father was sitting in the middle of the kitchen, holding my mother's head in his lap as though she had fainted." Carina's jaw clenched, and she swiped at the tears on her cheeks. "But she hadn't fainted. She had been shot through the heart. The gun was lying right beside them."

"Carina, I'm so sorry." Jay slid his hands around her waist and pulled her against him. She stepped into the embrace automatically, unable to remember the last time someone had held her close, the last time she had allowed anyone the opportunity.

They stood there in silence for a moment. Then Jay stepped back and stared down at her. "Who else was at your house besides your father?"

"I don't know." Her shoulders lifted restlessly. "I saw a guy standing guard at the front door when I drove by the house, but there wasn't any sign of him when I went inside."

Jay's eyes sharpened. "What about the two vehicles you saw? Were they still there when the cops arrived?"

"I don't remember."

"Talk me through it. After you went inside, what happened? Did your father say anything? Did you hear the police question him at all?"

"My dad looked up at me and said, 'She's gone. I can't believe she's really gone.'" Carina ran her fingers through her hair as she struggled against her emotions. "He looked lost, confused. Then the police came in, and he didn't say anything at all. One of the cops checked my mom for a pulse. The other pulled my dad away from her and handcuffed him."

"What did the room look like? Did it look like anyone had been fighting, stuff thrown around?"

She shook her head. "Why are you asking me about all of this? I was at the trial. My father never denied killing my mother."

"Did he ever confess?"

"What?"

"You said he never denied the accusation that he killed your mother," Jay said, his eyes focused on hers. "Did he ever admit that he did it?"

Carina thought back to the long days of her father's trial, the days of testimony by various witnesses, including the police officers. She shook her head. "No. He never confessed. He didn't testify at his trial, and the police said he wouldn't answer any of their questions."

"Then it is possible that someone else killed your mother and he took the blame."

"Why would he do that?"

"I don't know, but I think it's worth asking the question. Where is your father now? Which prison?"

"Last I heard, he was still in Florence. It's about forty-five minutes outside of Colorado Springs."

"Are you up for a trip?"

Carina stared at him like he'd just invited her for a joyride in a space shuttle. "You aren't serious."

"Sure I am." Jay motioned to the papers spread out on the table. "We can look at these reports all day, but I'll bet fifteen minutes with your father will tell us what's really going on, especially if he's the one who sent Nick."

"Even if I wanted to go visit my father, I couldn't possibly do that, not right now."

"Why not?"

"For one thing, I can't leave Bianca here by herself, especially with Nick around. Not only that, but she wouldn't want to miss school and practice."

"She could always stay with my parents."

"I couldn't ask Pete to watch out for her." She shook her head. "Besides, I can't afford to throw money away on an airline ticket just so I can talk to my dad for fifteen minutes to see if maybe he didn't really murder my mother."

"I can take care of the travel arrangements." Jay shrugged absently. "I have a ton of frequent-flyer miles I never have the chance to use."

"Wouldn't it be easier for me to just talk to Nick?" Carina asked warily.

"Do you think he would tell you anything you don't already know?"

"Probably not."

"What about Lou?" Jay asked.

"What about him?"

"Do you think he can tell you what happened?"

Carina considered for a minute. "I'm not sure if he knows what really happened or not. He tries so hard to protect me from what my family is really like that he almost never talks about our life in Chicago."

Jay stared at her a moment before he asked, "Did you come to Miami right after your mom died?"

She shook her head. "No. We went to Phoenix first. Lou helped us find a place there that had a guest house for him to live in, and he took care of the sale of our old house in Colorado."

"How long ago did you leave Phoenix?"

"About five months ago, not long after my father was convicted."

"Why did you move?"

"A lot of reasons." Carina shrugged. "Bianca had heard about your dad and wanted to train with him. Lou wanted us to make a fresh start after the trial. As soon as I found a new job, we moved."

"What came first?"

"What do you mean?"

"Who was the first person to suggest that you move here?"

Carina thought for a minute. "Lou did. Or at least, he's the one who wanted us to move. He didn't seem to really care where, as long as it wasn't back to Chicago or Denver."

"We need to talk to him," Jay said with conviction. "I think he knows more than he's telling you, and I have a feeling he might even know what really happened between your mom and dad."

"He should be home. Did you want to go now?"

Jay shook his head. "I'd rather wait until tonight. I'll have my dad come over after he finishes with his evening practice, and then I'll go over and talk to him."

"Look, I know you're a Navy SEAL and all, but it would probably be a lot safer if I was the one to go talk to him. If Nick sees you around there, it's very likely you'll end up with a bullet in you."

"I don't want you anywhere near your apartment right now," Jay said as though he were oblivious to the potential consequences of another run-in with Nick.

"Jay, I'm not exaggerating. If Nick or his friends see you again, they will try to kill you. Even if they realize you aren't who they were looking for, they'll shoot you simply because you got in their way."

"Don't worry about me," Jay told her lightheartedly. "I'm pretty good at hiding in the shadows."

22

HE HAD TO TELL HER. Lou knew the time had come that Carina needed to know the truth, but he didn't know how he could possibly find the words. How could he explain his part in what had happened to her?

All day he had watched out the window, hoping she wouldn't come home yet. Nick had driven by twice already today. At least, he had been by twice that Lou had managed to see him. Nick had changed cars each time, and Lou couldn't be sure how many men had come with him. He had also noticed a second driver who had appeared with alarming regularity. Now that it was dark out, he could only guess at who was driving by each time he saw a new set of headlights.

Nick and his boys were being persistent. He would give them that. Unfortunately, he doubted they were going to give up until they got what they came for. Nick thought that taking the girls back to Chicago was the best way to protect them, but Lou knew better. No one understood Alex better than he did. And only three people were still alive who knew the identity of the man really running the Outfit. Four if you counted Carina, but she had no idea what she had seen. She also didn't know everything her father had done to protect her.

Then again, she knew a whole lot more about the family business than Lou had given her credit for.

He had thought he had been protecting her when he had intercepted the package from her father a few days ago, only a few short days before Nick had shown up. When Carina had shown him the note, he had contacted the courier who had delivered the package. After he found out Lou had taken possession of the package, the courier had admitted that Giovanni had instructed him to plant the message.

While the message might have been meant for Carina, Lou knew now that it had also contained a message intended for him. Giovanni was telling him that Carina needed to understand the truth. He knew now that he should have confided in Carina when the package had first arrived, but he had hoped Nick and his friends wouldn't be able to find her, that he could protect her from the past she came from a little while longer.

He understood that if Carina discovered the small fortune her grandfather had left her, she and her sisters would never have to worry about money again. He also understood that her inheritance came with a price: the truth about who was really running the Outfit as well as all of the danger that would come with that knowledge. He wished he had been able to hide the contents of the package better than he had, but at least he was sure it was safe for now. Carina's friend Jay had helped take care of that, even if he didn't know it.

The sound of metal scraping against metal broke through the silence. Lou's good hand immediately wrapped around the semiautomatic pistol on the table beside him, and he struggled to stand and turn.

A floorboard creaked in the bedroom. Lou took aim, expecting to see Nick or one of his boys emerge from the short hallway off of the living room.

A voice sounded before he saw the intruder. "Don't shoot. It's Jay Wellman. I just want to talk to you."

Jay wisely waited a moment for Lou to absorb his words before emerging from the hall, his hands cautiously held out to his side.

"You're lucky I didn't shoot you."

"Sorry for coming in the back, but I didn't want to be seen at your front door. You still have eyes on your place."

Lou nodded. "I had a feeling that was the case. I've already seen Nick a couple of times." He set his weapon back on the table and slowly lowered himself into his chair. "Might as well come sit down and tell me why you're here. Are the girls okay?"

"They're fine." Jay nodded and moved into the sparsely furnished room. He sat down on the worn sofa and seemed to gather his thoughts.

"What's on your mind?"

"I need to know why Nick and his friends are here."

"I don't know."

"You have an idea," Jay persisted. He hesitated and then added, "Look, I know we just met, but you can trust me. You know you can or you never would have let me take Carina out of your sight."

"What is she to you?"

Jay's eyes narrowed. "What do you mean?"

"People don't just turn their lives upside down for a stranger without a motive."

"I do," Jay said without hesitation. "I'm in the military. That's my job."

"Watching over the girls isn't some military mission."

"No, you're right," Jay agreed. "But they're friends of my father's so they're my friends too."

Lou stared at the younger man, impressed that he didn't flinch as he sized him up. Jay obviously believed his involvement was really simply part of who he was and a result of the career he had chosen, but Lou suspected there was more to it than that.

He considered for a long moment. Everything in him, everything he had learned in his seventy-three years of living, told him not to trust anyone, not to ever reveal the secrets of the past. But these secrets were no longer safe with him, and he knew it. Lou wasn't sure if it was the earnestness in Jay's face that made him willing to talk, or perhaps it was the knowledge that this young man had already risked his life once to protect Carina.

A sigh escaped him, and he forced himself to take a tentative step toward trusting Jay. "Nick thinks he's here to protect Carina, but I'm pretty sure he was really sent to bring her back to Chicago for leverage."

Jay leaned forward, concern lighting his eyes. "What kind of leverage?"

"Leverage against her father. Maybe against her uncle."

Jay stared at him, looking as though he too were going through some internal debate about how much information he was willing to share. "Giovanni Perelli didn't really kill his wife, did he?"

Surprise lit Lou's face. This man who had only appeared in their lives a few short days ago had already seen through the lies and had grasped at least a small shred of the truth from that horrible day. Slowly, Lou shook his head, the weight of the truth still pressing heavily upon him.

"What really happened? Why did he let himself get convicted for something he didn't do? And why didn't he tell his daughters the truth?"

"Donna was killed as a demonstration, a reminder of who was really in charge of the Outfit."

Jay looked at him skeptically. "I thought Carina's grandfather was the top man before he died."

"No." Lou's eyes met Jay's and held. "He was forced to step down three years ago when he started having health issues. Alzheimer's. That's when Carina's father became number two."

"Who was number one?"

"I don't know his full name, but I knew him as Alex. He was pretty good at keeping a thick barrier between himself and the rest of the organization. Unfortunately, I'm one of the few who knows him personally." Lou flexed his fingers on his good hand. "Giovanni and the top man had a falling out on how things should be run, and Marciano made a comment that maybe they should let the FBI know that one of their own wasn't just on the mob's payroll but was also the man writing the checks."

Jay's eyebrows shot up. "Seriously?"

"He's FBI. Or at least, he was," Lou told him.

"Is that why Carina's mother was killed? Because the top guy thought someone was going to turn him in?"

Lou nodded. "The threat against Donna and the girls started years earlier. That's why Giovanni sent them away."

"Sent them away?" Jay's brows furrowed. "Carina thought her mother ran away with them."

"That's what she and her sisters were supposed to think," Lou said with a shrug. "Giovanni knew the girls needed to be afraid of him and the family. They needed to think there had been a clean break between their parents."

"I gather they kept in touch even after they separated."

Lou nodded. "I was their go-between. I had been Donna's bodyguard since Bianca was born." He hesitated now, his guilt all but consuming him. He looked down at his hand, rubbing at the stubs where his missing fingers had once been. "It was my fault she died."

Jay's eyes followed his movement, staring at his mangled hand. "Alex tortured you. You can't blame yourself for giving out their location."

"I never told anyone where they were," Lou said, straightening in his seat. "I would have died first."

"Then why did you say it was your fault?"

"Someone told Giovanni that I had talked when they delivered one of my fingers to him in a box. He believed it. I was in bad shape, too beat up to travel. By the time I got to Giovanni's house, he was already on his way to Denver."

"I gather he was followed."

Lou nodded. "From what I've been able to piece together, the top man got there right after Giovanni."

"Why didn't Giovanni turn him in?"

"It doesn't work that way," Lou told him. "You don't get to the top without having some very powerful allies. If Giovanni had talked, he had to know that someone would come after his family. He stayed quiet and took the blame to protect his children."

"And you've been encouraging Carina and her sisters to move every time someone got too close."

"Yes," Lou admitted. "And now I need your help to get them to move again. They aren't safe here. Not anymore."

"I doubt I have any influence on Carina or Bianca."

"I think Carina will listen to you. And Bianca will listen to your father."

"Carina hardly knows me," Jay said with a shake of his head. "Tell me what you know about the man in charge. Describe him to me."

"Dark hair, balding, average height. He's probably about fifty now."

"Anything more specific? Scars, tattoos?"

Lou shook his head. "All I know for sure is that he's a Fed."

Jay took a moment to absorb the new information. "Was he from Chicago, or was he assigned there?"

"He was assigned there," Lou said with certainty. "Rumor has it that he was from somewhere down south originally. Texas, I think. He came to Chicago as part of the organized crime unit. I don't think he was in town even twenty-four hours before he was on the payroll and moving up quickly."

"I know the mob has been known to pay off judges and people in law enforcement to protect their interests, but I've never heard of anyone going from being on the take to heading up the operation."

"Neither had I," Lou admitted. "I'm still not sure how he managed to make the transition, but I do know that he had a knack for taking care of anyone in his way."

"How?" Jay asked.

"You have to understand that this man was more of a ghost story than reality for most of us. Only a handful of people had ever met him in person, and even fewer knew his name. One by one, the people above him in the mob's hierarchy started getting arrested. Not just arrested. Convicted."

"He used his position with the FBI to clear his way to the top?"

"Exactly." Lou considered for a minute how much more information he could afford to share. "From where I stood, it looked like Sergio Perelli knew what he was doing and supported the changes. I never could figure out why he let someone from the outside rise to the same level as his own sons, much less pass them up."

"This is all fascinating, but what I don't understand is why someone would come after Carina and Bianca now."

Though Lou knew deep down that the package intended for Carina was the likely catalyst, he couldn't bring himself to trust Jay with it, at least not before he had the chance to explain things to Carina first. Instead, he lied, as he had done so often throughout his life. "I don't know. I've been trying to figure that out since Nick showed up."

"Maybe you should pack up a few things and come stay with us."

Lou's eyes narrowed. "Us? Are you staying with the girls?"

Jay met Lou's suspicious stare without flinching. "I am. Carina's friends thought it would be wise to have me stay at their house to look after them."

"I see." Lou considered his options. He didn't like the idea of his girls staying at a house alone with any man, especially not one who appeared to have broken through the invisible wall Carina had erected against men in general. He also didn't want to be responsible for leading Nick to the girls for a second time. "I think it's best for me to steer clear of the girls until they're safely away from here."

"Are you sure?" Jay asked skeptically.

"I'm sure." Lou nodded. He hesitated a moment before adding, "But if anything happens to me, tell Carina that she needs to take her sisters out for pizza."

Lou saw the concern on the younger man's face, and his confusion. "Pizza?"

"And make sure she keeps up the maintenance on her mom's car." He nodded again. "Hopefully she'll understand."

"I really think you should come with me."

Lou shook his head. "I don't want to take the chance that they'll find the girls through me again."

"I can get you out of here without being seen."

"I think I'm a bit old to be climbing out of bedroom windows." Lou shot him a sarcastic look. "Just keep my girls safe."

Jay hesitated and then nodded. "I will."

Lou watched the younger man disappear back the way he had come and heard the scratchy sound of the window closing. He listened for a long moment, impressed that Jay seemed to possess the capability of moving silently through the night. After a minute or two, he let himself relax in his chair once more. He lifted his eyes to look out the front window just as his door burst open. A familiar figure stepped inside and closed the door behind him.

"You." Lou felt a bead of sweat form on his brow as he looked into the cold, dark eyes.

"Tell me where they are," he demanded, his voice carrying the slightest hint of a Texan drawl.

"Never."

He reached down for Lou's damaged hand. A cool smile stretched across his chiseled face. "Should I remind you of what happens when people don't tell me what I want to know?"

"I didn't talk last time, and nothing you do to me will give you better results this time around."

"Tell me where they are."

"I'd rather die."

"That can be arranged."

23

CURTIS GRAHAM RIFLED THROUGH THE scatter of papers on his desk in search of a pen. His already demanding caseload seemed to multiply while he was out of the office that morning, including a new stack of case reports he needed to sign. He probably should have followed his instincts and told his old friend from the Academy to look into the database search himself, but he'd owed him a favor and couldn't find a way to easily refuse.

His insistence that Graham handle the matter in person was a bit odd, but then, Alex had always been a bit of an odd one. Besides, he had needed to go to Virginia Beach to follow up a lead on another case anyway. He dug his mouse out from beneath a stack of phone messages and updated his case notes on his computer.

He was just standing to leave for the day when his phone rang.

"What did you find?" Alex asked over the phone, his clipped tone hiding the Texan drawl that seemed to have faded over the past twenty-five years with the Bureau.

Resigned that his long night was about to get longer, he settled back down into his chair. "Let me see here." Graham shifted the phone to his left hand so his right hand was free to push at papers until he found his notes. "The person who accessed those names on the FBI database was a Lieutenant Seth Johnson."

"Who is he?"

"It's hard to say. All I'm sure about is that he's navy and he's stationed out of Virginia Beach." With his notepad in his lap, he leaned back in his desk chair and propped both feet up on his desk.

"You have to at least know what unit he's with."

"I have a partial copy of his service file, but just about everything in it is classified. Apparently the navy wasn't willing to share more than the basics," Graham told him. "From what I can tell, he went through flight training shortly after he was commissioned, but everything after that is a mystery."

"Did you put a trace on his phone?"

"Yeah, but he hasn't used it since I went to see him."

"What about the numbers he called before you talked to him?"

"There were a couple of calls from an encrypted government number that I haven't been able to identify and some calls to other cell phone numbers." He read over the phone logs, noticing the way the lieutenant used his phone in spurts, sometimes not making any calls for days or even weeks at a time.

The tension coming over the line broke into his thoughts. "Who did those numbers belong to?"

"Let me see if I have that yet." He shifted his computer keyboard into his lap so he could type while still keeping his feet up on his desk. "He made a couple to Vanessa Johnson. It looks like that's his wife. The only other number that is repeated recently is Jay Wellman's. In fact, Wellman was the last call he received before I paid him a visit."

"Run a background check on him too and let me know what you find out."

"All right. I'll give you a call." Graham jotted down the request on his growing to-do list. "Oh, there was one more thing. I have the list of all of the names Seth Johnson ran through our database. I don't know why he was looking up all of these people, but there are quite a few of them he was interested in."

"How many?"

"Thirty-eight."

"Are you sure they're all related to the same case?"

"Several of them aren't in our system, but all of them are from Chicago," he said. "I'll e-mail you the list and CC the organized crime unit. Maybe Lieutenant Johnson stumbled on some other members of the mafia up there."

"It sounds like some of this information might be sensitive. I was going to head down to DC in a couple of days. I'll come down a day or two early and visit Norfolk first. We can go grab some lunch and catch up."

"Are you sure you don't want me to e-mail the list to you? I can have my secretary type it up and get it out to you first thing in the morning."

"No, I want this information considered top secret until I can see it for myself. We don't want to take a chance of it getting into the wrong hands," he insisted. "In fact, I'd like for you to keep the file with you until I get a chance to come get it."

"Okay. You know more about this stuff than I do." Graham pulled open his top desk drawer and grabbed a candy bar out of it before dropping the file inside beside his car keys. "Let me know when you get your travel plans firmed up, and I'll make sure I'm here in the office to meet with you."

"I'll make sure you know when I arrive."

* * *

Jay stared down at his phone, surprised that when he called Seth's number it went straight to voicemail. Even though the Saint Squad was on leave, they all knew that if an international crisis broke out somewhere, they could very easily be called back in on a moment's notice. He dialed the number a second time, but his efforts yielded the same results.

He looked up at the Whitmores' home, not sure if he was ready to face Carina with the truth. How would she react, he wondered, when she found out that her family had been lying to her for years, that the man she had chosen to hate had sacrificed his freedom to protect her? He couldn't begin to put himself in her shoes, couldn't even imagine what it would be like to know that his father was flawed, much less a lifelong criminal.

Pete emerged through the front door, illuminated by the glow of the porch light. "Is everything okay?"

Jay took a step toward him and immediately felt some of the burden of the truth shift off of his shoulders. "I don't know." He held up his cell phone. "Seth isn't answering, which isn't like him, and I'm not sure how Carina is going to take the news that I have for her."

"Do you want me to stay for a while longer?" Pete asked.

Jay considered a minute but then shook his head. If he was being told his past wasn't what he thought it was, he doubted he would want an audience. "I'll be okay. Where are Carina and Bianca?"

"Bianca is already in bed." Pete glanced up at the side of the house, where the main level guest rooms were located. "At least, she'd better be in bed."

His father's sarcastic tone eased a little more of Jay's tension, and he gave a slight smile. "And Carina?"

"She's in the living room pretending to watch the news."

"Thanks." Jay put a hand on his dad's shoulder. "And thanks for always being there for me."

Jay didn't miss the surprise in his father's eyes before he controlled it. He gave a curt nod and took a step toward his car. "Give me a call if you have any problems. And make sure you keep those girls safe."

"I will, Dad." Jay managed a full smile this time. "I learned from the best."

* * *

"What did you find out?" Carina asked anxiously the moment Jay walked into the living room. She pushed off of the couch and turned to face him. She noticed Jay hesitate for the briefest moment, and her impatience and nerves went to battle in her stomach. "Well?"

Jay's eyes met hers. "We need to go see your dad."

"What?"

Jay closed the distance between them, an odd look of sympathy on his face. He put his hand on her arm and sat down on the couch, gently pulling her down to sit beside him. "I had a long talk with Lou. He doesn't believe your father is guilty either."

Carina stared at him blankly, trying to decipher his words. "That doesn't make any sense. Why wouldn't Lou have told me if he thought my father was innocent?"

"Because Lou knew your father went to jail to protect you and your sisters."

Carina shook her head in denial. "Why would my father need to protect us? No one would be insane enough to come anywhere near our family, much less kill my mother. Going after the family of the man in charge of the Outfit is suicide. Who would do that?"

"The man who is really in charge of the Chicago mob. The man who saw your father as a threat."

"What?" Confusion filled her. "But I thought . . ."

"You thought what you were supposed to think," Jay said quietly. He took her hand in his. "Your mother didn't leave your father, at least not the way you thought. Your father sent all of you away so no one would try to hurt you to get to him."

Carina shook her head, her reality shifting and falling around her in a dozen pieces. She tried to put them back together in a way that made sense but couldn't quite manage it. "I don't believe that."

Jay didn't say anything, as though he knew she needed some time to sort out her thoughts and memories. The image of her fifth birthday party flashed into her mind, her father grinning at her as she rode a pony in her grandfather's huge backyard. The yard had been crowded with family and friends, balloons tied to the chairs set up on the patio. Even in the memory, she could recognize the men standing near the gates, undoubtedly armed and assigned to keep them all safe. Lou was there too, never too far away but never in the middle of the action.

A recent conversation with Lou replayed in her mind, and she thought of how he too tried so hard to protect her from a truth she so desperately wanted to understand. Her voice was soft, barely louder than a whisper when she finally spoke. "I always wondered how my mom managed to support us without working."

Jay squeezed her hand, as though encouraging her to open her mind to the truth. "Lou gave me a lot of background information, and it all makes sense, except for why Nick is here now. We need to know what has changed recently that would affect you."

"Maybe it has something to do with my grandfather's death," Carina suggested. "I got the feeling Nick had been searching for me for a while."

"I don't know. Lou said your grandfather was suffering from Alzheimer's and that someone else has been in charge for the past few years."

"Is there any chance Nick was lying about the death of my grandfather?" Carina asked hesitantly.

"I'm afraid not," Jay said, sympathy humming through his voice. "Seth confirmed it when he ran the background checks."

Carina swallowed hard and drew a steadying breath. Her eyes met Jay's, and she forced herself to speak her thoughts aloud. "If it wasn't my father who was in charge, then it was probably my uncle."

"Not according to Lou."

"Do you really think my dad would have any idea of what's going on? As far as I know, he hasn't had any contact with anyone from the family since he was convicted."

"You don't think your uncle would have kept in touch?"

"Maybe." Carina shrugged. "It's hard to say. From what I've been able to tell, when someone in the Outfit goes to jail, ties are kept pretty loose so the associations don't become obvious to the police. Since my uncle was family, it's possible he might have visited him. I doubt any letters would be revealing since all of my father's mail is probably screened."

She pressed two fingers against her left temple, where a headache was forming. "Do you really think my dad would talk to me? Do you think he would tell me what really happened?"

"You'd know the answer to that better than I would."

"Not really." Carina shook her head. "I don't know him. Not anymore."

"But you did know him." Jay pulled his phone free of his pocket. "A friend of mine said he could come down here tomorrow after his wife gets off work. I'd like to have him stay and watch after Bianca this weekend. That will give us the chance to fly out to Colorado to talk to your dad in person."

Carina watched him dial a number, unsettled when his eyebrows furrowed in concern. "Is something wrong?"

"Seth isn't answering." Jay stood up and went into the kitchen to use his laptop. He powered it on and took a couple of minutes to log onto his e-mail. Carina assumed he was making sure his signal couldn't be traced. She followed him to the kitchen table and looked over his shoulder as he opened an e-mail. The content was simply a string of numbers.

"What is that?"

"A message from Seth."

"How can you tell?"

"I recognize his code."

"His code?"

"It's like a code word with numbers. A certain string of numbers tells me which one of my teammates sent the message and includes some other basic information." To Carina's surprise, he turned off his cell phone and crossed the room to retrieve the house phone.

Jay dialed, and Carina could hear a man's voice answer after only one ring. "Seth, what's wrong?"

Jay listened to the other man speak for a minute and then stood to pace across the room. Jay's side of the conversation was mostly one-word phrases. Then he ended the call, saying simply, "E-mail me when you get into town, or call me on this number."

After he hung up, Carina stepped into his path to force him to stop and look at her. "Is everything okay?"

"I'm not sure." Jay put the phone back on the charger and then stared down at her. "Not long after my friend ran all of those background checks for me, someone from the FBI showed up at our office."

The mention of the FBI caused a ripple of anxiety to pulse through her. More than once, her father had taken her out to a park or the circus only to meet up with someone from the FBI, always handing off one of those thick envelopes that was undoubtedly stuffed with cash. "What did they want?"

"He wanted to know why Seth had run those names," Jay told her. "I have to think that one of the names was flagged, but Seth said he hasn't been able to figure out why. The agent also took Seth's printout of the background so he has access to the complete list of names you gave me."

"You think it was someone on my family's payroll."

"Oh yeah." Jay motioned toward the guest rooms. "Why don't you go get some sleep. I'll talk to you in the morning."

Carina shook her head and crossed her arms. "I'm not going to be able to sleep. Besides, I want to help."

24

Jay should have known Carina wasn't going to be satisfied with just sitting back and letting him handle things without her help. She didn't just dress the part of some businesswoman; she possessed the tenacity to climb her way to the top of whatever ladder she chose. Despite the jeans and T-shirt she currently wore, she was all business when she followed him to the kitchen where he'd left his computer. "Does it really matter that my family knows their background checks were run?"

"It might," Jay said with a shrug. He set about connecting to the Internet the way Seth had taught him so his signal couldn't be traced.

"Why would it matter?" Carina persisted.

"For one thing, some of those names didn't come back with any hits."

"So?" She put a hand on the serving bar and looked over his shoulder.

He stopped typing and turned to face her. "So the fact that those names were lumped in with known criminals would tell anyone on the mob's payroll that someone on the inside is feeding the government information."

Her eyebrows lifted. "Someone thinks I'm an informant?"

"Possibly," Jay said, the latest information rolling through his thoughts as he tried to put it all in a logical order. "Lou also told me that the person in charge of the Chicago mafia is with the FBI. Or at least, he was."

"What?" Fear vibrated in her voice, and Jay looked over to see that her face had paled. He couldn't say why the look of vulnerability tugged at him when it had been her independence that had first impressed him.

He reached out a hand and ran it down her arm. "I'm sorry. I didn't mean to scare you, but you need to understand what we're up against. If someone shows up flashing an FBI badge, that doesn't necessarily mean he's a good guy."

"I thought I was free of that life." Despair hung in Carina's voice, and her eyes were moist. She looked as though the past was drowning her, pulling her under until she could no longer see her future.

Without thinking, Jay stood up and turned her into his arms. Her arms wrapped around his waist as he pulled her close in a comforting embrace. He could feel the way her fingers curled into the soft cotton of his shirt, her grip tightening like she was afraid to let go.

Jay simply held her for a long moment, trying not to think about how well she fit into his arms. He tried to remind himself that she was only looking for comfort and tried to think of her as an assignment, someone he was sworn to protect. He breathed in the scent of her perfume, the spicy scent that reminded him too well that she was a beautiful woman, who, under normal circumstances, he would want to spend time with.

He considered her emotions and the confusion she must be feeling right now. He shifted so he could look down at her, and his voice was sympathetic. "It may be that the only way to truly be free of your family's past is to find out exactly why your father is in prison."

Carina blinked back tears that threatened but kept her hands linked loosely at his waist. Then she took a deep breath and nodded before taking a step back. "I'll call my boss in the morning and tell her I need a few days off. When do you want to leave for Colorado?"

"Seth will be here tomorrow afternoon."

"I don't know about having some stranger watch after my sister," Carina said hesitantly.

"You can trust Seth. Besides, his wife is coming with him. Having another woman around should help Bianca feel a bit more comfortable." Jay nodded toward his computer. "Come on. Let's see when we can get a flight out."

Carina slid onto a barstool at the counter beside Jay. Her eyes narrowed, and she looked at him, surprised. "Why are you looking up flights out of Tampa Bay? That's more than four hours away from here."

"I know, but if someone really is looking for you, they might keep an eye on flights from the local airports. Our best bet is to fly out of Tampa or Orlando."

"Orlando is closer."

Jay considered for a minute. "If you were going to leave town and go somewhere to hide out, where would it be?"

"I'd either go stay with friends in New York or I'd go to Provo to stay with Gianna. Why?"

"We'll use New York." Jay gave a definite nod. Carina watched him, confused when he opened another screen on his computer and made a reservation for her and Bianca from Miami to New York.

"Wait a minute. Why are you booking us on a flight to New York? And what about you? I thought you were coming with me."

"This one is just in case someone is monitoring airline reservations," Jay told her. He then proceeded to make two more sets of reservations for her and Bianca, one from Tampa Bay to Philadelphia and the other from Orlando to Washington.

"I'm confused. Why are you booking all of these reservations?"

"Because I don't want anyone to know which flight you're really on," Jay told her. He then booked himself on the flights out of Orlando and Tampa. "When we figure out which flight we really want, I'll cancel the others and book us another flight out to Denver."

"Are you sure you're not being paranoid? How would anyone even be able to access flight information? I thought that was supposed to be confidential."

"It is . . . unless the FBI puts you on a watch list," Jay told her. "If whoever is looking for you really is with the FBI, you'll be flagged at the airport."

"Maybe this isn't such a good idea."

Jay looked over his shoulder and spoke with confidence. "Trust me. I know what I'm doing."

Carina stared at him, and Jay was surprised to see the trust in her eyes. When they first met, she would barely look at him, yet, somehow, over the past few days, he had managed to break down barriers that he suspected had been surrounding her for years.

Color rose to her cheeks, and she let out a sigh. "What can I do to help?"

"Look around and see if you can find Matt's parents' phone number."

"You want to call Senator Whitmore?"

"Actually, I want to call his daughter or son-in-law. They're supposed to be staying with the senator this week. If they aren't, the senator or Mrs. Whitmore should know where they are."

Although she still looked confused, Carina crossed into CJ's kitchen, picked up the house phone, and started scrolling through the caller ID.

"I think I found it," Carina told him.

He reached his hand out to take the phone from her. He glanced down at the screen to see a phone number listed under the name James Whitmore. Jay pressed the button to dial the number, wondering if Jim would even remember him. Jay had met him a couple of times over the past year, always when his whole squad was together for some type of social function in the DC area.

Jay tried to force some confidence into his voice when the senator answered the phone himself. "Senator Whitmore, this is Jay Wellman," Jay began.

"Hi, Jay. What can I do for you?" Jim asked as though they were old friends. "Am I correct in assuming you're looking for Brent or Amy?"

"Yes, sir." Jay's lips curved slightly. "I'd prefer to speak to the commander if he's available."

"I hope you aren't just calling to get him out of doing the dishes."

"No, sir." Jay's smile widened. "I actually need to ask him a favor."

"Here he is."

"Thank you." Jay could hear the senator speak to Brent briefly before the commander came on the phone.

"Hey, Jay. What's up?"

Jay balanced the phone on his shoulder so his hands were free to continue his search for flights. "Any chance you might be available tomorrow night to give me a ride to the airport?"

"In DC?"

"Yeah," Jay said as he confirmed another airline reservation. "I'm coming into Dulles around six tomorrow evening, but I need to get over to Baltimore to catch a flight out at ten."

"I should be able to do that. Where are you headed?" Brent asked.

"It's a long story," Jay said, his eyes shifting to look at Carina. "I'll fill you in when I get there."

"Okay. I'll see you tomorrow night."

When Jay finally said his good-byes and hung up, Carina asked, "What was that all about?"

"The commander is going to help us out with some of our travel plans."

"This seems like an awful lot of trouble just so I can talk to my father for a few minutes."

"If we can get answers, it'll be worth it." Jay finished booking their airline tickets and shut off his laptop.

"Are you sure you have enough frequent-flyer miles for all of this?"

Jay nodded. "I travel a lot for work. I'm usually on a military transport, but before I joined my current unit, I used to fly commercial most of the time. The miles really added up."

"I still don't understand why you're doing all of this," Carina said. "You barely know me."

Jay looked up at her, and he forced himself to consider the same question. He tried to convince himself that he would try to help any friend in need, but he had to admit that Carina wasn't exactly a friend. She was more the promise of one. He smiled. "I guess I like a fun challenge."

"Figuring out my life is *fun?*"

Jay shook his head. "No, figuring out who's after you is necessary." He stood up and looked down at her. "Convincing you to go out with me is the fun part."

Carina eyed him warily. "You could have just asked me out instead of coming to my rescue like this."

"I already did, but you never actually said yes," Jay reminded her. "Besides, coming to people's rescue is what I do."

"It's what you do?"

"Yeah. Volunteering to help you out just kind of happened." Jay reached for her hand. "You do understand that I jump out of moving vehicles for a living, right? I already know that my idea of fun isn't exactly the same as the next guy's."

"You may want to rethink your definition of fun."

Jay simply shrugged. "We're going to have a busy day tomorrow. You should really get some sleep."

"What about you? Where are you going to sleep?"

"I'm just going to crash on the couch." He waved absently toward the long leather sofa in front of the television. "Don't worry. I'll keep you safe."

"Thanks, Jay." Carina looked up at him. "I'm really glad you're here."

"Me too."

25

"You know, I could just stay with Amber this week. Or Lou," Bianca suggested as she toweled off her hair from her morning practice.

Carina shook her head and continued to pack her suitcase. "Sorry, Bianca, but I want you somewhere that I know you'll be safe."

Bianca draped the towel over her shoulder, and her eyes narrowed. "Don't you think you're acting a bit paranoid? No one is after me. I'm perfectly fine."

"And it's my job to make sure you stay that way," Carina insisted. She zipped up her suitcase and turned to face her sister. "I know all of these security measures may seem extreme, but I need to make sure that if someone from our family really is looking for us, they can't find you."

"What's to say that someone wouldn't show up at my school?"

"For one thing, you go to school out of district, so anyone who knows where we live would look for you at the wrong school anyway." Carina gave her an apologetic look. "Besides, you'll have a bodyguard with you just to be safe."

"Seriously?" Bianca's voice came out with a huff of disbelief. "Do you have any idea how embarrassing it was yesterday having my coach follow me around?"

"Let me guess." Carina's tone dripped with sarcasm. "He didn't let you eat french fries at lunch."

"I'm serious, Carina."

"So am I." Carina tried to look past Bianca's defiant attitude and consider how she would have felt if someone had been assigned to follow her around when she was in high school. Her sympathy stirred, and she tried to find the balance between understanding and necessity. "Look, it's only for a couple more days. After I get back, hopefully everything will go back to normal."

"It had better." Bianca stepped toward the door. "Because I don't think I can stand this much longer."

"That makes two of us," Carina muttered.

* * *

Special Agent Curtis Graham pulled into the alley, surprised to see another car facing him. The plain dark sedan was similar to what his informant drove, but he couldn't remember him ever being so early for a meet. Then again, he had never received a message from him that sounded so urgent before.

Slowly, he pulled forward so he could talk to his snitch through the drivers' side windows. That's when he saw that the man in the driver's seat wasn't who he expected.

A smile lit his face when he recognized his friend, and his shoulders relaxed. "What are you doing here? I didn't think you were coming into town for a couple more days." He looked around the alley, and his eyes darkened with confusion. "And why are you parked back here? I'm supposed to meet an informant here in ten minutes."

"I was coming to look for you," Alex told him. "Any chance you have those background checks with you that I needed?"

"Yeah." He nodded. "They're locked in the trunk. I kept them with me like you asked."

"Good."

Alex's next movement was swift and unexpected as he leveled his gun at Graham's head.

* * *

"Are you all set?" Jay asked, shifting the duffel bag on his shoulder with one hand and lifting Carina's suitcase with the other.

"I think so." Carina gripped the strap of her briefcase.

Jay's eyes narrowed. "What did you do with your gun?"

"The ammunition is in the dresser in the bedroom," she told him, running her fingers back and forth over the leather strap of her briefcase. "I put the gun in the cabinet over the refrigerator. I wanted to make sure it was out of reach in case CJ comes home early."

Jay nodded his approval. "Just wanted to make sure you weren't trying to bring it with you. The airlines frown on that sort of thing."

"So I've heard." With a wry smile, she motioned to his full pack. "What all do you have in there? We're only going to be gone for a day or two."

"Just being prepared." Jay headed for the backyard. "Come on."

"Why are we going this way?"

"Just a safety precaution." Jay walked past the swimming pools and crossed the swatch of grass on his way to the dock where the Whitmores' boat was moored. He stepped nimbly into the boat, securing their luggage before turning and reaching out a hand to help Carina board.

"I thought we were going to the airport. Why are we on a boat?"

"Because I want to make sure no one follows my friends here." Jay cast off the lines. "Grab a seat."

"I thought I was being overly cautious, but you take paranoia to a new level."

"Never hurts to play it safe."

"After dealing with Bianca this morning, I'm not so sure." Carina shook her head. "She's not very happy about having a bodyguard, especially someone she doesn't know."

"If everything goes as planned, we'll arrive in Colorado early tomorrow morning and we'll be on a flight headed back here by tomorrow night." Jay turned the key and revved the engine to life. He slowly motored away from the dock and then started down the channel.

He navigated his way out to the ocean, the boat rocking violently as he transitioned from the calm waters out onto the waves. The water whipped up off of the sea and stung his eyes.

For the first time in weeks, Jay felt the freedom he had always found on the water, the freedom he had lost when his last assignment had ended so badly. He wasn't exactly sure when he had managed to shed the nightmares or the haunting images of that day, but somehow, over the past few days, his problems and struggles had taken a backseat to other concerns.

He glanced over at Carina, his breath catching at her raw beauty. Her hair blew into her face, but she didn't make any effort to tame it. Instead, she kept her eyes in front of her, a combination of uncertainty and a tentative trust visible on her face.

"It's just a little farther," Jay told her, motioning to a public dock in the distance. Even from almost a mile away, he could see Seth standing near an empty slip, waiting for them.

"Are you sure your friends will be there on time?"

"Yeah. I'm sure." Jay nodded. He maneuvered past a boat pulling a water skier and then made a wide turn as they approached the dock.

He scanned the area as he closed the distance, and he could see Seth doing the same. Vanessa wasn't anywhere in sight, but he imagined she was close by.

Jay cut the engine and glided into the empty spot beside Seth.

He noticed Seth's gaze shift over to Carina before he sent a questioning glance at Jay. "Seth, Carina," Jay said briefly. "Carina, Seth."

"Nice to meet you," Carina managed as she lifted a hand to shade her eyes, despite the sunglasses she wore.

Seth caught the line Jay threw him and secured the bow. As soon as the boat was tied off, Jay stepped onto the dock and held a hand out to Carina.

"Any trouble getting down here?"

Seth shook his head. "We weren't official."

Jay nodded in understanding. Seth and Vanessa had taken a military transport to Florida, but their names wouldn't appear on any flight manifests.

"Where is Vanessa?"

"In the parking lot. Blue sedan, second row back." Seth reached into his pocket and pulled two cell phones free. "These are for you."

"I assume your number is already programmed in."

"Yeah. Mine and Vanessa's. Kel's is in there too."

"Kel?"

Seth nodded. "He's the one who checked the phones out to me."

"Thanks, Seth. I really appreciate all of your help."

Seth just nodded. "Directions to the house we're staying at?"

Jay handed him a slip of paper along with a photograph he had printed of the backyard so Seth would recognize his destination. "My dad will drop off Bianca around three and will pick her up for her morning workout." He turned to make sure no one was within hearing distance. "Also, my sidearm is on the top shelf of the security room upstairs. If Vanessa needs one, there's another in the kitchen cabinet above the refrigerator. Ammunition is in the dresser in the downstairs guest room."

Seth looked down at his watch. "Do you have time to tell me what's going on?"

"Just for the short version."

"Which is?"

"Going to see Carina's father to find out who in the Chicago mob might have an interest in her." Jay reached in his pocket and pulled out the flash drive he had copied all of his notes onto. "Here is what I've found so far. I thought maybe you and Vanessa could take a look and help me do some more digging."

"We can do that." Seth nodded.

"Thanks, Seth." Jay took Carina's hand, signaling that they needed to leave.
"Check in when you get to the airport."

Jay nodded. "Will do."

Then, with Carina's hand still in his, Jay started toward the car that would take them on the next leg of their journey.

* * *

Carina kept her eyes closed, willing the nausea to subside. She didn't know why she'd thought she could make a four-hour car ride without getting carsick. Maybe she had deluded herself into thinking she could pray herself well when the queasiness started, but so far, nothing seemed to be helping.

"Are you okay?" Jay asked with obvious concern in his voice.

She desperately wanted to say yes, but she couldn't open her mouth to get the word out. Instead, she slowly shook her head, hoping the movement wouldn't create any unwanted consequences.

She heard the sound of the window opening and felt the blast of hot air circulate through the car. The fresh air helped her fight off the worst of the motion sickness, but she didn't know how much longer she would be able to go before her stomach protested completely. She estimated they were nearly halfway between Miami and Orlando. After getting caught in some weekend traffic, she knew that if they stopped, there was no way they were going to make their flight on time.

Just as she thought it, the car slowed, and then she felt it come to a stop.

"Come on. You'll feel better if you get out and walk around a bit," Jay said gently.

She didn't move for a minute, hoping that the lack of motion would allow her stomach to settle. Cautiously, she opened her eyes to see Jay standing outside of the car, his hand on her open door. He reached his other hand out to her.

Carina took a slow breath and set one foot on the pavement. She looked past Jay to see that they were in a Walmart parking lot, the scent of french fries from the fast food restaurant across the street sending another wave of nausea through her. Not sure she could stand on her own, she let Jay take her hand and managed to stand beside him.

"Why didn't you tell me you get carsick? We could have gotten you some Dramamine before we left Miami."

"Sorry. It hasn't been this bad in a long time."

"Going out on the boat before starting this drive probably didn't help."

"Just give me a minute, and then we can get back on the road."

"Carina, you're in no condition to travel right now." Jay shook his head and then motioned to the store. "We'll pick up some medicine for you and find someplace to rest for a while. We can always push our flight off until tomorrow."

"But what about your friend who was going to help us get from one airport to another?"

"He'll understand," Jay assured her. "And if he can't help us out tomorrow, then I've got a few other friends I can call. For now, let's get you out of the heat and find something to settle your stomach."

Carina nodded weakly. With her hand still caught in his, she followed Jay inside.

26

JAY LEANED AGAINST THE CINDERBLOCK wall outside of the women's restroom. He had already called Seth to let him know that their plans had been delayed, but thankfully, Seth was agreeable to extend his trip to Florida for as long as he was needed. Jay hoped he wouldn't change his mind once he met his reluctant charge.

Bianca was clearly unhappy about her current living arrangements, and Jay doubted Seth and Vanessa were going to be able to do much to change her mood. Hopefully his dad would be willing to step in if needed.

The door to the women's restroom creaked open, and Carina emerged, her face still pale. She looked up at Jay, and her cheeks flushed slightly.

"Feeling any better?"

She nodded, but it was obvious she was still trying to convince herself. She lifted one hand and held it to her stomach, as though willing it to settle. "If we leave now, we might still be able to make our flight."

"Carina, you're in no condition to make another two-hour drive." Jay shook his head. "I already talked to Seth, and he's more than willing to stay as long as we need him to with Bianca."

Carina looked relieved, but she shook her head. "I can't ask your friends to do that."

"It's really not a problem. They'll keep Bianca entertained today and tomorrow. If we aren't back by Sunday, they'll probably even take her to church."

"Where are we going to stay tonight?" Carina asked now. "I doubt you want me using my credit card right now in case someone might be able to track it, and I certainly don't want you to keep spending money on me."

"Don't worry. I have an idea." Jay motioned toward the front of the store. "I want to pick up a few things here, and then let's go find someplace that has Wi-Fi. We can make a new plan of attack."

"Plan of attack?" Carina looked at him warily. "You make it sound like we're about to go to war."

"I usually am about to go to war." Jay held out a hand and waited for her to take it. He nodded toward the pharmacy. "Come on. Let's find something to help you feel better."

"At this point, anything but driving in a car is sure to help."

* * *

"You're my bodyguard?" Bianca looked at the petite woman with dark skin and expressive eyes. "Seriously?"

"Actually, my husband is the bodyguard. I'm just here for fun."

"Fun." Bianca let her breath out in a huff and dropped her backpack on the couch. "Right."

Pete gave her a dark look that silently told her she'd better change her attitude.

"Look, I get it that you're all here to make sure I stay safe and everything, but don't you think this is overkill?" Bianca asked, hoping someone would listen to reason. "I mean, for all we know, the guys who showed up at my apartment are long gone."

"Stick it out for a few more days," Pete said mildly. "Hopefully, once Jay and Carina get back, things can go back to normal."

"Can't I at least go home and get some more of my stuff?" Bianca motioned to her backpack. "I thought I was only coming over here for one or two nights."

"I don't think that's a good idea." Vanessa shook her head.

The sliding glass door opened, and Bianca shifted to see the enormous black man entering the house. "What isn't a good idea?"

"Bianca going home to get some things," Vanessa answered for her. "Bianca, this is my husband, Seth."

"So you're the bodyguard."

"That's me." Seth nodded. "What's this about going home?"

"I just want to pack up some clothes and books and stuff." Bianca motioned to the pool. "And a few more swimsuits. It's kind of hard to practice two or three times a day when I only have two suits with me."

"Make a list," Seth told her. "I'll see what we can do."

"I have a couple of hours until practice. If you want to run over there now, I can stay here with Bianca," Pete offered. "Or I can go to her apartment for her."

"No one in her neighborhood knows me. It's probably best if I go." Seth motioned toward Vanessa. "Did you want to come with me?"

Vanessa shook her head. "I want to keep looking through Jay's notes."

Seth nodded and then looked back at Bianca. "Okay, kid. Give me a list, your address, and a key. I'll take it from there."

"I don't have a key with me, but if you stop and see Lou, he can let you in. He has our spare."

"Lou Rizzoni?" Vanessa asked.

"Yeah." Bianca's brows drew together. "How did you know?"

"Jay mentioned him in his notes." Vanessa glanced up at Seth. "It says here that he used to be a bodyguard for the family."

Bianca sensed Seth's skepticism and was immediately defensive. "You can trust Lou. He's been helping take care of things since my mother died."

"Give me that list, and I'll go check on Lou and get your things."

With a nod, Bianca turned and left her new bodyguard behind and prayed that this chaos in her life would end soon.

* * *

"This is where we're staying tonight?" Carina looked at Jay skeptically as she stepped out of the car. A cluster of trees edged a small clearing, the beach visible across an open stretch of grass.

Jay nodded and pulled a bag of charcoal out of the trunk of the car. He glanced over his shoulder and said, "Let me guess. You don't like camping."

"I don't know," Carina said hesitantly. "I've never been camping before."

"Never?" Jay turned and looked at her with such incredulity that she felt like she might as well have announced that she was actually from Jupiter rather than Chicago. "Not even in your backyard?"

Carina shook her head, and her voice turned defensive. "Not everyone goes camping when they're a kid."

"Sorry. It just never occurred to me that you wouldn't have done this before." He motioned to the very hard-looking ground. "Are you okay with this? If you want, we can try to find a hotel room."

"Which we would have to use a credit card for," Carina commented and shook her head. "Sorry, this just isn't what I was expecting. I'm sure it will be fine." She motioned toward the car. "What can I do to help?"

"Go ahead and grab that bag with the groceries in it. I thought I could start dinner, and then we can go sit on the beach while it cooks."

Carina glanced out at the water and then smiled back at him. "I like that idea."

Jay grinned in response. "I was hoping you would."

* * *

Seth pulled Jay's car into the shopping center parking lot down the street from Bianca's apartment and took another look around. He had already driven around the neighborhood twice and had taken the time to identify the people who might be watching the building. After reading through Jay's notes, he had expected to see at least one person keeping an eye on the place, but to his surprise, the only person who seemed to be in the same place both times he went through was the local drug dealer parked at the corner.

Though he was tempted to bypass Lou and pick the lock to get into Bianca's apartment, he decided it wouldn't hurt to meet the man who had provided Jay with so much information. He looked around again before knocking on the door. A minute passed, and Seth strained to hear any movement inside. Hearing none, he knocked again, this time with a little more force. Again, he didn't hear any response from within.

Assuming Lou must have gone out, Seth pulled a small case from his pocket and retrieved the tools he needed. Thirty seconds later, he managed to unlock Bianca's front door and step inside. He flipped on the light switch and froze. He didn't know what state Carina and Bianca had left their apartment in, but he was willing to bet it hadn't looked like this.

Couch cushions were pulled up and lay drunkenly on the floor. Papers were strewn everywhere, the bookshelf was empty, the books heaped on the floor beside it. A sewing mannequin hung a few inches off of the floor, tangled in the cords of the window blinds. Fabric was piled beneath it.

Instinctively, Seth reached for the weapon holstered in the back of his waistband and listened for any sound. Once he was satisfied that he was alone, he stepped through the living room, methodically checking the kitchenette, bathroom, and bedroom before securing his weapon once more.

He pulled his cell phone from his pocket and called Jay. "Jay, I think we have a problem."

Jay hesitated, making Seth think that Carina must be close by. "What kind of problem?"

"I came to Carina's apartment to pick a few things up for Bianca, and the place is trashed." Seth stepped closer to the desk in the corner and noted a drawer hanging open, the contents riffled through. Then he noticed the television hanging on the wall. "The television is still here, so it wasn't a robbery, but someone was definitely looking for something."

"I hate to do it, but you should probably call the cops," Jay said reluctantly. "First you might want to check with Lou. I'm surprised anyone got past him with the way he watches Carina's place. He might have seen something."

"I knocked on his door before I came here, but he didn't answer."

"That's odd." Jay hesitated. "Do me a favor and go check again. He's been there every time I've been by Carina's."

"Okay. Hold on." Seth walked outside and started toward Lou's apartment again. That's when he caught a glimpse of the older man through the crack in the curtains. "You were right. Lou was home."

"Did he see anything?"

"If he did, he isn't in a position to talk about it," Seth said bitterly. "Sorry, Jay. He's dead. From where I'm standing, I'd say it was a single bullet to the back of the head."

"No." Jay breathed the word, and Seth could only stare helplessly. Several seconds stretched out in silence before Jay spoke again. "Call the cops. Let me know what they find out."

"I will," Seth told him. "What do you want me to tell Bianca?"

"I don't know. I guess, tell her the same thing I'm about to tell Carina. The truth."

27

"THE TRUTH ABOUT WHAT?" CARINA asked, shifting on the sand beside him.

"About Lou," Jay told her, wondering how he could possibly find the right words. Until Seth's call had interrupted them, they had been sitting on the beach, talking about everything from their childhoods to their futures. Now he had the burden of telling Carina that her future would proceed without a friend who was clearly very important to her.

"What about Lou?" Carina's eyes narrowed. "Jay, what's wrong?"

He stared out at the waves rolling up on the beach and tried to find his voice. The sun wouldn't set for a couple more hours, but he pulled off his sunglasses despite the glare coming off of the water. With some difficulty, he forced himself to turn toward her and look her in the eye when he gave her the truth in the simplest terms he could manage. "Lou's dead."

"What?" Carina managed to ask before tears sprang to her eyes.

"I'm sorry, Carina." Jay slipped his arm around her shoulder and pulled her to his side. "Seth just found him."

"Someone killed him," she said with certainty, despite the tears spilling onto her cheeks.

"Yes," Jay nodded, leaning his cheek on top of her head, his fingers stroking her hair, "someone killed him."

They sat together in silence for several minutes. Then she shifted so she could look up at him. "Whoever did this is the same person who's looking for me, isn't it?"

"Maybe." Jay put his hand down on the sand behind her, turning so he was facing her. "But I'm not going to let anything happen to you. And my friends will keep Bianca safe."

"I want to believe that, but I have to wonder if Lou's death is my fault." Carina wiped the tears off her cheeks. Her jaw clenched, and she looked like she was trying to fight off another wave of tears. "If I had gone to Chicago with Nick, maybe the family would have left him alone."

"And maybe it isn't the family who's behind this." Jay tried to sort out the facts. The last time he had spoken to Lou, he had seemed resolved that something might happen to him. "If Nick and his friends had wanted to kill Lou, they would have done it when they took a shot at me. He was right there, out in the open, but they never aimed in his direction."

"I don't understand any of this."

"I know." Jay reached out and pushed a strand of hair away from her face. "But we'll figure it out together."

* * *

"What do you mean she wasn't there?" Alex demanded, fury vibrating through his voice. "Are you sure she didn't slip past you?"

"Positive. She wasn't there," Frank insisted. "I had someone at all of the airports that she was supposed to be flying out of. She wasn't at any of them."

"What about her car? Where is it?"

"I don't know. We hacked into the GPS system to search for it, but we didn't get anything. It's almost like someone is playing with us."

"Someone is helping her."

"It's got to be that guy who was at her apartment," Frank said with frustration. "I've been checking out everyone she's called on her cell phone in the past few days."

"You need to go back further than that."

"I can't," Frank told him. "Her phone was equipped with a scrambler. Probably Lou's doing. Nick disabled it when he got ahold of her phone a few days ago, but everything before then is blocked."

"Has Nick had any luck finding Carina?"

"No, but he thinks that you're behind her disappearance. At this point, since he's still loyal to Giovanni and Marciano, he's not going to be much use to us."

"What *do* you have?"

"So far, it doesn't look like she has any connections to the people she works with outside of normal business hours. I'm working on the other names now."

"How many more do you have to go through?"

"Only four. I should be able to work through them by tomorrow."

"I'm not waiting until tomorrow. Give me the names, and I'll run traces on their cell phones so you can locate them. Hopefully one of them will lead you to Carina."

"Okay." Frank shifted the handwritten list and rattled off the four names. "Shelby Peterson, Victoria Quinn, Jay Wellman, and Matt Whitmore."

"I'll run these names and get back to you," Alex told him. "I want eyes on every airport within a five-hour drive of Miami. We can't take a chance of one of those girls stumbling onto my identity."

"Are you even sure they have access to the information?"

"I'm sure." His voice was even. "They may not know it yet, but I can't afford to take the chance that they'll put it all together."

"Okay. You're the boss."

* * *

Seth felt the impending danger looming, like an itch on his back that he couldn't quite reach. He'd felt it before, usually moments before facing someone with a weapon aimed in his direction. Of course, he preferred that scenario over the prospect of telling Bianca that her friend had been murdered.

The police had confirmed what he had already suspected. Professional hit, single bullet to the back of the head. There weren't any unexpected fingerprints, nor was there any sign of a struggle. Either Lou never heard his killer sneak up behind him, or he knew the person who shot him.

The state of Bianca's apartment told him that whatever the intruder was looking for likely hadn't been found. Every inch of the place had been rummaged through and appeared to have been methodically searched. Logically, some part of the apartment would have been untouched if the wanted item had been discovered.

Always cautious, Seth drove in the opposite direction of the Whitmores' and then pulled into the covered parking garage of a nearby hospital. He circled for a couple of minutes before leaving through a different exit. He then drove to a shopping area and parked to make sure he wasn't being followed.

He pulled out his phone and called the secure phone he had given Vanessa.

Vanessa's voice came on after the second ring. "Hey, is everything okay?"

Seth could hear the underlying concern. "Not exactly." He shifted in his seat and searched for any familiar cars before continuing. "Bianca's friend Lou has been murdered, and her apartment was trashed when I got there."

"Oh no." Vanessa's voice was low and filled with concern.

"I don't know what Jay has gotten himself into, but I'm worried."

"Me too." Seth heard Vanessa speak quietly to Bianca, and he suspected she was moving out of earshot. "Seth, I've been reading over Jay's notes since you left, and one thing has me really worried."

"What's that?"

"According to what Lou Rizzoni told Jay, the person in charge of the Chicago mafia is actually someone in the FBI."

"Someone from the FBI came and visited me right after I started running names for Jay. He said his name was Curtis Graham."

"I wish I was in my office so I could run his background."

"Me too. This is getting pretty scary."

"Not as scary as Jay and Carina trying to get on a commercial airplane tomorrow," Vanessa surmised.

"You think this head guy flagged Carina?"

"I would if I were him."

"Is there any way you could check?"

"I can't from here, especially after hours on a Friday evening. Do you have any contacts with the FBI or the airlines?"

"I don't, but maybe Amy can help us out," Seth said, referring to the squad's intelligence officer. "Her brother is FBI out in Phoenix. Maybe he could run Carina's name and see if she's flagged. I can also see if she can connect Curtis Graham with any of this."

"That's a good idea. Do you want to call, or do you want me to?"

"I will. I want to drive around a bit more before I come back. I don't want to take the chance that I'm being followed."

"Okay. I'll see you when you get back."

"And Vanessa?"

"Yeah?"

"Keep that sidearm Jay left you in reach."

"I will."

* * *

Jay's eyes narrowed when he looked at the unfamiliar phone number illuminating the screen. Carina, still nestled beside him, shifted and looked up with swollen eyes. "Who is it?"

"I don't know." Jay hit the talk button and answered with a tentative, "Hello?"

"Jay, it's Amy."

"What's up?"

"You can't go to the airport tomorrow."

His eyebrows drew together, and he braced himself against what was certainly not going to be welcome news. "Why not?"

"After talking to Seth about what's been going on, I called up my brother, Charlie. As a favor to me, he ran your friend's name to see if she was flagged for air travel."

"Are you telling me she is?" Jay asked, his heartbeat quickening.

"Yes." Amy paused briefly. "And so are you."

"What?" Jay sat up straight, and he saw the concern on Carina's face. He shifted away from her and stood up to pace in the cooling sand. "That means someone has connected us."

"Yeah," Amy agreed, sympathy hanging in her voice. "Seth is heading over to your parents' house right now. He wants them to stay somewhere else for a few days to make sure no one comes looking for you there."

Jay took a few steps before turning back to look at Carina's frightened face. "I can't believe this."

"I'm sorry, Jay," Amy told him before rushing on. "Seth gave me the basics of what's going on. I called up the prison to see if there was any way Carina could talk to her father on the phone, but he's in the infirmary. They're saying it was food poisoning, but the doctor I talked to couldn't be sure if it was really something he ate or if someone slipped something to him. Apparently, he was the only person who got sick after dinner two nights ago."

"Is he going to be okay?"

"It looks like it, but he's still in pretty bad shape," Amy told him. "Charlie is seeing if he can pull some strings to have him transferred quietly out of there. He thinks he can get him moved to another prison using an alias since there's a chance it's an FBI agent who's targeting him."

"Do you really think he can do that?"

"This is one time that it will probably be helpful to have a father who is a US senator."

"I appreciate all of your help, Amy."

"Anytime," she told him. "Hold on a second. Brent wants to talk to you."

Jay heard Amy hand the phone off to her husband. Then Brent's voice came over the line. "Hey, Jay. I just got off the phone with Kel."

"And?" Jay prompted, afraid to know what was going to come at him next.

"He thinks it's time for you and your friends to get out of Florida."

"Any suggestions? If my name has been flagged, my apartment isn't going to be safe," Jay said, his stomach churning as he felt his life spiraling out of control. "And Seth has already been visited by the FBI, so we have to assume he's on someone's radar."

"I agree, which is why Kel set you up with a place in the Outer Banks."

"What?"

"A friend of his has a house there you can stay at. Seth is going to meet you there with your friend's sister," Brent told him. "It's on one of the more secluded islands. In fact, you'll have to take a ferry to get there. It's definitely somewhere you can get off the radar while we try to figure out what's going on."

"Brent, I don't know if I want you to keep digging. I asked Seth to help out and succeeded in putting him right in the middle of all of this."

"We're a team," Brent reminded him. "Trust us. We have your back."

"Okay." Jay sighed, too exhausted to argue. "Where am I going?"

"I'm sending the directions in an encrypted e-mail to your phone," Brent told him. "But first, you need to head over to the Naval Air Warfare Center. Turn in the car you're driving. I have another vehicle reserved for you there. You'll need four-wheel drive to get to where you're going."

"When can I pick it up?"

"It'll be ready for you at oh five hundred."

"Okay. Thanks, Brent."

"Keep your head down."

"I will."

28

"I CAN'T BELIEVE ALL OF this is happening." Carina stared blindly out at the waves and shook her head as she fought back another bout of tears. "Everyone who's tried to help me is now in danger. I should have known better than to let anyone get too close to me."

"Hey, don't do that." Jay put a hand on her arm and stepped in front of her, where she couldn't help but look at him. "Don't take the blame for something you can't control."

"Don't you understand?" Carina's voice rose with her emotions. "Your own family is in danger now because of me. Your friends too." She shook her head in frustration. "I can't believe you would let any of them keep trying to help."

"They'll be careful, especially now that they know what we're dealing with." Jay reached for her and pulled her into his arms. Tentatively, she lifted her arms to encircle his waist.

She wanted to trust him. She desperately wanted to believe that someday everything would be okay. But how could she believe that? Everyone she had ever depended on was gone. Her mother, Lou, even her father and grandfather.

"If you were smart, you'd get in that car and drive as far away from me as possible."

He shifted back enough that he could see her face. "I am smart." He gave her a little half smile when he added, "Smart enough to be standing here on a beach alone with you." Then his eyes darkened and his hand trailed down to rest at the small of her back. "And smart enough to want to be with you after all of this is over."

He leaned down and kissed her cheek. Then his mouth found hers, and she was lost. She knew the waves were crashing behind her, but she couldn't hear them over the buzzing in her head. His lips were soft, persuasive, and his kiss left her head swimming. Emotions rushed through her, the newness of not only feeling wanted but being understood. When he broke the kiss, he stared down at her, looking as dazed as she felt.

She looked at him, unable to find any words. Then she instinctively pushed up on her toes so she could press her lips to his once more. It was the same dizzying, overwhelming sensation.

A seagull let out a lonely cry in the distance, and the scent of the sea mixed with the lingering smell of the charcoal Jay had left cooling in the nearby grill. Her heartbeat raced as her fingers curled into the cotton of his shirt.

When she dropped back down onto her heels, Jay's expression warmed and softened. Then he smiled down at her as though he had learned a secret about her. When his arms tightened around her once more, Carina let herself enjoy the now familiar embrace and let herself revel in the sensation of feeling cherished.

* * *

Pete understood the danger, but he wasn't about to be chased out of his own home. He had seen his wife off an hour earlier, sending her to spend a few days with her sister before she would head to California to visit their youngest son. She hadn't objected to the idea of a couple of weeks enjoying the San Diego weather, even though he knew she would have preferred it if he had joined her.

He hadn't told her everything, just enough to convince her that it would be best if she finally visited the Tampa Bay side of the family for a while before she took advantage of some of their son's frequent-flyer miles. She already worried about having two children in the military, and the last thing he needed was for her to know that their oldest son's visit home may have very well put him in more danger than a tour in Afghanistan.

The security in his home might be understated compared to the fortress the Whitmores had created out of their house, but he had installed enough of his toys over the years to be sure no one was going to show up unannounced. He heard a car engine and glanced out the window. He recognized the dark SUV as the same one he had seen drive by twice in the past half hour.

A firm believer that the best defense was a good offense, Pete headed for the front door and walked out in the fading sunlight as the vehicle slowed near his house. He gave a friendly wave, even though he was braced to dive for the bushes if the need arose.

The driver pulled to the curb and rolled down the window. Pete relaxed slightly when he saw that the twenty-something-year-old man was alone and both of his hands were visible as he shifted the car into park. "Hey, is this the Wellman residence?"

"That's right. Can I help you?"

"I'm looking for Jay Wellman."

"That's my son, but I'm afraid he isn't here," Pete announced casually.

"Any idea when he might be back?"

Pete shook his head. "He's active duty military. I'm afraid we only get to see him once or twice a year if we're lucky. He had to head back to base this afternoon."

"I'm sorry I missed him." The man reached out and put the car back in gear. "Thanks for your help."

"No problem," Pete told him. He watched the SUV pull away and memorized the license plate before it was gone. Then he pulled open the mailbox as though checking for mail before casually walking back inside.

With a last glance down the street, he closed the door and prepared to let his son's friends decide how to use this latest tidbit of information.

* * *

"What do you mean, we're leaving right now?" Bianca asked. Lou was dead, her world was spinning out of control, and now this Navy SEAL was insisting that she go with him to who knows where in the middle of the night.

"I'm sorry, Bianca, but something doesn't feel right," Seth told her, his expression serious.

"Nothing has felt right since Carina made me come over here," Bianca countered.

"Whether you like it or not, your sister is only doing what she thinks is best to protect you," Vanessa interjected. "After what Seth found at your apartment, her instincts must have been right."

"I just want to have a normal life, where nobody I love gets killed."

"We know you do." Vanessa's tone softened. "And we understand how hard it is to walk away from everything familiar right now, but we can't be sure that whoever killed Lou might not have figured out that you are friends with the Whitmores."

"How do I know that this is really what my sister would want?" Bianca asked now, fighting her fears and confusion. She believed Seth when he said something didn't feel right, but that didn't mean she had to fall in line with whatever he said. She barely knew this man or his wife.

"Would you feel better if you could talk to her first?" Vanessa asked.

Bianca thought a moment and then nodded. "Yeah, I would."

"Okay." Vanessa dialed a number on her cell phone and then asked for Carina. She then handed the phone to Bianca.

"Carina?"

"Bianca." Carina's voice came over the phone in a combination of relief and concern. "Are you okay?"

"I don't know." Bianca bit down on the inside of her cheek to keep the tears from coming. She didn't want to admit that all she wanted was to have her mother there to give her a hug and tell her that everything was going to be okay. Her mother was no longer an option, but Carina made a pretty good second choice. "Seth and Vanessa want me to leave here."

"I know. Jay is going to bring me to the same place they're taking you."

"I don't want to go." Bianca could hear the whine in her voice and hated that she was so vulnerable and that her freedom was being controlled by so many others without her input or consent.

"Bianca, please do this for me." Carina hesitated and then added, "It's kind of like when Mom sent us out for pizza. It didn't seem like a big deal, but it was."

"Okay." She took a deep breath and tried to sound strong. "But I'm going to see you tomorrow, right?"

"Yes. I'll see you tomorrow," Carina assured her. "I love you."

"I love you too."

* * *

Pizza. Jay stared at Carina as his last conversation with Lou replayed in his mind. "What did you mean by going out for pizza?"

"I just wanted her to understand how serious all of this is."

"But why did you say *pizza*?"

"That's where we were right before my mom died," Carina told him. "She had sent us out for pizza. I've always wondered if maybe she knew someone was coming to the house and maybe she sent us away on purpose."

"Why would you think that?"

"Pizza was her favorite food. It was odd that she sent us out to get some instead of coming with us or ordering out. She didn't even ask us to bring her something back." Carina's eyes narrowed. "Is something wrong?"

"When you said that, it reminded me that when I talked to Lou, he told me that if something happened to him, I should tell you to take your sisters out for pizza. Then he said something about keeping up the maintenance on your mom's car."

"What?" Fear and confusion flashed in her eyes. "What do you think he meant by that?"

"I think he was telling you that if something happened to him, then you're all in danger." Jay pulled out his cell phone and texted Seth a simple message. *Leave now.*

The response was almost immediate. *Be on the road in five.*

"Who were you texting?"

"Seth. I wanted to make sure they were really leaving now," Jay told her. "He said they're leaving in five minutes."

Carina looked at him with a new sense of panic. "Do you think there's any way the family could have found Gianna?"

"I don't know. If someone is tracking you down through your cell phone calls, it might be possible." Jay handed her his cell phone. "Call her up and tell her you want her to get out of her apartment right now. And also tell her to leave her cell phone at home."

"Why?"

"Just trust me. Have her write down this number and then call us on a friend's phone. That way we can call her back and let her know what to do next." Jay used his finger and wrote the number for his cell phone in the sand.

"If someone knows her phone number, wouldn't they be able to trace a call back to this phone?"

"It's blocked. Even another government agency wouldn't be able to trace it," Jay assured her.

Carina did as he asked, but he could tell that Gianna was resisting her request.

Jay put a hand on her arm and whispered softly, "Tell her about Lou."

Tears instantly sprang to her eyes, but she nodded. "Gianna, someone killed Lou. The last thing he said was that if something happened to him for us to go out for pizza."

Jay could tell by the way Carina's body position changed that Gianna was now more receptive to her sister's demands. While Carina continued to talk to her sister, Jay jogged over to the car to retrieve the second cell phone Seth had given him.

He considered who he might call for help. He knew anyone on his team would drop everything to help a friend in need, but all of them were currently on the east coast. Gianna was all the way across the country.

Out of options, he muttered a prayer, using words he had often heard come out of his teammates' mouths. "Okay, Heavenly Father, what do I do?"

Mentally, he went through a checklist of his teammates. Brent and Quinn had both grown up in Virginia, and Tristan had lived there since his teenage years. Then there was Seth, who was currently keeping Carina's other sister safe. He thought of Amy. Unlike the members of the squad, who had all attended college in the east, Amy had graduated from Brigham Young University, the same school Gianna was currently attending.

Jay dialed her number, relieved when he heard her voice come on the line despite the late hour. "Amy, I need a huge favor."

"What can I do?" Amy asked without hesitation.

"I think my friend's sister could be in danger, and I need some help getting her off the grid for at least a couple of days," Jay told her. "She's out at BYU. I thought that since you went to school there, you might know someone who could help."

"Let me think," Amy said, and Jay could visualize that look of concentration she always had when she was determined to find a solution to what often seemed to be an unsolvable puzzle. "There's got to be someone."

"Carina is talking to her right now. I told her to have Gianna pack up some things and go stay with a friend for now. She's going to leave her cell phone in her dorm room and then call us from another phone to let us know where she is."

"I know who I can call. My old roommate and her husband still live in Provo. He teaches history at the Y."

"Do you think they would be willing to help? Without asking too many questions?"

"I think so," Amy told him. "Let me call them, and I'll call you right back."

"Thanks, Amy." Jay walked back over to where Carina still sat on the beach, the phone still to her ear. He could tell she was trying to sound positive as she reassured Gianna, even though he could tell Carina was terrified. After another minute or two, Carina said her good-byes and then turned to Jay with tears in her eyes.

"I don't know what I would do if something happened to one of my sisters."

"My friend Amy is trying to find someone to help her out there." Jay gathered Carina close and then simply held her while they both waited for their phones to ring. Carina's rang first. She followed Jay's previous example and drew the phone number Gianna gave him in the sand. A moment later, Amy called.

"Okay, Jay. You're all set. My friend is going to swing by the store and pick up a burn phone so Gianna will have a way to communicate with you. Then they're going to take her up to Park City with them for the weekend. Their family has a condo up there they can use," Amy told him. "I didn't give them details, but I told them I really don't want them to take Gianna to their home. I don't want to put them at risk."

Jay thought of his own parents and nodded. "That's probably wise."

"You know, if we can't put our finger on what's going on by Sunday, we might want to consider something more permanent."

"Are you thinking about WITSEC?" Jay asked.

"We're dealing with the mob, Jay. It's something you need to consider."

"Yeah, but I can't take the chance that some FBI agent on the mob's payroll will be able to find them."

"Let me talk to my brother in the FBI and see if he has any ideas."

"I appreciate anything you can do."

29

THEY WERE ALL STANDING IN the kitchen when the deafening blare of the alarm sounded. Seth looked over at his wife, a silent question reflecting in his eyes. They had a choice to make. They could flee, or they could fight.

His protective instincts told him to slip out into the night and get Vanessa and Bianca to safety as quickly as possible. Logic told him that while fleeing would solve the immediate danger, fighting might help them understand it.

Vanessa stared at him during that split second of indecision, and then she reached into her purse where her weapon was stored. Seth nodded his approval and motioned to the stairwell door in the kitchen, a doorway that appeared to be little more than a pantry. He then signaled for her to call the cops.

Bianca stared up at him, utterly terrified. He put a hand on her shoulder and motioned to Vanessa. He didn't speak, but he mouthed the words. "Stay with Vanessa." Then he held one finger over his lips and motioned to the door once more.

Vanessa put a hand on Bianca's arm to escort her into their hiding place. Trusting that his wife would protect Bianca and keep her out of sight, Seth moved through the house toward the backyard, where the alarm had been tripped.

Jay had set up proximity alarms several yards beyond where a series of motion sensors protected the grounds. As expected, the sound of the proximity alarms startled the intruder enough to cause him to change direction.

Seth stepped out into the night, avoiding the infrared beam that would trip another motion sensor. He could see the movement behind some shrubbery, and he silently started in that direction.

Part of him wanted to believe that it was just a stray dog or a neighbor who was cutting through the wrong yard. Odds were against it, and he reached for his weapon as he disappeared into the shadows.

Seth caught the scent of someone, sweat mixed with traces of deodorant. The alarms stopped sounding, and Seth assumed that whoever was weaving his way toward the house had figured out how to disable the system.

Seth pressed himself against the cinderblock wall that separated the Whitmores' yard from the next-door neighbor's and waited. With his dark clothing and dark skin, he knew he was all but invisible beneath the moonless sky. Footsteps padded toward him quietly. He doubted someone without his intensive SEAL training would even hear the person approaching.

In his mind, he counted down the steps, calculating the angle that the intruder would take as he passed by. Then in a flurry of movement, Seth left the safety of the shadows and struck out. A kick to the midsection, an elbow to the jaw, and the figure clad in black clothing dropped to the ground.

The gunshot that sounded a second later startled Seth and sent him diving for cover behind a cluster of palm trees. He returned fire, now able to make out another figure near the boat. He didn't take the time to consider how the second man had escaped his notice. A spray of bullets impacted the trees and the wall behind him.

He squatted down and squeezed off a burst of gunfire of his own. Even in the darkness, he could see his bullets impact the ground in a line following the path of the shooter. Unprepared for a lengthy gun battle and nearly out of ammunition, Seth rushed back toward the house. He headed straight for the main level guest room where the extra clips were stored and quickly reloaded his gun.

A door creaked open, but Seth wasn't able to tell which direction the intruder was headed. Then he heard a jingle of something clattering down the main staircase followed by rapid footsteps.

Seth rushed down the short hallway into the living area just as the intruder ran toward the sound. "Freeze right there!"

The man stopped, holding his hands even with his shoulders. The light from the kitchen silhouetted the man and the gun he held.

"Drop the weapon," Seth demanded.

He should have known it wouldn't be that easy. The man started to lower his right hand as though preparing to lay his gun down on the ground. Then he squatted and spun, taking aim as he shot at Seth once again. Seth felt a bullet tear through the flesh of his left arm just as he fired. His target stumbled forward but remained on his feet and headed toward the stairs.

"Vanessa!" Seth shouted to make sure she knew it wasn't him coming toward her.

Stairs creaked, a door opened, and a gunshot sounded.

Seth prayed that his wife was the shooter, not the victim. "Vanessa? Are you okay?"

"We're okay," she called back. "We're both okay."

* * *

Bianca couldn't stop shaking. Vanessa had tried to get her to stay in one of the upstairs bedrooms while she and Seth talked to the police, but she was too afraid to be alone, even if she was only a few rooms away. Instead, she sat quietly at the kitchen table, watching and listening. And trembling.

A man's body was still sprawled in the front hallway, now covered with a plain white sheet, as though that could hide the reality that this person had broken in and tried to kill them.

Shifting, Bianca looked out the window. All of the floodlights were on, and the ripples the breeze made in the swimming pools looked so peaceful. The setting would have been soothing except for the coroner who was currently loading another body onto a stretcher, the black body bag confirming that he too was dead.

In the living room, Vanessa finished bandaging the gunshot wound on Seth's arm. Gunshot. Seth claimed it wasn't serious, just a flesh wound, but that didn't discount the fact that a bullet had caused the damage.

Bianca took a breath and felt another shudder rack her body. An hour ago, she had been so annoyed about her life being turned upside down that she hadn't considered that Jay and his friends were risking their lives to keep her safe. She wouldn't make that mistake again.

"Can you take me through what happened outside?" a policeman asked Seth once Vanessa had finished giving him first aid.

"Yeah." Seth nodded. He didn't even glance down at the bright white bandage that contrasted against his dark skin but instead took the policeman through the night's events, starting with when the alarm had sounded.

"Wait a minute." The policeman looked at Seth, confused. "You said you knocked him out with an elbow to the head?"

"That's right."

"Was that before or after you shot him?"

Seth shook his head, and for the first time, Bianca saw confusion on Seth's face. "I didn't shoot him."

"Someone did."

"Yeah." Seth nodded. "Right after I knocked the first guy out, someone shot in my direction. That's when I took cover and worked my way back into the house."

"Where was the second shooter?"

"From the sound of the shot, I'd say he was hiding down by the dock." Seth waved toward the front hall where the body still lay. "I don't know who that guy is, but I'd bet he had some kind of military or law enforcement training."

"Why do you say that?"

"Because I didn't hear him."

The police officer turned and looked out the window at the well-lit yard. "If you were standing over by that wall, how would you expect to hear someone who was all the way down at the dock?"

"I'm a Navy SEAL. I should have known he was there. Heard him, sensed him, smelled him." Seth shook his head, his voice filled with conviction. "The fact that I didn't tells me something."

The police officer shrugged as though he wasn't sure he believed Seth. The older man made some notes in a notepad. When a younger policeman came in from outside, the older one asked, "Do you have an ID on that one?"

"His name is Guido Manchione. Thirty-eight years old from Chicago."

Bianca didn't recognize the name, but it was definitely Italian. She was sure Carina would assume he had been sent by *the family.*

Bianca didn't know why Carina always seemed to be so liberal with the term, as though everyone who had ever worked with their father was really related to them, but she had to admit that she was starting to believe her sister wasn't nearly as paranoid as she had always thought.

She could also admit that her mother and Carina had succeeded in sheltering her from their past. In theory, she understood her background, but her memories didn't reflect any of the dangers or evils they had always been so afraid of. Her understanding of the mob was straight out of Hollywood, learned from the golden screen and television. Now she knew that reality was a lot scarier and a whole lot more personal.

The detective scribbled some more notes and motioned to the hall as he issued a command to his partner. "Get an ID on that one."

Bianca watched the younger detective shift the sheet so he could press the dead man's thumb to a handheld device. The detective's eyes narrowed when he read the little screen. He repeated the process, concern and confusion evident on his face. Slowly, he stood up and faced Seth.

"Did this man identify himself to you before you shot him?"

"No." Seth shook his head. "As I told your partner here, I ran into the bedroom down that hall to get more ammunition. I heard him enter but couldn't tell where he was until Vanessa threw something down the stairs to draw his attention. That's when I saw him go into the hall."

"Then what?"

"I told him to freeze. He stopped and acted like he was going to put the gun down." Seth nodded down at his bandaged arm. "That's when he shot me."

"And you managed to shoot and kill him *after* he shot you?"

Vanessa stepped forward and put her hand on her husband's shoulder. "Seth's shot wounded him. I'm the one who killed him."

"And he never identified himself?" the detective asked again.

"No, why?" Vanessa asked. "Who was he?"

"Frank Tesan. FBI."

"Let me guess," Bianca spoke up now, her voice wavering as she fought against reality. "He was from Chicago."

Everyone looked at her, understanding flashing in Seth's and Vanessa's expressions, confusion alighting the detectives'.

The younger detective regained his composure first. "How did you know that?"

She looked from the detective to Seth, an unspoken apology on her face. "Lucky guess."

30

Jay glanced over at Carina in the passenger seat. Her eyes were closed and her body relaxed as they approached the little town of Swan Quarter, North Carolina. The window was cracked, Carina's hair tousled from the wind. Her classic beauty was softer now, her golden skin free of make-up and contrasting against her long, dark lashes.

Even though she slept, Jay could still see the little line of worry between her brows. The invisible shield she had so fiercely cloaked around her when they had first met was gone, destroyed in that moment last night when he had kissed her. He supposed he had been chipping away at it long before he had held her in his arms last night, and looking back, he was a little surprised to realize he had been driven to understand her almost from the first moment he had met her.

He couldn't say when she had gone from just another pretty face to someone he truly cared about, but he'd been serious when he'd told her last night that he planned to be around for her after this whole ordeal ended. He just hoped for her sake that it ended soon.

Carina hadn't been able to relax last night until Gianna called on her new cell phone to let her know she had arrived safely in Park City. After she had ended the call, she and Jay had stayed up late, sitting on the beach and talking.

She had shared a lot of her memories of Lou, from her childhood as well as the last few years. The way she spoke of him, it was obvious that Lou was just as close as a family member and was likely the person she had visualized as her father figure for most of her life.

Jay hated seeing her life so unsettled, and he had found himself praying once more that he and his friends could help her find a sense of comfort and safety soon. That prayer hadn't been answered as immediately as he had hoped.

Shortly after Carina had fallen asleep, Seth had called to tell him what had transpired at the Whitmores' house. Jay had deliberately neglected to tell Carina about the shooting, not wanting to give her any more stress than necessary. Besides, Seth had been so concerned about getting Vanessa and Bianca safely away from the Whitmores' that he had only given him the short version of what had happened.

Now Jay was eager to get to their temporary safe house to find out what other information Seth might have uncovered.

He had deliberately left before dawn, hoping to get past Jacksonville ahead of the inevitable weekend traffic. Jay had expected Carina to complain when he woke her shortly before four a.m., but she had simply dug her little make-up case out of her suitcase, disappeared into the public bathroom for five minutes, and returned to help him finish loading the car.

They had successfully switched vehicles at the naval base in Orlando and had only hit one major slowdown outside of Savannah. The Dramamine Carina had taken before starting the long drive seemed to be working, although he suspected she was using sleep to escape any lingering symptoms.

She shifted in her seat, her eyelids still half closed when she turned toward him. She offered him a timid smile and sat up straighter. "Where are we?"

"Almost to the ferry."

"We're almost there?" She looked out the window just as he made the final turn toward the ferry landing.

Jay glanced down at the clock on the dashboard. "We've still got about an hour before the ferry leaves. Let's check in, and then we can see if there's someplace we can grab a bite to eat. You must be starving."

"Actually, I don't think I want to eat much right before going out on the ferry," Carina admitted.

"Then we'll go find someplace that has saltine crackers and ginger ale."

"That sounds like a great idea." Carina chuckled. She looked out the window and then turned back toward Jay. "I was just thinking, what am I going to do about my car?"

"I think my dad still has your car keys."

Carina nodded. "I haven't seen my keys since this whole thing started."

"Any chance you would consider selling your car? Trading it in for something else?"

Carina immediately shook her head, her expression adamant. "That car was my mother's. I don't want to drive anything else."

"Okay," Jay conceded. "I can see if my dad can pick it up in a couple of days. With the jamming device I had him put in it, either he or CJ can probably keep it parked at their house until we figure out what to do."

Jay hesitated as he thought of Carina's car and the obvious lack of maintenance before he had worked on it. "Remember how I told you that Lou said something about having you keep up the maintenance on your mom's car?"

She nodded. "I have no idea what he meant by that."

"Did Lou normally take care of the car's maintenance? Or did he ever remind you about that before?"

"He must have thought that I knew how to take care of the car." Carina shook her head. "That was a pretty big assumption on his part. The only thing I know about cars is that they need gas to run."

"They need a little more than just gas."

"I guess I should have paid more attention to the maintenance log my mom kept in the glove box," she admitted. "It was just one of those things I didn't worry about since everything seemed to be working."

Jay's eyes sharpened. "Did Lou know about the maintenance log?"

"I don't know," Carina told him. "He never mentioned it."

Jay replayed the older man's last words through his mind, wondering if there was more to the message than he had originally thought.

"What?" Carina asked.

"I'm not sure." Jay pulled the car to a stop by the ferry landing. "But I think I'm going to have my dad take a closer look at your car."

* * *

Carina gripped the dashboard to steady herself as Jay drove through the sand dunes near the beach. She could see why four-wheel drive was necessary to get to the beach house. There was no way a car would make it through what could only loosely be termed a dirt road. She had the window down, and the wind whipped through her hair, the scent of the water rushing over her.

"Are you doing okay?" Jay asked, clearly keeping his speed down to keep their car from jostling her any more than necessary.

"I'm fine," Carina told him. "The ferry wasn't nearly as bad I'd expected."

"Or your medicine worked better than you thought it would."

"That's probably it," she agreed with a smile. "How much farther?"

"I think that's it up there." Jay pointed to the white clapboard house nestled on the beach of Pamlico Sound. The front of the house faced the water, and an old Jeep was parked near the entrance at the back. Jay slowed down, a look of indecision on his face.

"What's wrong?"

"I don't recognize that vehicle." He glanced down at his directions again, and his eyebrows drew together. "I want you to stay in the car until I check the place out."

"Okay." Carina nodded. Then Seth stepped out onto the back porch and lifted a hand in greeting. "I guess it's safe."

Jay nodded and parked in the gravel driveway.

"I was hoping you were on the last ferry," Seth said as soon as Jay and Carina got out of the car. "A storm's supposed to be coming in, and there isn't going to be another one to this island until tomorrow at the earliest."

"Glad we got up early, then." Jay pointed at the Jeep in the driveway. "Whose car is that?"

"The guy who owns this place. He keeps it garaged in town for when he comes here. We picked it up when we got the house keys from a friend of his. That's where we left your car for now." Seth's jaw tightened, and he asked Jay, "Did you hear the news?"

"What news?"

"Double suicide bombing in Islamabad. Apparently the Taliban are retaliating against the bin Laden attack."

Jay looked grim, and Carina felt his tension level rise when he asked, "Are we going active?"

"Not yet." Seth shook his head. "We're in the wait-and-see mode right now."

"Hopefully we'll stay in that mode for a few more days."

"I don't think we're joining in on this one quite yet." Seth motioned toward the house. "Come on in and check the place out."

Carina stepped through the door Seth held open for them. She was immediately drawn to the view of the water. Windows lined the entire far wall of the living room. A couch and several chairs made up a cozy conversation area, and a wooden table and two matching chairs were tucked into the corner of the room, where someone could sit and watch the waves.

"This is gorgeous," Carina said, turning back to look at Jay. Then she heard footsteps on the stairs, and Bianca rushed into the room.

"Carina!" Bianca rushed into her arms, clinging to her as though they hadn't seen each other in months. "I'm so glad you're here. I was so scared."

Carina's hold tightened on her sister, her eyes meeting Jay's over Bianca's shoulder. Something had happened. She could see it on Jay's face and feel it in the way her sister trembled. Though she wanted to demand an explanation, for now her sister had to be her primary concern. "It's okay, Bianca. We're together now. Everything's going to be okay."

"I'm so sorry I gave you such a hard time." Bianca released her now and stepped back to look at her with an earnest face. "I know you were only trying to keep me safe."

"It's okay. I know what it's like to be pulled away from friends," Carina told her. "It's not easy."

Vanessa stepped into the room from a doorway opposite the expansive kitchen. "Carina, I know you've been in a car most of the day. Why don't you and Jay take a walk on the beach before the storm comes in? Seth can bring in your luggage while Bianca and I start dinner."

Realizing Vanessa was giving her the opportunity to talk to Jay alone, away from Bianca, she nodded. "That would be great, thanks."

Jay led the way to the front door, and she followed him out onto the porch and then down the half dozen steps onto the beach.

They started down the stretch of sand that led away from the windows overlooking the sound, away from where anyone could glance out and see them. Carina waited until they had walked several yards before she turned and demanded, "What happened?"

Jay stopped walking and shifted so he was facing her. He looked concerned, and his tone was apologetic. "There was an incident at the Whitmores' house last night when they were getting ready to leave. I didn't find out about it until after you had fallen asleep last night, and I haven't had a chance to talk to Seth to get all of the details."

"But you know something," Carina surmised. "Exactly what kind of incident are we talking about?"

"All Seth told me was that someone broke in. Apparently, it didn't end well."

Carina's eyes widened. "Are you saying there was a shooting? While my sister was in the house?"

Jay nodded. "Look, obviously Bianca is still shaken up about this, and I really think we should wait until she's not around to talk about it."

Carina folded her arms across her chest. "She's not around right now."

"I meant that we should wait until she goes to bed before we get the whole story from Seth," Jay corrected.

The idea of Bianca in the same house with someone trying to hurt her sent a ripple of terror through Carina. "Why didn't you tell me any of this before? You could have told me about it this morning."

"You're right. I could have, and I didn't," Jay said matter-of-factly. His voice was calm as he continued his explanation. "By the time we got on the road this morning, Seth and Vanessa were already on their way here. There wasn't anything you could do except worry, and I wanted to spare you that. I knew that making such a long drive was going to be hard enough, and I didn't want to add any more stress any sooner than I had to."

"I had a right to know," Carina said evenly.

"I'm sorry," he said, though he looked anything but remorseful. "I was just trying to protect you."

"Maybe I don't want to be *protected*." She let out a frustrated sigh, a well of emotions bubbling up inside her. "All my life, someone has been *protecting* me. My mother, Lou, maybe even my father."

"And in turn, you try to protect your sisters."

"I'm the oldest. They're my responsibility."

"You care about them."

"Of course," Carina said with an exasperated sigh.

Jay reached out and ran his hand down her arm before linking his fingers with hers. "And I care about you."

Carina stared at him, not sure what surprised her more, the words he had spoken or the way he had so neatly turned the argument around on her. Her voice no longer held any heat when she spoke again. "You should have told me."

Jay looked at her a moment, as though gauging her mood. "Come here." He tugged her gently toward him and pulled her against the solid warmth of his chest.

She leaned into him, settling her head beneath his chin. She held on for a long moment before asking the question still forefront in her mind. "Is this ever going to end?"

"It is." Jay pulled back so she could see the certainty in his eyes. "We're going to get through this. Life may not go back to the way it was before, but we'll find a way for you to be able to live your life again without interference. We'll find a way to make you feel safe."

"You sound so convinced that I almost believe you."

"Believe me."

When Jay lowered his lips to hers, Carina let herself believe.

31

NICK HELD HIS PHONE IN his hand, debating what to do next. He had failed to complete his assignment, and the man who had sent him here was now dead. He couldn't contact Giovanni Perelli directly for fear that the authorities would connect him to the Perelli family, and the only liaison that had communicated between them was Frank Tesan.

He flexed his free hand, hoping that his fingers would remain intact after he made the phone call he was currently dreading. He dialed the number, holding his breath until Marciano Perelli answered.

"Marciano, it's Nick Baldino," he said tentatively. "I'm sorry to bother you, but I didn't know who else to call."

"What's wrong?"

"I'm sorry. I tried everything I could think of, but I couldn't convince Carina to come back to Chicago."

The voice on the phone turned sharp. "Who sent you after her?"

"Your brother, Giovanni."

"But who actually gave you the order?" he demanded. "I know you didn't talk to my brother directly."

"Frank Tesan gave me the message," Nick told him, growing more confused by the second. Surely Marciano would have known that his brother had sent him. Or had he? "He told me to talk to Carina and convince her and her sisters to come back to Chicago. He said that someone might be after her, that she needed to come back to the family so we could keep her safe."

"Where is Frank now?"

"He's dead. He was shot and killed last night. So was Guido Manchione."

"Where are you now?"

"Miami. This is where Carina has been living for the past few months."

"I know exactly where she's been," Marciano said shortly. "I want you to tell me everything that's happened since Tesan sent you down there. And I mean everything."

Nick swallowed hard and nodded to his empty hotel room. Then he proceeded to tell Marciano everything.

* * *

Carina stood on the balcony and stared out at the water and the clouds threatening in the distance. The bedroom behind her was simply furnished with a queen-sized bed and an oak dresser. A long storage bench ran beneath the windows in the corner of the room, and Carina had found an abundance of quilts and blankets inside. French doors led to the balcony she was standing on now. Another door across the room led to the Jack-and-Jill bathroom that connected her room to Bianca's.

Downstairs she could hear chatter while the men cleaned up the kitchen. Carina had offered to help after dinner, but Jay had insisted that she take some time to settle in. He seemed to understand that she needed a few minutes to herself; Carina was amazed that he was so perceptive when it came to her needs.

Her heart ached a little when she thought about his admission that he wasn't LDS. She hadn't thought something like that would be that important to her, not with how casual she had been about religion lately. Finding out what had happened with Bianca, hearing her sister's account of Seth's inspiration in defending her, gave her a sense of gratitude and a realization that the Lord had been watching over Bianca when she herself hadn't been able to.

With that realization came new questions, this time not about her past but about her future. She wondered if it would have mattered had she known sooner that Jay wasn't Mormon, if she would have somehow been able to stop herself from falling for him.

She heard a door open and turned to see Vanessa walk out onto the balcony from the bedroom next to hers.

"Hey, there," Vanessa greeted her and then held out the gun that Carina recognized as her own. "I wanted to give this back to you. Jay said it's yours."

Carina nodded. "Thanks." She took the weapon from Vanessa and motioned to her room. "Let me just put this in my bag."

She went inside and secured her gun before joining Vanessa on the balcony once more.

As soon as she returned Vanessa asked, "How are you holding up?"

"Okay, I guess." Carina rested a hand on the railing.

Vanessa looked at her intuitively. "Is something wrong?"

"I was just thinking," Carina said, hearing the wistfulness in her tone. She shrugged her shoulders and shared her thoughts. "I was just wishing that Jay was Mormon."

"You're LDS?" Vanessa asked, surprise sounding in her voice. "I didn't realize that."

Carina nodded.

"I gather you have feelings for Jay."

Again, she nodded.

"It's a challenge when you realize you're in love with someone who can't take you to the temple."

Shock came first, pure and simple. Shock at Vanessa's words and shock that they might hold a thread of truth. "I never said I was in love with him. I hardly know him."

"I think you know him better than you realize," Vanessa said gently. "I've been in your shoes before, and I know how hard it can be. If you need to talk, I'm here."

Carina stared at her. Her instinct was to keep her feelings to herself, but the truth was, she needed someone to confide in, someone who might understand. She saw the sincerity in Vanessa's face and felt the first stirrings of friendship. "You got married in the temple, right?"

"I did." Vanessa nodded. "But it took me twelve years to get there."

"What do you mean?"

"Seth's a convert. I dated him for six years and was on the verge of marrying him when I realized I couldn't do it." Vanessa's narrow shoulders lifted. "Walking away from him was the hardest thing I ever did."

"What happened?"

"A few years after we broke up, he was assigned to work with the Saint Squad. Of the five people in the unit, four of them were LDS. Working with them so closely, he found the gospel on his own. After he converted, we stumbled across each other and realized we still loved each other."

Vanessa put her hand on the rail and looked out at the water. "It wasn't easy when we were first dating. I kept praying for Seth to open himself up to the gospel. I wanted it so badly but always felt like it would never happen. It took a long time for me to understand that we don't always get to operate on our own timetable. The Lord has a tendency of putting us on His."

"Right now, I'm afraid to hope for anything beyond finding a way to keep me and my sisters safe." Carina sighed and searched for the seeds of her testimony. "I'm trying to find my faith, but I keep wondering why the Lord is letting all of this happen to us. I've tried so hard to escape my past and protect my sisters from it, but it always comes back to me no matter what I do or where I go."

"I don't know either, but I do know from my own experience that the Lord is with us as long as we allow Him to be."

Carina felt tears sting her eyes as an arrow of hope pierced her despair. She took a deep breath, followed by another. When she finally found her voice again, she asked, "Do you think Seth would be willing to give me a blessing?"

Vanessa reached out and put her hand on her arm. "I'm sure he would."

* * *

Jay sat beside Carina on the wicker couch on the sun porch and listened to Seth and Vanessa recount the events of the night before. Fat raindrops splattered against the windows, a flash of lightning illuminating the crashing waves outside. Not for the first time, Jay felt a rush of gratitude that he had followed his instincts and left so early that morning. He couldn't imagine trying to camp out in this weather, and if they had missed the ferry, he and Carina wouldn't have had a whole lot of options of where to stay.

Eating a real meal that someone else had prepared had been just as much of a treat as the prospect of a real bed to sleep in. Vanessa had made them chicken and dumplings, and Bianca had contributed by baking a pan of brownies. Jay figured his father would understand her need for junk food, considering what she'd been through over the past twenty-four hours.

After they had finished eating, Seth had given both Carina and Bianca a blessing, one of those odd rituals Jay was getting used to when it came to Mormons. He had observed the practice before. With his teammates, it was an expected custom if someone was ill or injured. This was the first time, though, that he had seen one given for something that wasn't health related, except for when Kel had blessed his baby.

He had to admit that both Carina and Bianca had seemed more accepting of their situation after Seth had laid his hands on their heads. They also seemed more hopeful. As Seth reached the point in his story where an intruder had made it into the house, he could feel Carina's tension level rising again. Gently, he put his hand over hers, finding an odd comfort of his own when she turned her hand over and linked her fingers with his.

When Seth finished talking, Carina asked, "Who were the two men that were killed? What were their names?"

"One was Guido Manchione."

Carina straightened in her seat and spoke before he could continue. "From Chicago."

Surprised by her certainty, Jay's eyes narrowed. "You knew him?"

She nodded. "He worked for my grandfather."

"Doing what?"

"I'm not exactly sure." Carina shrugged. "I know he ran messages sometimes. That's how I remember him. He came to the house to meet with my father, sometimes carrying packages, other times just to talk to him."

"Do you remember anything else?"

Carina pressed her lips together and nodded. She took a moment, as though gathering her strength before speaking. "There was one night that I came home early from a party. I wasn't supposed to, but it was just down the block and my mom was busy talking to people. He was there with my father and a couple of other people." Carina looked up at Jay with a wounded look and tightened her grip on his hand. "I heard a gunshot. A few minutes later, the door opened and I saw the body of the man who was killed."

"You think he might have been the killer?"

"I don't know who actually pulled the trigger, but he was definitely involved." Carina turned her attention back to Seth. "What about the other man? Who was he?"

"Frank Tesan." Seth looked from Carina to Jay before he added, "He was FBI."

"Lou said that he thinks the top person in the Chicago mafia is FBI, but he said the guy's name was Alex," Jay said.

Seth nodded. "Vanessa and I were talking about that. Maybe this is the guy he was talking about. He could have been using multiple names."

"Maybe," Jay conceded.

"I did some digging into this Tesan guy's background after we got here," Vanessa told them now. "He's the one who flagged your names and put you on the no-fly list."

"At least now we know how that happened," Jay said. "I still don't understand why he was coming after Carina and Bianca though. And also, why did Nick keep trying to get them to go back to Chicago but never try to hurt them?"

"It also doesn't make sense that the top man would go out and do his own dirty work," Carina put in. "It just doesn't work that way."

"Maybe looking for you at the Whitmores' was a last resort."

"Again, for what purpose?" Jay asked. "And if someone really did go after Carina's father in prison, why now? He's been in prison since he was arrested two years ago. Surely, if someone wanted him dead, they could have tried earlier."

"The other question is what were they looking for in Carina's apartment?" Vanessa commented. "Seth said that it looked like whoever trashed the place didn't find what they were looking for."

"Was Lou's apartment ransacked too?" Carina asked, her eyebrows drawing together.

Seth nodded. "It didn't look as bad as yours but only because he didn't have very much stuff. Why do you ask?"

"I was just thinking—wondering, really—if whatever they were looking for was something that I was supposed to have or something of Lou's." Carina shrugged. "I have to think that if Lou was killed in his apartment, the search must have started there."

Jay nodded in agreement. "She's right. Lou was like a watchdog. There's no way he would have been sitting in his apartment if someone had broken into Carina's."

"You don't know what they were looking for?" Seth asked.

Carina shook her head. "I have no idea."

"I think at this point we have to start looking for connections between Tesan and the names of the people Carina gave us. Maybe from there we can find some answers," Seth said. He looked over at Carina and added, "You and Bianca will be safe here."

"What about Gianna? Your friend Amy found her a place to hide for this weekend, but then what?" Carina asked. "She's already halfway through her summer semester at BYU. I know she's not going to want to quit, but I'm afraid if she keeps going to class, someone might find her."

"Actually, I have an idea on that one," Jay told her. "I think we should see if there's any way we can set up surveillance on Gianna's apartment."

"Quinn and Tristan?" Seth suggested.

Jay's shoulders lifted. "Or Charlie Whitmore."

Vanessa looked from Seth to Jay, and then she smiled. "Or maybe both."

32

Jay circled the house, determined to check the perimeter one last time before heading to bed. The wind was blowing full force now, the rain beating down steadily as the wind whipped over the water, pounding it onto the sand.

Even though Jay knew this island could only be accessed by air or sea, he wanted to make sure everything was secure.

By the time he had circled the house, the rain had soaked through his clothes. Once he was satisfied that the main level was secure, he stepped onto the porch railing and pulled himself up onto the second-floor balcony that ran along the front of the house.

Satisfied that no one was at the house who wasn't supposed to be, Jay started toward the door leading to the upstairs den. That's when he saw her.

Though Carina's room was dark, a glimmer of light from the bathroom silhouetted her by the bed, where she had knelt to pray.

She looked so earnest just then, as though she was talking to a parent or older sibling rather than a higher being. Despite the biting wind and sheeting rain, an unexpected warmth seeped through him, starting in the center of his chest and spreading out until it filled his whole body. He stood there for a moment, trying to decipher this strange feeling. Then he stepped back to give Carina her privacy.

Oddly unsettled, he walked through the door leading to the den and made his way to his bedroom at the end of the hall. He kicked off his shoes, stripped out of his wet clothes, and fished a towel out of his duffel. After pulling on a pair of sweatpants and a T-shirt, he headed downstairs.

When he entered the living room, he came upon another touching scene, one that pulled at him nearly as much as the sight of Carina praying.

Vanessa was curled up on the couch beside Seth as he read from the book he held. Though his instinct was to leave them alone, he found himself caught by the words Seth spoke.

"'If any of you lack wisdom, let him ask of God . . .'"

When he finished the passage, Seth glanced up and motioned to Jay. "Everything okay out there?"

"Yeah." Jay nodded, undecided if he should move farther into the room or turn and go back the way he had come.

Seth marked his place in his scriptures and motioned for him to sit with them. "I assume Carina already went to bed."

The image of her kneeling immediately flashed into his mind. "She's heading there anyway."

"You two seem to be getting pretty close," Seth commented.

Jay lowered into a chair. "I guess so."

"How long have you known her?"

"I just met her when I got home. My dad coaches Bianca," Jay said and then corrected himself. "Or coached her. I doubt they'll be able to stay in Miami."

Seth's eyebrows lifted. "With the way you two are together, I figured you had known each other for a while."

Vanessa put her hand on Seth's leg. "You know as well as I do that everyone falls in love on their own timetable."

Jay stiffened at Vanessa's casual mention of love. "I never said I was in love with her."

"You never said you weren't," Vanessa countered. She stared at him for a long moment, like she was trying to gather her thoughts while Jay let her words roll through his mind. He was just coming to terms with the possibility of being in love when her next words hit him like a ton of bricks. "You realize you're about to break her heart, don't you?"

"What are you talking about?" Jay asked, immediately defensive. "I already told her that I'm going to be here for her and that I want to keep seeing her after all of this is over." He let out a sigh. "If all of this is *ever* over."

Vanessa looked up at Seth, silently asking permission to share her thoughts. Seth's eyes were serious, but he gave her a subtle nod. Then Vanessa shifted her attention back to Jay. "One of the most important things in our religion is temple marriage. Carina's fallen for you, but at some point, she'll have to choose between you and what she really wants for her future."

He dropped his mouth open in shock. "I never said anything about marriage."

"No, but you can't see the way you look at her either."

"Wait a minute." Jay shook his head as the rest of Vanessa's words caught up with him. "You're telling me it's that big a deal to her that I'm not Mormon?"

Vanessa nodded. "I'm telling you that I think her feelings for you are already strong enough that she doesn't feel like there's a way she can win."

Jay considered for a minute, trying to imagine what it would be like if he couldn't see Carina again, if she didn't give them the chance to explore these feelings that were growing between them. A seed of terror took hold deep inside him and started to bloom. "You don't really think she'd walk away from me, do you?"

"Vanessa did."

"Huh?" Jay looked at Seth, completely out at sea.

"I wasn't LDS when we first dated. We'd been together for *six years* when I asked her to marry me the first time." Seth said the words, and Jay could see the hurt flash in his friend's eyes. "She said no."

Vanessa reached for Seth's hand and spoke with complete sincerity. "I knew that if I'd pushed, Seth might have gotten baptized and gone through the necessary steps to take me to the temple, but I wanted more for him than that. I wanted more than that for both of us. I needed him to find out for himself that the gospel was true."

Jay felt that inner warmth start to spread through him again.

She continued. "If you do love Carina or think you could be falling in love with her, you owe it to yourself to save both of you a lot of heartache."

"How?"

"Read the Book of Mormon," Seth said with conviction. "Pray about it. Find out for yourself if it's true."

"I know the guys have bugged you about reading it before," Vanessa continued for Seth, "but before, they were just trying to share the peace and happiness we have all found. Now it's not just your happiness at stake. Carina's future and happiness depend on what you choose to do."

"What if I don't think it's true?" Jay asked and felt some of that warmth fade away.

"Then at least Carina will know that you took the time to explore her religion, that you tried to understand."

* * *

Carina walked along the beach, stepping through the icy water as waves rolled over the narrow strip of sand. The sky was crystal clear, the air crisp as it only is right after a storm. In the distance, she could see Seth and Jay swimming in the sound, both of them wearing only a pair of swimming trunks rather than wetsuits. How they could stand the cold water was beyond her, but they seemed determined to get in a workout this morning before breakfast.

Bianca was still sound asleep in her room, and Vanessa was working on her laptop at the kitchen table. Carina heard her mention something to the men about starting her analysis, but she wasn't quite sure exactly what Vanessa was analyzing or why she felt she would be able to figure out who was after Carina any better than a couple of Navy SEALs.

A piece of driftwood washed up onto the sand, and strings of seaweed caught on one jagged edge. Everything was so peaceful here, so isolated, so safe. She started at the ringing of a cell phone. Jay had insisted she hold on to the one he had given her yesterday, but she hadn't expected anyone to call her on it. The only person who had the number was Gianna, and with the time difference, it was unlikely that she was awake yet.

Carina answered it with a tentative hello.

"Carina?" A woman's voice came over the line. "This is Amy Miller. I'm a friend of Jay's."

"Yes, he told me about you. You're Matt's sister."

"That's right," she answered, and Carina could hear the smile in her voice.

"I tried calling Jay, but he wasn't answering his phone. I'm guessing he's out for a swim."

Carina looked out at where Jay was just turning back toward the shore. "You must know him well."

"One of my jobs is to coordinate all of the squad's training. About the only time the guys don't answer the phone is if they're wet or in hostile territory."

Carina considered the thought of Jay being behind enemy lines somewhere, and a shudder worked through her. She supposed she had never really let herself think about what Jay normally did for work. So far, she had only seen him as the nice guy who was always helping her out, the guy who listened in a way that made her want to confide in him.

She tried to keep her voice casual when she said, "It looks like Jay and Seth are heading toward shore, but they're still a ways out. Do you want me to have one of them call you?"

"Actually, Jay doesn't need to call me if you can just pass along a message. Tell him that I e-mailed him a lot of information for the two of you to go over. Also, can you let him know the surveillance is in place?"

"Are you talking about the surveillance for Gianna?"

"Yeah." Amy seemed to hesitate before offering her more details. "My brother's boss helped him set it up through the FBI's Salt Lake office."

"But what if someone on my family's payroll finds out? Amy, my family has people in a lot more places than you might think."

"Trust me. There's no way anyone would think that this case has anything to do with the mob."

"How can you be so sure?"

"Because my brother had it classified under the hate crimes unit."

"Seriously?" Carina's eyebrows lifted, and a little smile tugged at her mouth. "That's one thing the family definitely wouldn't worry about."

"That's what we figured," Amy told her. "I have to run, but if you need anything, feel free to give me a call."

"There is one thing I'd like your advice on."

"What's that?"

"I'm worried about Matt and CJ. What happens if someone goes back there looking for me? I couldn't stand it if anyone hurt them or their kids."

"Don't worry about them. They're going to stay away from the house for a couple of weeks. One of CJ's old friends from when she was in witness protection, a US Marshall, is going to stay there to make sure there aren't any problems."

"Thanks." Carina breathed a sigh of relief. "That makes me feel so much better."

"Don't worry," Amy assured her. "We've got your back."

33

"You sent someone after my nieces. After my own flesh and blood." Marciano Perelli's voice simmered with violence.

"Carina knows who I am," Alex stated simply. "And Giovanni broke our agreement. He sent something to her, something that might help her understand what she knows."

"You broke the agreement first." Marciano shook his head. "He never would have tried to contact her if you hadn't tried to kill him. Isn't it enough that he's in prison for a crime you committed? That he watched you kill his wife?"

Alex didn't address Donna Perelli's murder; instead, he casually leaned back in his chair. "I heard Giovanni had a bout with food poisoning, but that didn't have anything to do with me."

"We both know it wasn't food poisoning, just like we both know it wasn't your first attempt. You didn't really think we wouldn't find out about it, did you?"

"I'd be careful about throwing those kinds of accusations around." His voice turned cold, and he leaned forward on his desk. "Don't forget who's running this organization. I would hate for you to find yourself in less-than-favorable circumstances—to have to learn a hard lesson like your brother did."

"My father would never have approved of how you are running this business."

"Our father," Alex corrected. "And let's not forget that if anything happens to me, you're going to have a war on your hands. My son has just as much right to succeed me as you do."

"You may be the oldest, but my father was a fool to ever trust the son he walked away from so many years ago," Marciano said sharply. "He should have turned his back on you just like he did your mother."

Alex's dark eyes flashed with a barely leashed fury. "My mother isn't any of your concern."

"No, but you are. And so is my brother. My real brother."

* * *

Pete took a moment to look around the parking garage before unlocking the door to Carina's car. He had taken three buses and then jogged two miles to get back to where he and Jay had left it, but at least he was sure he hadn't been followed. The man who had come by looking for Jay had driven by twice after talking to him the day before, but since then, he seemed to have given up on staking out his house.

After talking to Jay, Pete had agreed to come search the car. Then he was going to drive it over and leave it in the Whitmores' garage. CJ's friend from the US Marshalls, Tara Baldino, had agreed to stay and watch the place for a few weeks to make sure it was safe before the family returned. She hadn't seemed to mind the additional request of using Carina's car while she was there.

If someone was tracking the car, Tara would find out soon enough. Assuming there weren't any problems, Carina could make arrangements to get the car to wherever she ended up. But first, Pete was going to check the car out. He opened up the passenger door and sat down before opening the glove compartment.

He started pulling out the contents—an envelope with the insurance and registration information inside, a box of tissues, a pair of scissors, two small notepads, and an array of pens and pencils. Finally, he found what he was looking for. Pete picked up the maintenance log, a simple black book with a rubber band around it. He slipped the rubber band off and opened it up.

His eyes narrowed. Taped to the inside front cover was a key. From the shape and size, he guessed it was a house key. He flipped through the pages of the maintenance log and read the dates of the car's oil changes marked neatly inside.

Not sure what to think of his discovery, Pete put everything back into the glove compartment, except for the maintenance log. After circling around to the driver's side, he drove straight to the hardware store. Copying the key only took a few minutes, and he immediately put one of the two copies he had made onto his key ring.

Then he started toward the Whitmores', where he would leave the car and find a way to get the log and original key into Jay's hands.

* * *

Seth cradled the cell phone between his shoulder and his ear while he dried off his hands from the dishwater and then moved outside onto the porch to ensure some privacy. "Why did Jay's dad call you?" Seth asked with concern. "Is everything all right?"

"Everything's fine," Kel assured him. "He knew not to try to contact any of you directly since someone's been watching him, but he wanted you guys to know that he searched Carina's car and found a key taped to the inside of the maintenance log."

"Jay mentioned that Lou had made a specific mention of the maintenance log," Seth said. "Any idea what the key goes to?"

"It looks like a house key."

"You have it already? How?"

"Pete had it pouched up here to me on a military transport last night. He said he made a couple of copies. He has one, and the other he put into his safe deposit box."

"It doesn't matter how many copies he has. If we don't know where the lock is, none of them is going to do us any good."

"I know," Kel agreed. "There's one more thing I wanted to let you know about."

"What's that?"

"You know that FBI agent who came to visit you last week?"

"Yeah," Seth nodded. "What about him?"

"He's dead."

"What? How?"

"Murdered," Kel told him. "He was found this morning."

"Any suspects?"

"Not yet. It looked like a meeting gone bad, but there's one thing that's troubling me," Kel admitted.

"What's that?"

"Another agent came and questioned me when he found some of Graham's notes. I told him that he had taken the copies of some background checks you had run. When he called back a couple of hours later, he said that they didn't find anything like that in his files."

"You think someone killed him for the information?"

"I think someone killed him so he couldn't talk about the information," Kel said. "This looks to me like a mob hit."

"Great," Seth muttered. "What do you want me to tell Jay?"

"Tell him the truth," Kel said simply. "And tell him to pray."

* * *

"Good news," Tristan Crowther's western drawl came over Jay's phone.

"I could use some of that," Jay muttered, pushing aside the latest batch of background checks. He had just finished talking to Carina about the key his father had found in her car. Unfortunately, she was as confused by it as they were. His dad had sent the maintenance log and the key to Kel, but for now, Lou's message to Carina remained a mystery.

"Quinn and I went out to Provo and did a surveillance run at the dorm like you wanted."

"And?"

"No activity at all," Tristan told him. "We didn't see anything, and neither have the FBI guys who staked out the place."

"I'm still worried that someone might show up. Before all of this happened, Carina said she and Gianna used to talk and text all the time."

"That's the other thing. We brought Gianna's phone back with us to Virginia to see if anyone was following the signal," Tristan continued. "Not only did we not see anyone following the phone, but when we tried tracking calls to and from the phone, we couldn't."

"Why couldn't you? Gianna certainly wouldn't have access to a secure phone."

"No, but it was modified with a blocker. Amy did some digging into the technology for us and said the FBI confiscated some phones with similar modifications at a raid in Chicago a few years ago. The arrests were all mob related."

"It must have been Lou. He must have fixed her phone to make sure no one could find her."

"That would make sense," Tristan agreed. "It looks like it worked. Best we can tell, no one knows where she is."

"Thanks, Tristan. That is good news." Jay hung up the phone as Carina walked into the room carrying two plates laden with chicken salad sandwiches.

"What's good news?" she asked, sliding one of the plates in front of him.

"It looks like Gianna's apartment is safe."

"Really?" Carina asked with a mixture of hope and skepticism.

Jay considered the information about Gianna's phone. "Where did you and your sisters get your cell phones?"

"I'm not sure." Carina shrugged. "Lou bought them for us."

"That's what I thought you were going to say." Jay reached for his sandwich and took a bite.

"Why?"

"Gianna's phone had been modified so that no one can track the GPS signal on it. Apparently, the technology also interferes with anyone being able to accurately pull a call log from the phone." Jay took a sip of water and contemplated for a moment. "If that were the case, I don't know how anyone was able to track Bianca to the Whitmores' house. Logically, they would have tracked phone calls from one of your phones to CJ or Matt, but if Lou modified all of your phones, that shouldn't have been possible."

Carina thought for a minute, and Jay could see the moment when she figured out the missing piece of the puzzle. "Nick."

"What about him?"

"He grabbed my phone from me when he showed up at the pool last week. He must have done something so he could track my calls."

"That would make sense," Jay said, feeling more confident about Tristan's assessment that Gianna really hadn't been found. "In that case, you might want to go call Gianna. Let her know that everything is safe and that she can go back home."

Relief and gratitude shone in Carina's eyes. "Thank you." She leaned down and gave Jay a quick kiss. "I'm going to go call her right now."

* * *

"You shouldn't be calling me here," Marciano said the moment he heard his brother's voice on the phone. "I don't know how you managed to get transferred to another prison, but I don't want Alex to be able to find you through me."

"He's out of control," Giovanni said, his voice raspy, like he was fighting a cold and couldn't quite catch his breath.

Marciano heard the unspoken words hanging on the line, the line that was most surely being monitored. *He's out of control* translated to *stop him now.*

"You need to tell the cops who really killed Donna," Marciano insisted boldly. They both knew Alex could no longer be trusted. Giovanni had gone to prison to protect the rest of his family. Marciano had fallen in line in the family business for the same reason. Now Alex seemed determined to eliminate them—to eliminate his own family—to make sure that control remained unequivocally his. Now determined to fight the man who had set out to destroy them, Marciano dared to speak their older half-brother's name out loud. "It's time Raymond Alexander is the one behind bars, not you."

"My day will come."

"It needs to come now. Together we can put things back the way they used to be."

"The girls come first," Giovanni countered. "They'll understand everything someday."

"I hope you know what you're doing."

"I do."

34

CARINA SAT AT THE LITTLE table by the window, her sketch pad open in front of her. She tried to work on the design that had come to her earlier that morning but found her concentration was too scattered. So much had happened over the last few days, and she was still trying to make sense of it all.

Jay and Seth had shown her a photo of Frank Tesan, the FBI agent who had been killed at the Whitmores' house, but she hadn't recognized him. Even though everyone seemed determined to spend most of their time researching every angle possible, so far they hadn't gotten any closer to figuring out what had renewed her family's interest in her or why anyone would try to hurt her or her sisters.

Her father had been successfully transferred to another prison, and she had been told that he was apparently well on the road to recovering from whatever had caused his sickness. Amy's brother, Charlie, had interviewed him personally in the hopes of uncovering the truth about her mother's murder. Unfortunately, her dad still refused to talk about the events of that day.

Carina had to wonder if he would tell her the truth if she could meet with him face to face, but Jay was insistent that it would be too dangerous right now. Even though everyone seemed pretty confident that her father was safe now, Jay was proving to be quite protective of her. Many of their conversations over the past few days had revolved around what she should do next, where she would go when his leave ended in a few more days.

It scared her a little at how easily she had shifted from only considering her sisters in her future plans to including Jay as well. She also worried that the closer she felt to him, the more confused she became.

She watched Seth and Vanessa together, and her heart yearned for what they had, the same thing that was so evident in CJ and Matt

Whitmore's relationship: love and eternity. The more she felt like she was discovering love with Jay, the more it terrified her that she wouldn't be able to have eternity.

Footsteps sounded behind her, followed by voices.

"I don't care if my dad's not here to see it; I am not taking you out for a hamburger and french fries." Jay's voice held both humor and conviction.

"Oh, come on, Jay. We swam like three miles this morning. In freezing water," Bianca said. Carina recognized by her tone that she already knew she had lost the battle but was still holding out a seed of hope. "Besides, if we go out to eat, you won't have to cook tonight."

Carina turned and couldn't help but smile when she saw the knowing look Jay gave Bianca. "You mean, you won't have to do the dishes tonight." Jay reached out and rubbed his hand teasingly over her head. "I'm on to you, kid."

"I thought it was Carina's turn to do the dishes," Bianca countered mischievously.

"Nice try," Carina said. "Besides, I think Jay was going to cook up that fish Seth caught this morning."

Bianca turned toward her and wrinkled her nose. "Yet another good reason to go out to dinner tonight."

"Tell you what," Jay started. "If you help Vanessa with lunch today, I'll take you with me into town afterward for some supplies."

Bianca looked at him, surprised. "You're really going to let me go into town with you? In public?"

"Weren't you just bugging me about going out to a restaurant?" Jay asked. "That's pretty public."

"Yeah, but I knew you were going to say no," Bianca admitted. Then she gave him a sheepish grin. "I was just hoping you would go out and bring me something back." Her eyes lit with humor. "With paper plates."

"Seth and I have checked out the village for the past few days. If someone knew where you were hiding, they would have shown up by now." He turned toward Carina. "I actually thought that maybe I could take you out for ice cream or something after dinner tonight if you're up for it."

Carina smiled. "I'd like that."

"Hey!" Bianca protested. "How come she gets ice cream?"

"She never swam for my dad," Jay told her with a grin. Then he tugged on her ponytail. "If you're nice to me, maybe we'll bring you something back."

* * *

Jay jogged along the beach with Seth by his side. Their routine had fallen into place easily enough, and he was a bit surprised at how well the five of them had come to coexist over the past six days.

Bianca had taken to swimming with him and Seth each morning. Jay suspected she went with them more to work out her stress than to train for any future competition. Creating new designs appeared to be Carina's release, although she was always quick to make time for him when they could steal a few moments together.

Seth and Vanessa now included the rest of them in their nightly scripture reading and what they called "family prayer." It was odd to think that he was finally reading the Book of Mormon, both with Seth and on his own. He supposed with all of the copies he had stacked up over the past year, he should have known it was inevitable.

The more he read, the more questions he seemed to have. Ironically, when he talked to Carina about the Church, he discovered that she freely admitted she didn't know all of the answers. Oddly enough, he found comfort in the fact that Carina seemed to still have questions of her own.

He supposed he always thought his teammates had all achieved some spiritual pinnacle the moment they joined their church. Now he was beginning to understand that the Mormons seemed to think that everyone was always growing, always learning more about God and His plan for them.

Jay found he looked forward to the prayers they had together at each meal, still amazed after almost a year that Mormons talked to God like He was a personal friend who was really listening. He even found himself offering prayers of his own as he went to bed each night, always including a request for answers and surprisingly expecting to get some.

Those answers hadn't been forthcoming nearly as quickly as any of them had hoped. They still didn't have any idea who had killed Lou or the motivations of the two men who had shown up at the Whitmores'.

Little by little, Jay felt like he was beginning to understand Carina's family and their business, but the pressure of time was starting to wear down on him now that his leave was coming to an end.

For the past few days, he had been trying to figure out some way to bring Carina with him to Virginia Beach. He had thought of having her and Bianca stay at his apartment or even seeing if she could stay with one of his teammates, but the risk was too great. He had already been linked to them, as had Seth. Maybe after some time had passed, Carina could come to Virginia, but for now, she needed to keep her distance from him until they were sure she and Bianca were safe.

The possibility that they wouldn't find the answers they were looking for had never occurred to him when this ordeal had first started, but now Jay was wondering if they would ever understand the truth. The more time he spent with Carina, the more he realized she wasn't going to be easy to leave behind.

He had considered putting in for some more leave so he could stay with her a bit longer, ideally helping her find someplace to hide out that wasn't too far from his home; unfortunately, Jay knew the request wouldn't be approved. It was a minor miracle that his squad hadn't gone active the minute the news came in about the retaliation bombing in Islamabad last week. He also knew he didn't want to watch his teammates go into action without him by their side.

The itch to get to work was back, tempered only by his desire to stay and spend more time with Carina. He saw the door open as he and Seth approached the house. Carina emerged onto the deck and looked out over the beach until she saw him. Then her eyes locked with his, and she smiled.

Her hair was pulled back into a short ponytail, and he suspected that the sundress she wore was one of her designs. Over the past week, he had seen enough of her sketches to know she rarely wore anything besides jeans that she hadn't made herself. He also suspected that if she had not found herself caring for her sisters, she would likely be succeeding in the fashion industry in New York instead of barely scraping by.

Jay slowed to a walk a few yards from the house. Seth jogged past him and took the porch steps two at a time. Seth glanced back at Jay when he reached the door. "I'm going to grab a shower before dinner."

Jay nodded in response and then waited on the sand while Carina closed the distance between them. She reached up and gave him a brief kiss. "How was your run?"

"Fine." Jay motioned toward the house. "What have you been up to?"

"Looking for a job."

"Excuse me?"

"Somebody named Kel called and talked to Vanessa right after you guys left. I guess he's the one who knows the owner of this house."

Jay nodded. "What did Kel want?"

"He said the owner won't be using this house until the first of August, and he's willing to let us housesit for him until then."

"Really?" Jay asked, his emotions mixed. He had hoped to get her settled a little closer to Virginia Beach, but he couldn't deny that she was safely off the grid here. His concern for her safety overshadowed the convenience he had hoped for, and he gave her a slow smile. "That solves one problem, at least for now. Any luck so far with jobs?"

"I found a few possibilities. Bianca already has an interview tomorrow for a lifeguarding position at one of the local hotels. There aren't a lot of businesses here on the island, but I think I can probably do pretty well if I can get a job waitressing at one of the higher-end restaurants."

"You shouldn't have to waitress," Jay said, not pleased with the image of her standing on her feet for hours, knowing that she had already put her talent and her education on hold for the past two years.

"It's only for a couple of months." She shrugged. "Besides, from what I hear, tourist season is pretty good here. Since I won't be paying rent, I should be able to save up for a new place by August."

"Any chance you might consider moving to Virginia?" Jay couldn't stop the question from coming out of his mouth, even understanding the risks.

"I was hoping you might want me to."

"Absolutely." Jay smiled at her. "And I hope you don't mind if I come down here to visit you every chance I get."

She wrapped her arms around his waist and looked up at him with complete sincerity. "Come as often as you can."

She reached up, and her lips met his in a kiss filled with warmth and promise. Jay fell into the kiss, drawing her closer, wishing this moment could go on forever.

He heard the rumble in the distance, at first too lost in Carina to worry about the source of the sound. Then the back door opened, and Seth's voice broke into the moment.

"Jay, we've got to move. We've been called in, and our ride is almost here."

A new sense of adrenaline rushed through him when he turned and saw the military helicopter closing in fast. "That's for us?"

Seth nodded. "The landing zone is just down the beach."

"I've got to go grab my gear," Jay told Carina, pulling away and rushing into the house. He packed up the contents of his room in less than a minute and then raced back downstairs, where everyone was waiting on the back porch. He pressed his car keys into her hand. "Here are the keys to my car in case you need them. You should be able to keep using the Jeep while you're staying here though."

"What will you do for a car?"

"I'll have my dad ship your car to Virginia on the train. We can switch when you come up."

Carina nodded, and she glanced hesitantly at the helicopter lowering onto the beach a few hundred yards away. She pressed her lips together and looked up at him like she wasn't quite sure what to do. Then she said simply, "Be safe."

"You too." Jay leaned down and kissed her, lingering longer than he had planned. "I'll call you as soon as I can."

Carina nodded as Jay moved down the stairs onto the beach. He fell into step with Seth as they both started toward the helicopter. Sand whipped up into the air, and they both shielded their eyes as they jogged over the beach grass and climbed aboard.

As they strapped in and ascended into the air, Jay looked down at Carina standing on the porch with Bianca and Vanessa. All three women were waving, and he was struck with the odd sensation that he now had someone to come home to when this mission ended.

35

ALEX CHECKED THE LICENSE PLATE of the little coupe when it pulled into the parking lot, and he gritted his teeth in determination when the tall man stepped out of it and headed toward his apartment. He was tired of waiting, tired of trying to run the Outfit with only a portion of the tools he needed. Carina Perelli needed to be found, and he was resolved to make sure it happened soon.

Three different times, he had sent his underlings to find her and bring her back to him. Each time, they had failed. Their excuses had varied. First had been the unfortunate timing of Lieutenant Wellman's deployment. The next two attempts had been unsuccessful when his men had failed to keep the lieutenant in their sights when they'd suspected he was going to meet Carina.

He knew it was possible that Wellman wasn't going to see Carina at all on his weekends away from home, but the lengths that he was going to in order to make sure he wasn't being followed made Alex think the lieutenant was still in contact with his niece.

His niece. The term was laughable. Carina Perelli didn't even know he was family. All she knew was that he was one of the men with her father when Leone Hamilton had been silenced. He wasn't about to allow that knowledge to come back to haunt him. He also wasn't about to let Carina unravel the clues her father had sent her.

He couldn't be sure exactly where Giovanni had hidden the payoff records he had accumulated over the years, the records that could supposedly expose his true identity as an FBI agent. What he did know was that Giovanni had sent her a key to one of the apartments owned by the property management company their father had left to Giovanni's children, one of the legitimate companies he and his organization needed in order to hide their vast income from their less-than-legal sources.

Alex gritted his teeth as he thought of his father's last-minute changes to his will. It had been bad enough that a portion of family assets had gone to his younger half brothers, but he had been infuriated to find that his father had also singled out these girls who had lost their place in the family years before. The last straw was when he'd learned that both his father and Giovanni had reportedly locked away information about him, leaving those tidbits for the girls to find.

His birth certificate, payments to his mother, and correspondence between his parents would prove that he was a Perelli by birth. Copies of his old FBI cases could prove that he had used his position as an agent to pave his way to the top. The biggest concern, however, was the video that one of Giovanni's men had supposedly taken when Alex had killed Donna Perelli. That item, if it really existed, would put him in prison for life.

It wasn't going to happen, Alex promised himself. The Perelli girls were a loose end he couldn't afford to leave hanging, and he was now determined to take care of them himself.

Alex focused on the young man who would lead him to his objective. He waited until Jay was safely inside his apartment before pulling into the parking lot beside his car. Then he picked a handheld device off of his seat and read the data it displayed. As he suspected, the lieutenant's car was equipped with some type of GPS jamming equipment. Casually, he stepped out of the car and walked toward the apartment building, glancing down at the readings as though checking a phone for text messages.

When he reached the apartment building, he knocked on the door of one of the ground-floor apartments he knew to be empty. After waiting an appropriate amount of time, he continued toward the manager's apartment. He was nearly to the manager's door when his equipment confirmed that the jammer had finally lost its effectiveness. He checked the distance between himself and Wellman's car.

Then he pulled his cell phone from his pocket and put it to his ear as though he was answering a call. He turned and walked back to his car. As soon as he was again seated in the driver's seat, he dialed a number and prepared to utilize the Bureau's resources to help him achieve his goals. With the right tools, he was certain Wellman's car could be tracked without the lieutenant ever knowing about it. At least, he wouldn't find out about it until it was much too late for him to interfere again.

Alex slid the key into the ignition and put his car in gear. As he drove away, his lips curved slightly. His time was here. He could feel it. Finally, he was going to take back what was rightfully his.

* * *

"Hey, guys. We just got word." Brent leaned on the doorjamb leading into Seth and Jay's office. "We're shipping out again on Tuesday."

Seth looked up from his computer screen. "Where to this time?"

"Afghanistan."

"Any idea about how long?" Jay asked. Their last mission had only lasted a week, and he hoped this one would fall into a similar time frame. Carina had less than a month to find an apartment, and he wanted to help her get settled when the time came.

"Hard to say," Brent said, "but I'd guess a month."

Jay couldn't keep his disappointment from showing on his face.

"Don't worry, Jay," Seth told him sympathetically. "Vanessa can help Carina move if we aren't back in time."

"Amy isn't coming with us on this trip, so she'll be able to help too," Brent offered. "Did you ever figure out what to do with the stuff from her old apartment?"

Jay nodded. "Carina gave me a list of things she really wanted to keep, and my dad loaded everything into her car when he shipped it up here last month. She had him sell the rest of her stuff in a yard sale. She decided it would be easier to buy new furniture instead of paying to ship everything and taking the chance that someone might try to follow the movers to her new place."

"Smart." Brent nodded. "I'm looking forward to meeting her."

"You know, you and Amy could always come down with us this weekend," Jay offered. "Assuming that it's still okay for me to take off tomorrow."

"We wouldn't want to intrude." Brent shook his head.

"You wouldn't be intruding," Jay assured him. "Seth and Vanessa are coming down with me too. Vanessa has been doing a bunch of research on Carina's family, and we're still trying to figure out what that key goes to."

"Did you give her the copy we made for her?"

Jay nodded. "Yeah. I gave her one, and I kept a copy for myself. We think the numbers on that note Carina got before this whole thing started might be a clue, but we haven't figured it out. Mostly, we're just going to spend this weekend searching through property records and the information Vanessa has on the Perelli family."

"In that case, maybe we will try to come. Amy would love a weekend at the beach."

* * *

"Carina, these are incredible." Amy flipped through Carina's wedding dress sketches, a look of amazement on her face.

"Thanks." Carina couldn't stop the smile from spreading over her face. "Formal dresses are actually my favorite thing to design."

"It shows. I wish I had known you when I got married. It was a nightmare trying to find something not too low-cut and that had sleeves."

"I wish I had known you then too," Carina agreed. "It's so hard to find that first person to trust you with such an important design. Once you have done a couple, people start to believe you know what you're doing."

Amy looked up from the sketches, an odd look on her face. "Is this what you want to do for a living? Design wedding gowns?"

"It's where I'd like to start," Carina admitted. "The dream is to design modest formal wear and eventually branch out to create a women's line too."

"How are you at keeping secrets?" Amy asked as though she was contemplating some top-secret mission.

Before Carina could answer, Vanessa spoke. "I think with her family background, keeping secrets is probably a requirement."

Amy's mouth widened into a grin. She pulled her cell phone out of her pocket and dialed. Her eyes still on Carina, Amy greeted the person who answered. "Hi, Kendra. It's Amy."

Amy laughed at something Kendra said before responding. "Hey, you know how we were talking about trying to find a new designer, someone you could trust to not leak any information? I think I may have found one for you." Amy nodded. "She's just starting out, but I'm looking at some of her designs, and they are incredible. I can e-mail you a couple to check out."

She looked down at the sketches again, sliding three from the stack. "Okay, I'm going to send you my favorites, and you can let me know what you think." Amy nodded again. "Sounds good. Tell Charlie I said hi next time you see him."

As soon as Amy hung up, Carina asked, "What was that all about?"

"That was my brother's fiancée. If it's okay with you, I'm going to scan these and send them to her. If she likes them, you may have your first commission."

"Seriously?" Carina's eyes lit with excitement. Then the puzzle pieces started to fall into place. "Wait a minute. Isn't your brother dating Kendra Blake? The singer?"

Amy nodded. "He's marrying Kendra, but that isn't public knowledge yet—thus the need for secrecy."

Carina's jaw dropped. She held up a hand and tried to formulate a cohesive sentence. "You're saying I might be able to design Kendra Blake's wedding dress?"

"That's exactly what I'm saying."

"That's . . . that's . . . *huge*!"

"It would definitely put you on the map as a designer." Amy nodded. "You might want to start thinking about company names. You probably don't want to use your own name with what's been going on."

Suddenly nervous, Carina motioned to her sketches. "I don't know if I want you to send these in to her yet. I'm sure I can do better."

"Relax." Amy laughed. "These are just a sample. If she doesn't like these, I'll have you send some others."

Carina pressed a hand to her jittery stomach and took a deep breath. "Okay."

Amy motioned to the stacks of files Vanessa had brought with her. "I know you two still have a lot of papers to look through. I think I'll grab Bianca and take her into town so we can pick up some dinner. Brent wanted to try out that seafood place in town."

"That sounds great," Vanessa said before Carina could say anything. "With any luck, the guys will be finished with their run by the time you get back."

A minute later, Amy and Bianca headed out the door. Still stunned by the possibility of designing a dress for a famous singer, Carina tried to turn her attention back to the papers in front of her but found herself rereading the same things two and three times. That's when she noticed something unexpected in the biographical sketch Vanessa had given her on her grandfather. "This is strange."

"What?"

"According to this, my grandmother was my grandfather's second wife. Apparently, he was married once before." Carina skimmed through the account of Sergio Perelli's brief six-month marriage to Helen Alexander.

"What happened to the first wife?" Vanessa asked, shifting so she too could read the information on the computer screen. "It looks like she moved to Houston right after they split up. I can't tell if she never used the last name Perelli or if she changed her name back, but she definitely was using her maiden name after the divorce."

"Let me try something." Vanessa reached for the laptop and shifted it so she could type a few keys. She opened up a new tab, entered a website through a secure login, and then ran an identity search using birthdates that started from right before Helen Alexander and Sergio Perelli divorced through nine months later. Six names popped up on the screen with the last name Alexander.

One by one, Vanessa opened them. On the fourth one, her eyes lit up with a combination of excitement and surprise. "I think this is it."

"What? I don't understand." Carina skimmed over the birth record. It was dated five months after the divorce, and the mother was listed as Helen Alexander. The father was listed as unknown.

"I know it sounds crazy, but I think it's possible that this baby is your uncle."

"Wait. You're saying…"

"I'm saying Sergio Perelli could have fathered a child with his first wife. I think this child is his oldest son."

Shock came first, followed by understanding. "Older than my father, which means if he is, my grandfather might have considered him to be the heir to the family business."

Vanessa nodded. "With the timing of the birth, I have to think the divorce was caused by one of two things: either Helen Alexander found out she was pregnant and didn't want to live life as a mafia wife."

"Or?" Carina prompted.

"Or she had an affair, and your grandfather divorced her because he knew the child wasn't his."

Carina shook her head. She hated the truth about her grandfather's dark side, but she understood it well enough to be certain she knew the answer. "If Helen Alexander had cheated on my grandfather, she wouldn't have lived long enough to give birth to another man's son."

Vanessa stared at her for a minute, as though trying to comprehend the truth. Then she said, "Let me check one more thing. I'll be right back."

She picked up her phone and started dialing a number as she walked outside onto the screen porch. Through the glass, Carina could see her talking to someone but couldn't hear the words over the constant rumble of waves crashing up on the beach.

Several minutes passed before Vanessa walked back inside. "It looks like you're right."

"What do you mean?"

"I had a friend check out Helen Alexander's financial records. She didn't have any assets to speak of when she married Sergio, but after the divorce, she had regular deposits to her bank account, even though she never held a job."

Carina looked at her suspiciously. "Vanessa, what exactly do you do for a living?"

"It's probably best if you don't ask me that question."

Carina crossed her arms and leaned back in her chair as she considered both the information and the source. "Maybe the payments were just alimony."

Vanessa shook her head. "These deposits seem too big to be alimony alone. Not only that, but right after the baby was born, Helen moved into a new house. She paid cash, but there's nothing to indicate she had a way to come up with that kind of money."

"That does sound like something my family would do." Carina nodded in agreement. "Real estate has always been a favorite way to hide cash."

Vanessa pointed at the computer screen. "I think this is the man we're looking for. 'Alex' is really Raymond Alexander."

* * *

"Who is Raymond Alexander?" Jay asked as they all sat around the dinner table Saturday night.

"If we're right, he's Carina's uncle," Vanessa told him. "It would make sense why her grandfather was helping him move up in the organization and grooming him to take control."

Jay looked from Vanessa to Carina and then back again. "You think her own uncle may be behind all of this?"

"He fits the description Lou gave you. Fifty-four years old, from Texas, FBI," Vanessa said. "According to his file, he's been assigned to Chicago for the majority of his career."

"How did he manage that?" Amy asked. "From what my brother has told me, FBI agents usually rotate every five years or so to a new city."

"Apparently, every time he was due for a rotation, he would convince his superiors that he was on the verge of some big mob bust. Since he kept producing results, it made sense to keep him around."

"Where is he now?" Jay asked.

"I don't know." Vanessa shrugged. "I left a message for his supervisor, but I probably won't hear back until Monday."

"I sure hope this is the person we've been looking for." Jay reached for Carina's hand and gave it a squeeze. "I am so ready for all of this to be over."

"We all are," Carina said.

36

CARINA SAT ON THE DECK, an umbrella overhead, shading her from the noonday sun. Her hand moved the pencil in long fluid lines over her sketchbook as another design took shape. A gentle breeze cooled the otherwise humid air, and she found the sound of the waves soothing. So many thoughts were rolling through her mind after the excitement of the weekend that she was surprised she could sketch anything, but the ideas were flowing, and she wanted to get these latest ones down on paper before she lost them.

She supposed her emotions were feeding this current frenzy, or perhaps it was the possibility that she was so much closer now to finding a new sense of security. Vanessa had talked to someone in the FBI earlier that morning. Carina didn't know how she had managed to uncover so much information, but according to Vanessa, Raymond Alexander had been on leave the day Lou was murdered. He had also been on vacation the day her mother was killed. The possibility that they had finally identified the person who had taken so much from her was overwhelming, as was the knowledge that her father was likely innocent.

With her emotions in such turmoil over the past couple of days, she was glad Jay and his friends had postponed their departure until this morning. They had planned to leave on Sunday, but bad weather had affected the ferry schedule, and they had decided to spend another night.

They had all been such a great source of emotional support to both her and Bianca that she knew she was really going to miss them over the next few weeks. She also found herself looking forward to moving to Virginia Beach, where she already felt like she had a built-in network of friends.

When everyone left a few minutes ago, Carina had found this good-bye with Jay to be a little easier than the last time he had deployed. She didn't know if it was because he had already proven to her that he was going to come back or if she was more accepting now that this was part of who he was.

Her pencil broke, and she reached into her briefcase on the chair beside her. She dug a fresh pencil out of her bag and started sketching once more. She was so absorbed in the details on her design that she didn't hear the footsteps.

A man's voice interrupted her thoughts. "Nice view you have here."

Carina's sketchbook dropped out of her hand, and her pencil went flying. She stood up and turned to see the man standing at the base of the porch steps and lifted one hand to her chest, where she could feel her heart racing. "You startled me."

She took a closer look at him. He was dressed like a tourist in khaki shorts and a polo, and appeared to be around fifty. His eyes were dark and unreadable, his graying hair receding. He looked vaguely familiar, but she couldn't place him. Carina tried to tell herself he was probably just lost and needed directions, but something in the way he was looking at her made her uneasy. She swallowed the lump in her throat.

"Can I help you?" she asked.

"I believe you can." He walked up the steps onto the porch, and Carina instinctively took a step back. She knocked into the chair she had just been sitting in, stumbling before she managed to put a hand on the table to steady herself.

"Who are you?"

"It doesn't matter." He glanced at her cell phone lying on the table and then looked back at her. "You have something that belongs to me."

"I don't know what you're talking about." Carina shook her head.

"Your father sent you something," he clarified. "I want it."

"You're Alex." The words escaped her the moment the thought entered her mind. She saw the truth in his eyes and asked, "Why are you here?"

"You've seen me."

Confusion came first. Memories pushed through her mind as she tried to place this man. Then she remembered the night Leone Hamilton was killed, or *silenced*, as someone in her father's office had said. This man had been there with her father and her uncle Marciano. "I just want to be left alone. I have been silent for all these years, and the family has left me alone. That's all I want."

"I might have been satisfied with that, but your grandfather's death complicated things," he told her. "Your father sent you a package. I need it."

"What are you talking about?" Carina asked. "I haven't communicated with my father in years."

His eyes grew cold, and his voice sharpened. "Don't play dumb with me. I know he sent it to you, and I know it wasn't in your apartment."

Carina remembered the information Vanessa had given her just that morning. "You killed Lou."

Alex reached beneath his shirt and pulled a pistol out of his waistband. "If you don't want to be next, I suggest you give me what I came for."

She stared in disbelief, unable at first to see past the gun. Then all she could think was that her past and present had finally collided. All of her preparations, everything Jay and his friends had done to help her hide from her family, hadn't been enough to prevent this moment. "Where is the package your father sent?" he repeated evenly. "You should have received it in the beginning of May."

"Someone did leave me an anonymous note on my windshield," Carina admitted, realizing now that Lou must have intercepted the package that had been meant for her. "Is that what you're talking about?"

His eyes sharpened. "What did it say?"

Carina tried to read this man's face, desperately trying to decipher whether he intended to let her live or whether she was destined to end up like Lou. She let out a shaky breath and gave him a portion of the truth. "It said 'remember who you really are.'"

"What else?"

"That was it."

"What about the key?"

"I don't know what you're talking about," Carina insisted.

He grabbed her arm, and fury lit his face as he rammed the gun beneath her chin. "Don't lie to me!"

Carina yelped in surprise and pain. The next thing she heard was the door opening and Bianca's voice.

"What's going on?"

Then suddenly, the pressure of the gun barrel eased, and Alex abandoned her for her sister. Carina stumbled back against the railing, helpless as Alex grabbed Bianca, his gun now aimed at her left temple. Tears threatened, mirroring the ones in Bianca's eyes. Her face was pale, confusion and terror evident in her expression.

"I'll repeat. Where is the key?"

"My boyfriend has it. He was trying to figure out what it was for."

"Call him. Tell him to bring it back here."

"He doesn't live here."

"No, but he only left ten minutes ago." Alex gave her a knowing look. He released his grip on Bianca and motioned toward the phone. "Actually, you call him. I'm not sure I trust your sister."

Carina nodded to Bianca, praying that she would know what to say to help Jay understand the danger.

37

Jay sat in the backseat of Brent's SUV with the strange sense that he was forgetting something. They were due to board the ferry any minute, but he was having trouble keeping his thoughts focused on shipping out tomorrow. Instead, he kept mentally going over everything that had happened that weekend, feeling like he had left something vital behind.

He tugged at the duffel bag at his feet and checked the outside pocket.

"That's the third time you've checked your bag. What's wrong?" Seth asked.

"I just keep feeling like I forgot something."

"Whatever it is, you're going to have to do without it," Brent said from the driver's seat. "The ferry is getting ready to load."

Jay's phone rang, and he saw Carina's number on the caller ID. He answered with a smile. "Hey, Carina. I was just about to call you. Did I forget something at the house?"

"Actually, it's Bianca."

"Oh, hey, Bianca. What's up?"

"Carina asked me to call you to see if you can bring her that key you were holding onto for her."

Jay opened his mouth to tell her that Carina already had a copy. Then he hesitated. He listened more closely to the background noise, realizing that he was on speaker phone. "Sure, I can do that." Then on impulse, he added, "You know, I think I know what I forgot. I was going to bring the leftover pizza from last night with me. Did I leave it in the fridge?"

Bianca's voice was shaky when she answered him. "Yeah, I think so."

Brent started to pull forward onto the ferry, and Jay tapped him on the shoulder and shook his head. Then he flashed him a hand signal to indicate that there was trouble and they needed to turn around.

Jay felt like his world had fallen out from under him. They were in trouble. The kind of trouble that ended in death. "Bianca, tell Carina that I'll be there in about fifteen minutes. My friends wanted to go out to eat before we catch the ferry, so I'm going to drop them off first before I head your way."

Her voice was more tentative when she said, "Okay. I'll tell her."

Jay hung up and saw that everyone in the car was staring at him. "They're in trouble. Alex must have found her."

Brent motioned to Amy. "I want you to stay here. Call in the local authorities and get them here fast."

Amy nodded and climbed out of the SUV. "Be careful."

"We will." Brent nodded. Then he motioned to Vanessa. "Come on, Vanessa. You're our driver. Let's see if we can put some of your CIA training to work."

"You got it." Vanessa scrambled out of her seat and slid into the driver's seat as Brent slid over. As she started back toward the house, the three members of the Saint Squad began formulating their plans.

* * *

"Why don't you ladies have a seat?" Alex waved his gun toward the patio chairs. "My associates will let us know when your navy friend arrives. And they'll make sure he's really alone."

Carina caught a glimpse of a man at the side of the house, undoubtedly a guard Alex had brought with him. She couldn't tell how many others there were and prayed that Jay would understand what he was coming back to. He had mentioned pizza, their personal code for danger. Surely he would be prepared.

Bianca stumbled toward a chair, the one farthest away from Alex. Carina chose the seat to the left of her briefcase, fully aware that the side pocket was open, her gun within reach. But she also knew that if she reached for her gun, her long-lost uncle might very well end her life before she had a chance to use the weapon.

Bianca reached for her hand and gripped it tightly. Carina could feel her fear. She shared it. When she looked up at Alex, clarity overshadowed all else as she realized this man held the answers she had been searching for. Her voice was surprisingly calm when she asked, "What is the key for?"

A ghost of a smile crossed his face, as though he found humor in the simple question. "It's the key to the family."

"I don't understand."

"Of course not. You've been gone for too long." Alex leaned back against the porch railing and lowered his weapon like the weight had become too much to bear.

"Why don't you explain how things are now?" Carina suggested mildly. "Jay said it would take him fifteen minutes to get here."

He seemed to contemplate for a moment before he shook his head. "This isn't something you need to worry about."

"You're holding us at gunpoint. I have every right to worry," Carina countered. "What I don't understand is why Nick helped you find us. I thought he worked for my father."

"Nick was naive enough to trust the wrong people." His lips curved slightly. "He knew I was looking for you. One of my associates suggested that he help find you to keep you safe."

"So he thought my father sent him to protect us, but he was really working for you without even knowing it."

"Ironic, isn't it?"

Carina tried to ignore the sinking feeling in her stomach. Her shoulders straightened slightly when she asked, "What do you want with us?"

"This is between your father and me. He's going to give me what I need, or he's going to find that he doesn't have any family left."

Carina swallowed hard, and she heard Bianca bite back a sob. "Was it you?" Carina asked. "Were you the one who really killed my mother?"

Alex didn't answer. He only stared at her with a look in his eyes that Carina knew too well. How often had she seen one of her father's men with that same awareness on his face, that understanding that they were about to kill the people standing in their way, just as soon as they got what they wanted.

"What now?" Carina forced herself to ask. "What happens after Jay brings the key?"

"I guess we'll just have to wait and see."

* * *

"Are you sure you don't want to try a water approach?" Seth asked when Vanessa stopped the car a quarter mile from the house. "It would be unexpected."

Jay shook his head. He was trying hard to think of this as just another mission, but he was failing miserably. "From the background noise, it sounded like Bianca was out on the deck. Besides, that house was designed with a ton of windows overlooking the beach. Someone would see us coming."

Brent passed his binoculars to Jay. "I counted three guards. We have to assume there's at least one with the girls, maybe more."

"I think we go with a 'play dumb' entrance. I go in with a key and neutralize anyone threatening the girls."

"And we watch your back," Seth finished for him. He shook his head skeptically. "The only problem with that is if those goons down there decide to shoot you first and look for the key later, you'll end up dead."

Jay gave him a wry look. "I'm trusting you to make sure that doesn't happen."

Brent nodded his approval before addressing Vanessa. "How are you on a rifle?"

"Not as good as Quinn, but I hit what I aim for," Vanessa told him.

"In that case, you can cover us from up here. My rifle is in the back." Brent motioned toward the trees on the side of the house and spoke to Jay. "Seth and I will work our way down into the yard and use the trees and shrubbery for cover. As soon as we're in position, drive to the house, nice and slow so we can make sure no one is planning to use you for target practice."

"How are we splitting up our entry points?" Jay asked.

"I'll take the back entrance. Seth can circle to the right side to the front door, and you can take the left side and go for the deck. Hopefully the girls are still outside in the open where they'll be easy to find."

Jay nodded even as his stomach clenched. He watched Brent and Seth move down the side of a sand dune, using the landscape to hide their approach. Vanessa retrieved the rifle from the back of the SUV and chose her position along the ridge overlooking the house. When everyone was in position, Jay sent up a silent prayer, slid into the driver's seat, and started the engine.

He felt the surge of adrenaline, the one signaling that his body was ready for action. Running alongside the familiar feeling was stone cold fear that reminded him that if this mission wasn't successful, his life would never be the same.

When he pulled over the ridge, the house looked quiet. The men who had been standing guard a moment ago were no longer visible, but Jay couldn't tell if his teammates had neutralized them or if they had taken cover when they heard him coming.

The Jeep was parked in the driveway, and suddenly, Jay sensed movement in front of it. A shadow shifted beneath the midday sun, and Jay considered what needed to be done. The longer they could remain silent, the better chance they had of getting Carina and Bianca out of there safely. Rather than take the space beside the Jeep, he stopped right behind it.

He swung the door open, deliberately making noise when he stepped out onto the gravel driveway. He then walked loudly toward the door. A moment later, he sensed someone coming up behind him, and he struggled not to react too quickly. He heard the stutter of footsteps and turned as Brent grabbed the man from behind, silencing him with a quick elbow to the side of his head. Brent scooped up the pistol the man had dropped and ducked closer to the side of the house.

Jay surveyed the yard in search of the other men they had seen through the binoculars a few moments before. That's when he saw Seth lower another man onto the ground in the trees and collect his weapon. He signaled to Brent to check the other side of the house. Brent nodded and started toward the corner.

A moment later, the back door opened and gunfire erupted. Jay dove for cover behind the Jeep as terror swept through him. Where was Carina, and was she now in even greater danger than before? Another burst of gunfire sounded, followed by a single rifle shot. The man dropped onto the porch, and Jay sprinted toward the deck.

38

THE SOUND OF GUNFIRE PIERCED the air, and pure evil swept over Alex's face. His words were filled with venom, his eyes focused on Carina. "Your friend must want you to die today."

He lifted his gun, at first taking aim at Carina. Then he smiled wickedly and swung the gun toward Bianca. "Let this be a lesson about what happens when people don't follow directions."

"No!" Carina screamed. Her heart racing, she reached into her briefcase with a single thought in her mind. Protect Bianca. She grabbed her gun, flipped the safety, and swung it toward Alex. Without hesitation, she squeezed the trigger. And missed.

Alex turned toward her, fury flaming in his eyes. His weapon swung toward Carina now, and Carina fired again. This time Alex stumbled back and grabbed his side, where the bullet had apparently grazed him along the rib cage.

"You'll die for that." He lifted his weapon, one-handed now, and Carina fired again, her shot ringing out in tandem with another.

All expression on Alex's face froze, and he crumpled onto the deck.

Her arms trembling, Carina lowered her weapon and immediately felt her body start to shake. She saw Seth rush toward Alex as Jay reached her and snaked one arm around her waist to pull her close as he reached his other hand toward Bianca. "Are you both okay?"

Carina couldn't speak. She clung to him, one arm reaching around Bianca as the three of them hugged and formed a single unit.

"I'm so scared," Bianca managed to say, voicing all of their thoughts.

"It's okay now," Jay assured them both.

Carina let herself glance over at Seth and the body of the man who shared her blood. "Is he . . . ?"

Seth nodded. "He's dead."

"It's over now," Jay added. He leaned back and kissed her forehead. "It's all over."

* * *

Marciano Perelli read the details about an upcoming trial, a trial he knew Alex was scheduled to testify at because of his position with the FBI. He considered the layout of the courthouse, the vantage point from the building across the street.

Alex had dropped out of sight over a week before, but Marciano was confident he would resurface for the trial. This could be the opportunity he had been waiting for, his chance to finally end this family war.

For months he had waited and plotted, quietly making arrangements while doing everything possible to protect his family and make sure Alex's influence didn't penetrate the tight circle of trusted associates he had surrounded himself with.

Nick Baldino had been instrumental in helping build that circle. After discovering that he had been used as an unwitting accomplice to Alex's plans, Nick had been more than willing to help the Perellis root out those who had allied with the enemy. One by one, those spies had been dealt with quietly and efficiently.

No one threatened his family and lived, even if the man issuing the threats carried the same blood that ran through his own veins.

He knew from some of his interrogations that Alex hadn't yet given up his search for Carina. Alex's obsession with finding his nieces had left him vulnerable and apparently unaware that Marciano's support within the organization was growing while Alex's was being eliminated.

Marciano smiled a little when he thought about how frustrated his half brother must have been when he realized that people he worked with in the government were now working against him. Alex must have been furious to find that someone on the inside understood the threat even if they didn't know his name.

A trusted associate within the FBI, one who had been on the family's payroll for years, had tried to locate his nieces for Marciano in an attempt to determine if they were still vulnerable. The associate had come back with the news that not only had they dropped off the grid, but his brother's location had also been sealed. Had Giovanni not called him, even Marciano wouldn't have been able to locate him.

"Marciano, you need to see this." Nick Baldino stood at his office door, a file folder in his hand.

"What is it?"

"A report from one of our friends at the Bureau." Nick entered the room and handed it to him. "Alex is dead."

"What?"

Nick handed the file to Marciano, but before he could open it, Nick added, "Carina killed him."

"Carina?" Marciano's eyes met Nick's. "Are the girls okay?"

Nick nodded. "They're fine. The file doesn't say where the incident happened. Apparently, that has been classified at a higher level than our source has access to, but it details that Carina and Bianca were both there and that they are both okay. From what we can tell, Gianna isn't living with them right now."

"They're safe." Marciano sighed the words. He read through the report, noting that the details were still sparse.

"Do you want me to try to find out where they are?"

Marciano considered for a moment. Carina still held the key to many of the family's secrets as well as a decent slice of their legitimate assets, but she had also accomplished what the rest of his associates had failed to do. She had rid him of Alex, the one person who had been destroying everything his father had built.

Slowly, Marciano shook his head. "If the girls want to come back to the family, they'll come when they're ready."

"What about the key you were looking for?"

"The information Carina has access to was only a threat to Alex, not the rest of us. As for the money and assets my father left for her, I think she's earned them."

"I thought you said she doesn't know where everything is locked up."

"She doesn't." His shoulders lifted. "But if she ever decides she wants to understand, she knows where to find me. For now, I want you to call our attorney. Let's see if anything can be done about getting Giovanni out of prison."

* * *

Carina sat in the living room of her new apartment, her phone gripped in her hand. Jay should have called by now. They had instant messaged online for more than an hour last night, and he had told her when he would be allowed to call her next.

Jay's squad had yet to return from the mission that had taken him away right after Raymond Alexander had shown up in North Carolina. It had been so hard to watch him go, her whole world still feeling like it was in a state of confusion. Thankfully, Vanessa and Amy had arranged to stay a few extra days with her. They had both visited twice afterward, both times bringing the wives of the other two SEALs on the Saint Squad.

It was due to one of those visits that she had managed to secure a job here in Virginia Beach so quickly. Riley Crowther, Tristan's wife, owned her own business and needed someone to help pick up the slack as she prepared for the birth of her first child. Even though the job was only guaranteed for six months, it paid well enough for her to find a modest apartment and still cover Gianna's next tuition payment.

Bianca had found a job of her own with one of the year-round swim teams, coaching their younger swimmers. It didn't pay much, but it offset all of her own swimming fees and gave her a little bit of spending money.

Together, they were making a new life, and so far, they hadn't seen any sign that the family knew where they were.

Bianca walked into the apartment with her swim bag over her shoulder and kicked the door closed behind her. She looked down at Carina's phone and gave her a sympathetic look. "He hasn't called yet?"

"Not yet."

"Maybe something came up," Bianca suggested. "It's happened before."

"I know." Carina sighed.

"Is he still reading the Book of Mormon?"

"He says he is." She nodded. "But he still won't commit to meeting with the missionaries."

"You know, six months ago, I was wondering if religion even mattered to you." Bianca's expression was a combination of sympathy and amusement. "I can't believe it took someone who isn't LDS to help you see what's important."

Carina's eyebrows drew together. "What do you mean?"

"Since Mom died, it's like you took your testimony for granted. Once Jay started asking questions, I think he reminded you that you knew the answers."

Even though she didn't like to admit it, Carina could see the truth in her sister's words. In Miami, she had struggled to get motivated to drive the few miles to church each Sunday; yet, when they were staying in the Outer Banks, she had made a point of attending every week, even though getting to church took more than two hours and included a ride on the ferry. "What am I going to do if he doesn't believe in the gospel?"

"I don't know." Bianca gave her a sympathetic look. "I guess we'll have to keep praying that he finds the truth."

Carina let out a sigh and nodded. Though she had tried repeatedly to deny her feelings for Jay, she knew that distance had accomplished what had started during that awful time in Florida. She had fallen in love with this man, and she was torn about what to do now. If Jay didn't accept the gospel, could she follow Vanessa's example and walk away from the person she had grown to depend on, the man she wanted in her future? Or did she try to make a future with Jay and hope for a miracle, knowing that it might never come?

The phone rang, and she answered it without waiting for the number to flash on her caller ID. "Hello?"

"Hi, Carina. It's Amy."

Carina couldn't keep the disappointment out of her voice. "Oh, hi, Amy."

"You were waiting for Jay to call," Amy said perceptively.

Carina let out a sigh. "He said he was going to call almost an hour ago."

"I heard through the grapevine that their mission was delayed. It's probably going to be a few hours before we hear from our guys."

"Thanks for letting me know. I was starting to go a little crazy."

"No problem," Amy said, and Carina could hear the smile in her voice. "I actually wanted to let you know that I talked to Kendra today."

Carina's heartbeat quickened. She had been waiting anxiously for weeks to find out if Kendra had chosen her to design her wedding gown. "What did she say?"

"She wanted to know if you could meet her at my parents' house in northern Virginia in two weeks to finalize the designs on her wedding dress."

"What?"

Amy's laughter carried over the line. "She loved the last design you sent her. She wants to get started as soon as possible."

"I can't believe it! Amy, thank you so much."

"I'm glad I could help," Amy said with humor in her voice. "But beware. I think you'll end up designing the bridesmaid dresses too. And my mom mentioned something about needing something for the wedding."

Carina thought of the whirl of excitement that would surround Kendra Blake's wedding, especially the news that a big star would be choosing a temple marriage over a traditional one. The thought popped into her head that she couldn't have that with Jay right now. "It sounds like I'm going to be very busy."

"With any luck, by the time Riley is ready to come back off of her maternity leave, she'll be able to teach you how to set up your own business."

Carina tried to keep her thoughts on her professional life rather than her personal one. "Sounds like a dream come true."

39

JAY HEADED STRAIGHT FOR A computer the minute he entered his squad's boardroom on the *USS Harry S. Truman*. He logged on quickly, praying that Carina would be online as his teammates scrambled to use the other computer terminals in the room. Undoubtedly, they too wanted to chat with the women they had left at home. The phone call Jay had hoped to make two days ago had never materialized, interrupted by a high-priority mission.

They only had a few hours before they would fly out again, this time on a helicopter bound for Afghanistan, but he needed to talk to Carina first. He didn't stop to wonder when talking to her had shifted from a want to a need. It didn't really matter when it had happened, just that it had. She had become the most important thing in his world, and he ached to see her.

For tonight, instant messaging was the best he could do. Assuming that she was at her computer. A smile crossed his face the minute he saw that she was online.

You there? Jay typed, hoping she hadn't just left herself logged on while she was off doing something else. A minute stretched into two while he waited impatiently for an answer.

I'm here. How are you?

Okay. Only have a few minutes but wanted to make sure you're okay.

I'm fine, but I miss you.

Jay smiled. *Miss you too.*

Any idea yet when you'll be back?

Nothing certain yet, but it should be sometime this week.

I hope so. I love you.

Jay read the words, the three simple words that resonated through him. He started typing his response, eager for Carina to know he shared her feelings. Before he could hit the send key, his Internet connection severed.

"You've got to be kidding me," Jay muttered.

"Did you get kicked off too?" Seth called from across the room.

"Yeah." Jay nodded.

"So did I," Tristan added. "Looks like we're under a communications blackout."

"I wonder why," Seth mused before the phone in the boardroom rang.

Brent answered it. He was only on the line for thirty seconds before he hung up and motioned to the rest of them. "Grab your gear. It's time to go."

* * *

Carina didn't know what to think. She had actually confessed her love to Jay, and what had she gotten in return? Nothing. Absolute silence. Seventeen hours and thirty-two minutes of absolute silence.

She couldn't count the number of times she had woken during the night to check her computer and cell phone only to find Jay still hadn't responded. She had started to call Vanessa this morning to ask her advice, but she couldn't bring herself to talk to someone else about Jay when the only thing she wanted to do right now was to talk *to* Jay.

Working today had been a trial as she struggled to concentrate on the various tasks that should already be second-nature to her. Carina supposed that Riley would probably understand her dilemma well enough, but it wasn't the same as having gone through it the way Vanessa had.

Carina finished filing the last batch of course evaluations in Riley's home office and started to sit at the round table where her laptop was set up. She glanced over at Riley, who was sitting at the desk across the room, her face pale. At first Carina thought maybe she had forgotten to eat again. Then Riley looked up at her with tears in her eyes.

"Riley, what's wrong?"

She didn't speak, only waved helplessly toward her computer.

Carina circled her desk and looked over Riley's shoulder. And her whole world dropped out from under her. She felt the color drain out of her own face when she saw the headlines on the screen dated today, August 6, 2011. *Helicopter crash in Afghanistan kills 38 including 31 US Special Forces.*

"You don't think . . . ?" Carina let the unspoken question hang in the air.

"I don't know." Riley's voice came out in a whisper.

Carina felt her chest tighten, and helplessness washed over her. What would she do if Jay was one of those thirty-one? She looked down at

Riley. What would Riley do if Tristan was among them? Would her child be born without a father? Would she ever be able to love someone again after finding the man who was so obviously perfect for her?

Carina barely recognized the silent prayers running through her head, but she felt a spurt of hope go to battle with the despair. "See if you can find any more details. I'm going to call Vanessa."

"I'll try Amy." Riley nodded as though her desire for answers now outweighed the shock of the news.

When neither Amy nor Vanessa answered, Carina and Riley both started searching for more information. The reports were vague, all of them saying essentially the same thing. Then she caught one with more details, and her world started spiraling out of control once more. *Helicopter crash reportedly kills members of SEAL Team Six.* "What SEAL team are the guys with?"

"Eight."

"Then it can't be them." Carina let out a sigh of relief. "It says here that the victims were from SEAL Team Six."

"Team Six doesn't actually exist. It's just what the press calls some of the top-secret units that they can't put a name on," Riley told her, her eyes moist. "Right now, I just want someone to tell me for sure that it wasn't Tristan."

"You're saying the Saint Squad could have been with them?"

"I don't know. Tristan and I got cut off last night when we were IMing. Usually that means they had a communications blackout."

"A communications blackout?"

Riley nodded. "They happen a lot, either right before or right after something major happens. It's the military's way of controlling information to make sure nothing slips out that might interfere with their operations."

Carina thought of the way Jay had just disappeared offline right after she had said she loved him. Could it have been because of the blackout that he hadn't responded? Again, she was faced with the horrifying thought of what she would do if Jay had been one of the men killed. She didn't have an eternal marriage like his teammates' wives. Even if he was okay, what was to say that something wouldn't happen to him in the future?

She thought of Vanessa's choice, realizing what she had gained by waiting so long for Seth to accept the gospel. If Seth was on that downed helicopter, she still had him for eternity. If Carina ended up with Jay and he didn't accept the gospel, she would never have that security.

A weight pressed in on her as tears welled up in her eyes. She was very likely going to lose Jay one way or another. For the moment, she could only pray that it wasn't today.

* * *

The entire Saint Squad took the news like they had been run over by a truck—one they hadn't seen coming. Thirty-one of their comrades were dead, shot down returning from a rescue mission. They stood together in the boardroom aboard ship, staring at the television screen mounted in the corner of the room.

"That could have been us." Tristan said the words quietly, echoing all of their thoughts. They had been out on a similar mission when the Chinook helicopter had been shot down, but they had returned to base safely, not a scratch on any of them.

"Our wives have got to be going crazy." Seth looked over at Jay and added, "And Carina."

"When is this communications blackout going to end?" Quinn asked impatiently. "This is crazy. The news has already gone viral."

"I'm trying to get a message out to Amy so she can call everyone," Brent told them. "Command says I should have a secure line within another fifteen minutes."

Jay considered what Carina must be going through right now. Only yesterday she had said that she loved him, and now she didn't know if he was alive or dead. She didn't even know how much he loved her in return.

The memory of another helicopter crash overwhelmed him. He remembered so vividly that moment before impact when he thought he was going to die. Emotions churning through him, he stepped toward the hatch. "I'm going to get some air."

Before anyone could respond, Jay quickly pushed his way out into the corridor and started toward the stairs leading to the upper decks. He heard someone come out behind him, but he didn't look back.

Not until they made it out into the fresh air did Seth speak. "You okay?"

Jay clenched his teeth together, not trusting himself to speak.

"Talk to me."

"I can't stop thinking about the crash. I try to fight it, but I can't stop thinking that I could have died."

"It's never easy when something like this happens." Seth put a hand on the railing and stared out at the ship's wake. "And it never makes any sense no matter how much we analyze it."

"Seth, it's not just today's crash. It was when *we* crashed." Jay turned to face him. "How come you and the rest of our squad were so calm?"

Seth's eyes widened. "We weren't calm."

"Yes, you were," Jay insisted. "There was something different about you four when we went down."

"Maybe it was just perspective," Seth suggested. "Trust me, we were all just as scared as you were. We just know a bit more about what comes after this life than most people."

"I want what you have," Jay said suddenly.

"What do you mean?"

The clarity of his thoughts surprised him as the words tumbled out of his mouth. "I want all of it. The peace. The Spirit. Whatever you call it. I want it all."

"Then you want the gospel," Seth said simply.

"Yeah." Jay nodded as the truth dawned on him. "I want the gospel."

40

I LOVE YOU TOO! CARINA remembered the message Jay had sent her the minute the communications blackout had been lifted. It had been followed with the explanation. *That's what I was trying to say before we were cut off last time.*

Carina's relief at seeing for herself that he was okay was complete, but the hours of worrying, of not knowing if he had lived or died, had helped her make up her mind. She was going to have to let him go.

Living with Jay's profession would have been hard enough had they found a future together, but she knew now that she couldn't do it. Not when she could only have him for this lifetime, however long that might be.

"Are you okay?" Vanessa asked beside her.

"I will be." Carina nodded. "Or at least I hope I will be."

Vanessa gave her arm an encouraging squeeze as they waited for the bus that would bring the men from the airfield to where the families were waiting. There were a dozen other families waiting with them, all of them eager for their loved ones' return. Several held handmade signs, "Welcome Home" being the central theme.

Vanessa and the other wives had been so sweet to include her in so many of their activities lately. After the scare the week before, she felt like she was one of them, but she knew it wouldn't last.

She still hadn't spoken to Jay on the phone or on video chat, but they had messaged several times since that first time he had professed his love. She had tried her best to act like everything was okay between them. After all, she owed it to him to talk to him in person when she broke things off. She owed him that and so much more.

Words ran through her mind, possibilities of what she might say to him, how she could make him understand. Each time she rehearsed their next meeting, she became more nervous.

A plain white bus came into view, and the crowd stirred with excitement. Carina's stomach tightened uncomfortably.

The bus pulled to a stop, and the doors opened with a whoosh of air. Men in fatigues started coming down the steps, their eyes sweeping the crowd until they found that special person in their lives. Then the footsteps quickened and long-awaited kisses of greeting were shared.

Tristan was the first member of the Saint Squad to step off of the bus. He zeroed in on Riley immediately and hurried toward her. His duffel dropped to the ground, and he swept his wife up in his arms and lowered his mouth to hers. Filled with envy and trying hard not to let it get to her, Carina tore her eyes away from the reunion. That's when she saw him.

Her heart stopped for a moment, and she couldn't stop the smile from forming. He was so handsome in his uniform, but she knew now that there was so much more to him than his looks and that confident air he had about him. He truly had a heart of gold, completely unaware of how deep his own well of generosity ran. She could see Jay smile as his eyes met hers and he started toward her.

Something seemed different about him, but she couldn't put her finger on what. All she could think about was her absolute relief that he was okay and that he was home. All of her rehearsed greetings were forgotten, and she opened her arms to him as he reached for her. He lifted her into the air and spun her around. "I have missed you so much."

"I missed you too," Carina admitted before she could censor her words. The delight in his eyes and the feeling of his arms around her overshadowed her intentions. Even though she knew the end would come sooner than she wanted, she wasn't ready for it now. Not quite yet.

Reunions continued around them as Jay kissed her briefly and then pulled her away from the crowd. "I have so much to tell you."

Carina's eyes narrowed. "I thought you couldn't talk about your missions or whatever."

"I can't." Jay shook his head and waved that away as a triviality. "That wasn't what I wanted to talk to you about."

"Then what?"

"I was hoping you could come over to Seth and Vanessa's house for dinner tomorrow night."

Carina considered. Maybe that would be the right time to talk to him about the future. To explain why things needed to change between them. "I can do that."

"Great." A smile crossed Jay's face. "Because that's when I'm having my first missionary lesson."

"What?"

Jay's smile faded, and his expression grew serious. "I get it now."

She shook her head. "I don't understand."

"I've had a lot to think about over the past few days. Past few months really," Jay told her. "With everything that's gone on, I finally found the answers to the questions I hadn't even realized I was asking."

Her jaw dropped, and emotions flooded through her: shock, disbelief, hope. "Are you saying that you're interested in learning about the Church?"

"No," Jay said, pausing briefly as her excitement faded. "I'm saying I'm interested in joining the LDS Church."

Carina's eyes widened. "Seriously?"

"Seriously." Jay nodded. "I love you. I want us to be together forever."

She gave herself a moment to feel loved and cherished, but a seed of doubt crept in. "Are you planning on getting baptized for you or for me?" She shook her head slowly. "I don't want you to join for me."

"It's for me," Jay assured her. "I told Seth I want what you all have. I want that sense of peace that I didn't realize I was missing."

"I love you." She reached up and kissed him, reveling in the feel of his arms around her.

When they shifted apart, Jay grinned down at her. "You know what this means, don't you?"

"What?"

"When I convince you to marry me, you're going to be stuck with me forever."

"I like the sound of that." Her eyes lit up, and her smile widened. "Forever."

ABOUT THE AUTHOR

ORIGINALLY FROM ARIZONA, TRACI HUNTER Abramson has spent most of her adult life in Virginia. She is a graduate of Brigham Young University and a former employee of the Central Intelligence Agency. Since leaving the CIA, Traci has written several novels, including the Undercurrents trilogy, *Royal Target*, *Royal Secrets*, *Obsession*, and the Saint Squad series.

When she's not writing, Traci enjoys spending time with her husband and four children, preferably on a nice, quiet beach. She also enjoys coaching North Stafford High School's swim team.